NINA

NINA

A NOVEL

LOUISE PHILLIPS

UNION
SQUARE
& CO.
NEW YORK

UNION SQUARE & CO. and the distinctive Union Square & Co. logo are trademarks of Hachette Book Group, Inc.

ISBN 978-1-4549-6258-8
ISBN 978-1-4549-6259-5 (e-book)

Library of Congress Cataloging-in-Publication Data

Names: Phillips, Louise (Fiction writer) author.
Title: Nina : a novel / Louise Phillips.
Description: New York : Union Square & Co., 2025. | Summary: "A feminist, redemptive crime novel about a woman, Elizabeth, who has never come to terms with the loss of her daughter who went missing twenty-five years ago, and why she is compelled to go back to the house where her little girl, Nina, disappeared"—Provided by publisher.
Identifiers: LCCN 2025019362 (print) | LCCN 2025019363 (ebook) | ISBN 9781454962588 (paperback) | ISBN 9781454962595 (ebook)
Subjects: LCGFT: Detective and mystery fiction. | Novels.
Classification: LCC PR6116.H488 N56 2025 (print) | LCC PR6116.H488 (ebook) | DDC 823/.92—dc23/eng/20250522
LC record available at https://lccn.loc.gov/2025019362
LC ebook record available at https://lccn.loc.gov/2025019363

Union Square & Co. books may be purchased in bulk for business, educational, or promotional use. For more information, please contact your local bookseller or the Hachette Book Group's Special Markets department at special.markets@hbgusa.com.

Printed in Canada

MRQ-T

1 2025

unionsquareandco.com

Cover design by Claire Sullivan
Cover image by Getty Images © Marco Bottigelli
Interior design by Rich Hazelton

For Caitríona

PROLOGUE

IT WAS ONLY BY CHANCE THAT HE LEARNT OF HER WHEREABOUTS, and watching her now, he thinks back to the first time he saw her, the image still vivid in his mind, her perfect frame, those long slim fingers, her hair shoulder-length, delicate, warmed by the evening sun. She wore jeans and a powder-pink shirt with tiny white daises, the top button open, revealing her lightly tanned skin.

He'd studied her for hours, long before he approached, and when he did, he said something funny. It made her laugh. He smiles at that, recalling her naive confidence, that sweet, uncertain vulnerability.

Her vulnerability was one of the things that drew him to her, and why she was finally chosen—that need of hers to appear strong, while deep down, all she ever wanted was for others to like her. It was her desperation that made her special, the defencelessness within the desire, including her attempts at awkward flirtation, as if she'd spent hours learning how to fall in love from some stupid, romantic TV show.

They say time is a healer. It isn't, it's just time, and if he tries hard enough, even now, he can reimagine it all, hearing her whimpers, his hands tight across her mouth, blocking out the screams. He feels her terror, the rise of adrenaline within him, and then, most pleasing of all, that unexpected stare, her eyes a combination of shock and uncertainty, but something else too, a hint of sadness, that somehow, she should have known it would come to this.

1

ELIZABETH

THE DAY I TURNED SIXTY, I DECIDED TO RUN AWAY FROM HOME. I GAVE myself a deadline. It needed to happen within a year. Tomorrow is my birthday, so today is the day. I live with my daughter Alison, her husband, and my three grandchildren. Right now, I'm in the kitchen. I feel both invisible and of little consequence.

There's a loud clattering of dishes, cereal bowls, cups and glasses being emptied into the sink, the cutlery crashing down on top, quickly followed by the sound of running tap water—splash—splash—splash. There are other noises too, the children's voices arguing with one another, thwarting, complaining about not wanting to go to school.

"I hate cereal," Emily moans. She's eight and the eldest.

I walk toward the large island unit with its black crushed marble top, ready to clear some spilt milk. My son-in-law trips over a schoolbag. "SHIT," he yells, annoyed. Mornings aren't his thing.

I suck in air, attempting the relaxing techniques I recently learned from Spotify, breathing in through my nostrils and out through my mouth. If everyone wasn't so busy, they might notice me—they don't. I count backward from one hundred too, filing the chaos into that part of my brain developed from necessity since moving in with my daughter five years ago. It had seemed like such a sensible idea at the time, amalgamating resources. That's what *she* called it. I wasn't so sure. I feel it is her house. I think she feels that too.

I love my daughter dearly, but all the years of unspoken words, especially since we moved in together, has created a messy and complicated maze. And now, it's as if every day, instead of real life, I'm living a kind of false existence, and on those rare occasions when I try to reach out to Alison, she's always beyond my grasp. Of late, I've finally learned to accept, we may no longer be capable of finding one another, because that's what happens when you stop connecting properly. A certain point is reached, one you dare not go beyond, because if you do, you risk losing whatever tentative relationship, no matter how small, you still have.

If this was the only problem, perhaps things wouldn't be so difficult, but the proverbial elephant in the room is my other daughter, Nina.

Nina is missing. She's been that way for a very long time, and the word "missing," with all its ramifications, has circled around in my head for over twenty-five years. It's part of who I am. I have to believe she's missing, because the alternative isn't acceptable.

Others think differently, including the Irish police. They look at it as something else—*missing presumed dead.* It's a cold case now. They don't call it "closed," only, it is. Last year, over 11,000 people went missing in Ireland. All but twenty-seven of them eventually turned up. The others, like Nina, form part of the statistics of the loved ones who never came home.

Sometimes, I think Alison is slightly threatened by her older sister, thinking, but not saying, that I might have loved her more.

Mostly, I try not to dwell on that part. When you spend half a lifetime fantasising about your daughter coming home, with all that unknowingness, pent-up anger, and grief, it defines you in ways you never wanted or intended it to. It affects your relationships with others. It affects everything.

My son-in-law, Ciaran, is still fuming over the schoolbag. His shirt is ruined with a coffee stain. He'll need to change it. He'll be late. Again, I place this information into that quiet part of my brain, the part that tries, mostly, not to give a shit.

My daughter is preparing three lunchboxes. I hand her the drink bottles, dutifully filled with water. Lucy, the black Labrador, darts into the kitchen barking at a stray cat who hoards the window ledge outside. The feline doesn't move. Like me, it appears oblivious, but finally, it leaps down and slinks off.

We've now reached the "schoolbags on the backs of children" point in the morning proceedings. My grandchildren are Emily; Oscar, who recently turned seven; and Katie, the baby, age four. She will always be "baby" because she was born last. I love them too.

On the clotheshorse by the double doors to the garden, the sun gleams down onto an array of socks, underpants, shirts, and pyjamas. I begin to fold them onto the cleared island unit, looking up periodically as one by one the children make their way out to the car for school. My son-in-law kisses my daughter on the cheek. Simultaneously, they both say "bye, honey," and I'm tempted to say "snap," like you do in that card game when two cards match.

Alison hovers, checking nothing important has been left behind. The "important" heading doesn't include me. At times like this, I feel like a tiny bird, small and easily dismissed. My daughter lovingly pats the dog on the head, while issuing final instructions to the children. She shouts back at me from the hallway. "Bye, Mom."

"Bye," I reply, too low for her to hear, but either way, she's already gone. Tomorrow, it'll happen all over again, the chaos within the ordinary, the repetitive grey mundane. Only tomorrow, I won't be here.

I place a half-finished carton of milk on the top shelf of the large, sleek fridge. There's an aroma of coffee lingering from the cafetiere.

I pick it up, draining the liquid into the sink, before emptying the discarded remains into the pedal bin on the floor. The dregs fall like chunky brown snow.

I carry the folded laundry upstairs. In the children's bedrooms, after putting everything away, I pick up dirty socks, pants, and inside-out pyjamas. This is my morning routine. When I enter my daughter and son-in-law's bedroom, I glimpse a reflection of myself in their dressing-table mirror. I don't look that old, I think. Regular visits to the hairdresser under Alison's instructions, topping up my hair colour, takes at least ten years off me. My skin, inherited from my mother, has few enough wrinkles, which is just as well, as skin care was never high on my priority list. I don't tidy up in here. Alison and Ciaran might think I'm meddling. Instead, I place the laundry at the end of their bed.

In my room, I stare at the wallpaper, like that actress once did in *Shirley Valentine*, when she talked to the wall. I don't say "Hello, wallpaper." I don't say anything. The wallpaper is purple with large white swirls. At night, I follow the pattern over and over. A couple of months ago, a face appeared. At first, I couldn't make it out, but then I solved the mystery. I realised the face was mine. She was calling out, wanting to know what had happened to me, where I'd gone? I didn't know how to answer her, which is another reason why I'm running away.

I pack enough clothes to ensure I don't have to return for a very long time. On top of my belongings, I place an envelope with newspaper clippings and an old photograph with the date 1992 written in pencil on the back. Flipping the photograph over, I stare at the image. In it, there's a house with a white rosebush in the front garden. The roses are large, fully in bloom, the petals delicate, as if they already know that soon, they too will perish. In the centre, a pebbled pathway sits behind a small black wrought iron gate with low concrete pillars on either side. Beyond them is the front door, which, like the window frames, boasts a shade of royal blue. I imagine the rooms behind windows. Even now, I can't help but shiver, remembering a place where, in so many ways, it all began. Finally, I study the left of the image, which lies in shadow. The shadow could be nothing, or something, or someone. Either way, I've kept it all these years, a clue if you like, because isn't that what they say you should do, if you want to find answers—go back to the beginning.

I place the photograph in the suitcase and slam it shut before scribbling a note to Alison.

Soon, like the rest of the family, I pull the front door closed behind me, my old Ford Fiesta waiting like a chariot in the drive. Once inside it, duly seat belted, I consider playing some music, something upbeat, but decide against it. Silence is best for now.

On the motorway, my head is filled with other sounds, cars whizzing past at speed, trucks honking their horns. When the car stalls in heavy traffic, a radio broadcast steeps in from another car. I need to block it out, so, despite the heat of the day, I close my driver's-side window.

I wondered a while back if I might be depressed. I looked it up online. I hadn't realised people could be depressed for years and not know it, so I completed a questionnaire.

- ❑ How often have you felt down, depressed, or hopeless?
- ❑ How often have you had little pleasure or interest in doing things?
- ❑ Do you have trouble sleeping?

- ❏ Do you ever feel like a failure?
- ❏ Or feel you've let yourself or others down?

You had to choose your answers from four options: (a) not at all, (b) several days, (c) more than half the days, or (d) nearly every day. I wasn't surprised by the result. I could tell by the number of D's from early on exactly where it was heading.

I'd looked up post-traumatic stress too. That can also last for years. Apparently, if you ignore it, it will worsen over time. War veterans suffer it a lot. Women who've experienced domestic abuse suffer it too. There wasn't a questionnaire for that one, but rather a list of symptoms—vivid flashbacks, negative thoughts, nightmares, intense feelings of distress at real or symbolic reminders of the trauma, alongside experiencing physical sensations such as pain, sweating, nausea, or trembling. Tick—tick—tick—tick—and tick.

The traffic eases. The car is travelling at speed again. I look up. Above me is a cloudless blue sky. It catches me unawares, and for the briefest moment, I feel more like a girl than a woman, as if temporarily unburdened. I breathe in deep, wanting to hold on to that feeling, but it's already slipping away.

The large blue signs on the motorway tell me how many kilometres it is to my destination. I need to keep focused on the task at hand. There's no going back now. I've waited too long for this, because I also know this *thing* I'm doing isn't only about running away. It's also about returning.

2

ELIZABETH

IT'S NOT LONG BEFORE I REACH MY DESTINATION. I PARK THE CAR IN the small driveway to the front of the house. Tall, dense laurel bushes separate this garden from the one next door, recalling as a young bride moving into this street, and those laurels being newly planted. Now, they're a large wall of greenery.

My friend Ellie, who's lending me her house while she's away, has already told me about April, the little girl who lives next door. She describes her as an utter joy, although I've already received several specific instructions about how I should act with her. How I need to be careful the way I phrase things, idioms, metaphors or other common expressions. I've also been told she's very intelligent, talkative, and if we become friends, and at any point she decides to use the bathroom upstairs, I should only ever leave one toilet roll in the room at a time. Apparently, the child is obsessed with cleanliness, an obsession that has resulted in blocked drains on several occasions. I didn't question it too much, but if Ellie mentioned it, I'm going to assume it's important. The girl is ten, and I also understand she may call on a regular basis. Acceptance of this is an unsaid condition of our arrangement. It's not ideal, but if my needs were purely about accommodation, I could have gone elsewhere. Only, they're not. The location is important. I lived on this street as a young mother, ten doors up from Ellie's, the year Nina went missing.

I open the car door, still partly surprised I'm here, and that somehow, after all these months of silently thinking about it, it's actually happening. If someone was interviewing me right now, I'd say I feel a combination of two things. Firstly, knowing it's the absolute right thing to do. While, secondly, also knowing I'm running a risk with Alison. If Alison was being interviewed, she'd probably say I'm misbehaving like some silly child. One who should be spoken to with absolute determination and clarity for fear I might repeat something stupid like this again. Daring to overstep the mark, behaving wholly irresponsibly, and that the risk of this action being repeated would need to be constantly guarded against.

I breathe out, taking in my surroundings, realising something else too. I'm nervous. Sometimes, I think there's another person inside of me, a stranger, and that somehow, instead of me doing certain things, I'm watching her doing them instead. What would this stranger be thinking now? She might, like Alison, consider me crazy to be back here, playing some kind of amateur detective, recklessly returning to the scene of the crime. I try to shut that voice down, but the stranger inside me isn't having any of it. She knows I'm afraid, and that fear, the one that has kept me awake at night in the days and years building up to this, will never go away. It too is always there, because both the stranger and I know there's always the risk he might find me, watch me, and wait his time to make his move. The stranger inside me dismisses it as paranoia, but I'm not so sure, not on this street so full of memories.

Clutching my car keys, I stare at the cherry blossom trees on either side of the road, thick and heavy, although no longer in bloom. They camouflage the low garden walls as my eyes are drawn downward toward the road markings: DRIVE SLOW. BEWARE OF CHILDREN. And despite the current emptiness of the street, I hear children playing—loud, happy cries, unafraid, as if the years since Nina's disappearance have simply vanished.

I also know there's another reason why I'm here. The stranger inside me knows it too. Like me, she's felt it for some time, but unless you've experienced it, it's hard to understand. Often, I feel choked, trapped, especially around other people. I'd wondered if it was part of the post-traumatic stress list of symptoms, the ones that gradually escalate over time, because over time, I've found it increasingly difficult to be around other people, including Alison. People try to make me better, but I'm not ready for that.

At the front door, I lift the key toward the lock. Again, the movement feels surreal, as if the "stranger" me, the one who usually plays the part of Elizabeth, is doing it instead. I'm so caught up in my own thoughts, I jump when I hear footsteps behind me, dropping the keys to the ground.

"Hello," says a young girl's voice, and for a second, I wonder if I might be imagining her too.

I pick up the keys, still startled.

"Are you Elizabeth?" she asks, looking inquisitive.

"Yes," I reply.

The child has ebony-black hair and wears thick bifocals with crimson frames. She stares at me with such intensity, I blink, as I notice one of her eyes turns inward.

"I'm April," she says. "I'm very friendly."

"I can see that."

"I'm also autistic."

"Right."

"My friend got a new rabbit today."

"Oh?"

"Do you want to know her name?"

"The friend or the rabbit?"

"The rabbit," she laughs.

"Okay then."

"It's Charlie, and she makes me and my friend very happy. My friend's name is Jasmine, by the way." Her stare intensifies. "Ellie says you're nice. Are you?"

"I try to be."

"Hmm . . . ," she says, looking uncertain. "I try to be nice too, but it can be hard."

"Sometimes, I find it hard too."

"They say I get overwhelmed."

"They?"

"My mam and dad, and the teachers at school."

"I see," I reply, although I'm not sure where this conversation is going.

"I cry a lot too. I can be really loud."

"I'm sorry to hear that. About the crying I mean."

"It's okay. It's because my brain's too big."

"Too big?"

"I think about everything all the time."

"I think about things too."

"Everything?"

"No, not everything, but there are certain things I think about a lot."

"Like a fixation."

"I guess you could call it that," I say, aware of all the things I've been fixated on for years, mostly Nina, but also the fear, the kind that keeps you paralysed.

"I'm fixated about Pokémon."

"That's nice," I reply, sounding only half-interested. Children hate it when you do that to them. "Do you want to come inside?" I ask, attempting to make amends. "I know you're a friend of Ellie's."

"No," she replies, completely deadpan.

"Maybe another time then," I say, placing the key in the lock, relieved this conversation will soon end and I can be alone again, inside and away from all distractions.

"A stray cat scratched me yesterday."

"Oh?"

"Do you think I'll get rabies?"

"I don't think . . ."

"What are the symptoms?"

"I'm not . . ."

"Can you die from it? I don't want to die."

"I'm sure you'll be . . ."

"I mean, has anyone ever died from rabies in Ireland? It would be important to know that."

"Maybe, a hundred years ago," I say, trying to keep my anxiety in check.

"Are you sure?"

"No, but . . ."

"Ellie looks things up on Google. Google is very good with questions."

"I'll bear that in mind."

"So, you don't think I'll die from this?" She holds up her arm, displaying a minor scratch.

"I'm sure you won't." The key turns in the lock.

"Okay then. I better go." She begins to walk away, and she's already in the garden next door when she adds, "I hurt my head yesterday."

"How did you do that?" I ask through the thick laurel bushes, curious now.

"I was banging it off the radiator making music."

I hear her close the front door.

A smile attempts to emerge on my face, but I shut it down.

I stand motionless for a second, unsure what to do next. Finally, I open the front door.

Once inside Ellie's house, my mood immediately shifts downward. I look around the hallway, one similar in design to the house ten doors up, the house where we as a family once lived. If I try really hard, I can imagine everything as it once was, the children's coats layering the end of the banisters, the old familiar sounds and smells, the younger me, standing in the hallway with a view directly out to the back garden, as two swings are temporarily abandoned.

I tell myself again I've made the right decision to come here, even if I'll need to remain vigilant, because outside of my desire to find Nina, the fear, the one that paralyzes you, is also part of moving forward, and piecing all the information together is complicated, because the truth is rarely easy to find, especially when others want to ensure it's kept from you.

I think about the newspaper clippings too, the ones I packed with that old photograph. In them, the headlines are all about Rachel Meadows's abduction and murder. She was thirty when she disappeared, the same age Nina would be now, and if Rachel Meadows is part of this, I've no choice but to dig deeper, because my life, and the lives of others, could depend on it.

3

NICK

NICK MATTHEWS LEANS BACK IN HIS CHAIR, SCRUNCHING HIS EYES tight, tired and in need of caffeine, staring at the images of Rachel Meadows on the laptop screen. The night-lights of Terenure village shine in at him through the top-floor window of the police station, the office dark now except for a lone desk lamp and the reflective glare of the laptop illuminating his face. Flicking through the crime scene images, questions ricochet against one another. He knows how to solve a crime, ten years as a detective has taught him that, but he also knows studying these images could reveal something others have missed.

He presses two fingers to the bridge of his nose, staring at the street life below. A couple hail a cab, the rain drizzling down after a day of intense heat. In the shadows, a group of women huddle beneath a red umbrella while traffic whizzes past, fast and furious, in much the same way as the crime scene images invade his sleep, disjointed, like a kaleidoscope revealing only slithers of themselves.

His phone buzzes an alarm, telling him his shift ended two hours ago. He's no intention of leaving; his apartment, devoid of company, has already lost the battle against the images on-screen. He zooms in on a photograph of Rachel Meadows, the earliest known victim, her sprawled body lifeless in a darkened laneway—hair tangled, muddied, and partly covering her face. Rachel had a life, family and friends who cared about her. A father who never thought he'd see his daughter this way, and a mother with a broken heart so huge, she'll spend the rest of her life reliving snapshots of her daughter's life. All because some son of a bitch took their daughter from them.

Nick examines the long slim fingers, another tentative link between the victims, like a calling card telling him to take note, as he flicks to the image of the lone navy shoe, the heel broken, as if at some point Rachel lost her balance or was pushed. The next set of images are the ligature marks on her wrists and ankles. He zooms in again, studying the abrasions consistent with scratches caused by a rope. Another victim had similar markings, from being restrained in a face-down position.

The final set of photographs reveal the contents of Rachel's bag, discarded off the N8 motorway, containing a smashed compact mirror, makeup, and miniature perfume samples. The samples could be important, but in truth, every detail mattered.

Rachel, like the other three victims, was in her thirties, all killed over a fifteen-year time frame, and all within the investigation formally called Operation Shadow. Some in the force believed the perpetrator was a kind of *sleeper*, a guy who otherwise lived a normal life. He could even be married, resisting the urge to strike until there was some form of trigger, something tempting him to walk temporarily out of his so-called *normal* life to kill again.

But Nick knows the start of a story is seldom the first killing. With guys like this, escalation happens over time. At first, the killer might have been content following his victims, or peeping in at them through their bedroom windows, and most likely, his first offence would have been close to home. Only soon, he'd have needed more, breaking and entering the likely next step, quickly followed by a desire for his victims to know he existed.

Nick opens the original missing persons photographs of all four women, their eyes staring back at him. *It's been too long,* they seem to say, as Nick considers if he, like his colleagues before him, could mess up.

At first, he hated the idea of the Cold Case Unit. He thought he'd miss the adrenaline rush of arriving at crime scenes, his mind assessing every detail—an unlocked window, a TV humming in the corner, or a countertop obviously wiped down. It all mattered, as did the study of the victim, their age, profile, bruises or marks, entry and exit wounds, position of the body, and what, if anything, all of it could tell him. Cold cases, he figured, wouldn't be for him, but he was wrong. Which is why he finds himself, long past his shift, scanning case files created long before he became a detective, and the reason why is simple. The killer is still out there.

Operation Shadow, the brainchild of Assistant Deputy Commissioner Christopher Norris, was born out of many factors. The lack of a firm suspect was one. The unproven link between the victims was another. These, alongside the endless television documentaries and news headlines teasing the public, questioning the police, all reflected badly on the force. The point of Operation Shadow was to establish a solid link across the four female victims, and that, right now, was still uncertain. Sitting upright, Nick wonders about other potential victims out there, those stalked or attacked before killing became part of the killer's MO, and, with such a long time span, a copycat killer couldn't be ruled out either—imitation being a form of flattery. But despite the time lapse since the last victim, the clock was still ticking. This killer, or killers, is capable of the worst of crimes. They will strike again, including taking down whoever gets in their way.

4

ELIZABETH

I WAS SCARED LAST NIGHT, LISTENING FOR EVERY MINOR CREAK and sound, knowing being here in this house not only brings back memories of Nina going missing but also, by being alone, makes me vulnerable if he decides to terrorise me again . . . it's like I'm purposely placing myself in danger, goading him to harm me. I've already received a dozen text messages from Alison. She's tried to phone me too. I should call her back and behave like a grown-up, taking whatever lecture or anything else she decides to dish out, but I'm not ready for that. In part, I'm being selfish, and most likely unfair. Only, despite all the risks, I know being here is exactly where I need to be. It wouldn't take a genius to work out that for a long time I've been living a half-life, drifting without purpose, eroding any sense of self. So, for now, I need to sever all ties with my daughter, even if it risks losing whatever tentative relationship I still have with her.

Equally, though, I know this isn't all Alison's fault. She's tried. We've both tried, but unfortunately, I've realised a part of me wanted to remain stuck, because by staying that way, I could hold on to the hope that one day, if everything stayed the same, Nina would return.

Earlier, I thought about those facial reconstructions the police did ten years after Nina's disappearance, and then again five years later. How I'd looked into the eyes of this familiar stranger, reimagining

Nina as a teenager, and then as an adult, hoping I might see her out walking one day, or sitting at an open window, or even standing in a doorway, perhaps behind a door partially cracked open, finding my missing child in a stranger's face. That's one of the things you do when you lose someone, you keep reimagining the life they might be living. The one they might be living without you.

I send Alison a text message telling her I'm okay, and that I don't want her to fret, that I'm fine, and how it's not about her, it's about me, a form of cliché ex-lovers might use. I give her Ellie's address too, not wanting her to worry, but the significance of the location, ten doors up from her first childhood home, won't be lost on her. She won't be happy. So I wait until I see the two blue ticks telling me she's read it before I switch off my mobile phone.

I wonder if I'm the only woman in her sixties who has ever run away from home. Although, if I were actually missing, instead of a runaway, it would be a totally different scenario. There would be a police red alert of some kind, the missing person, me, being an older individual, and deemed high-risk, akin to people with disabilities or young children. They had something like that when Nina disappeared, which is one of the reasons I left a note for Alison—no family needs to live that twice.

The silence was weird waking up this morning—no clatter of dishes, or children being woken from sleep. There was no barking dog either, or the sound of multiple showers, Ciaran always having his first, feeling entitled, followed by Alison, then Emily, the others preferring baths. I wasn't sure how I felt about this new lack of sound, but I didn't dwell on it.

I've already made plans for today, something I've rehearsed so many times in my head, I've almost tricked myself into believing I've already gone back there.

Now, parking the car across the road from Massey Woods, this time I know it's for real. There aren't too many cars about, which also means the woods will be near empty. I want them that way, because it's within the solitude that I hope to remember.

As a young girl growing up, I used to run through these woods, full of fever, looking upward, umbrellaed by the trees, at times the clear blue sky winking through, as if to say, nothing bad can happen here, but that wasn't true. Bad things can happen anywhere.

Today, the sky is bright blue. It was that way when Nina went missing too. I take it as a sign, as if something is aligned, a nod to my belief that this reliving will have the perfect backdrop, just like that terrible day all those years ago, when the loveliness of a summer's afternoon offered its false safety.

The farther I go into the woods, the more I've the sense of years slipping by. Underfoot, there's the same dry mulch, as overhead I hear a scattering of birdsong. The trees sway too, breathing in deep, brittle branches, kissing one another, recounting the secrets of the woods, of others who've travelled the same path—young lovers, old friends, families on a day out, schoolchildren on a visit, but today it's only me. A woman who has walked the same path in her mind for over twenty-five years, who still remembers being a young mother with two little girls in tow, Nina, age five, and Alison, two years younger. Nina was always so protective of her younger sister, never thinking anything bad could happen to her—that was another mistake.

That day, both of them had dolls. Nina's doll had dark hair, identical to her own. Alison's doll was blonde, mirroring her soft curls. I remember how Alison used to carry her doll by the hair, her fist grabbing chunks of it, the unwitting creature bobbing along with no choice in the matter. Nina held her doll differently, cradling it in her arms, affectionate, caring.

Soon, I'll reach the clearing in the woods. This is the point where both girls decided to play a game, hiding behind bushes, before jumping out and saying boo, followed by shrieks of laughter.

A familiar pain pinches my chest, a form of twisted knot, as in my mind's eye I see Nina, her hair tied in a long dark plait resting on her shoulder. I see the doll too. Its eyes are blinking. I stop, attempting stillness, wanting to keep Nina's image in front of me, but I'm already too late, because the image is slipping away, and now, Nina is chasing Alison as part of the game. I call out as they get farther away from me, neither of them listening. The knot in my chest tightens.

Alison runs to her left, darting into a covert of bushes and small trees. Nina is a few steps behind her, pretending for Alison's sake that she can't catch up. Nina calls out to her sister. "Hold on. It's dark in there. I won't be able to find you." And soon, like her sister, she too is gone. I'm running now, toward the same group of trees, my body less agile with age, the limbs of an older woman, calling out, repeating their names over and over, the same way I did over twenty-five years before. And then I stop, staring into the darkness, both girls invisible, the birds suddenly silent. The trees are silent too, because now, all I can hear is my voice, screaming loudly, repeating their names, imagining them cuddled together, laughing, hoping that soon they'll jump out and scare me, and how afterward, I'll laugh too, and everything will be okay. Only, I'm not laughing. I'm terrified, and then I spot Alison's blonde curls, clutching her doll, looking scared.

"Where's Nina?" I scream, a part of me already knowing something bad has happened.

She shakes her head, crying now, losing her breath, gulping.

I look past the bushes and trees, hoping I'll spot Nina. Perhaps she's still hiding.

Alison can't stop crying, pulling my attention back to her.

"Where's Nina?" I repeat, angry now.

She shakes her head again.

I grip her by the shoulders, her panic escalating mine.

"She . . . went . . . with . . ."

"With what?"

"The man."

My mind flips, zillions of thoughts rattling forward, hard, terrifying memories of a truth I needed to keep buried.

"What man? Who?"

Alison shakes her head again.

"Nina," I scream, the sound somehow separated from me.

I'm running again. I don't know what else to do, but no matter how hard I search, or where I look, Nina isn't there. She's gone.

The knot inside me is now the size of my chest.

Time skips another beat, and then I stare down at my hands, the hands of an older person, a sixty-one-year-old woman, no longer a young mother. Today is my birthday, and when I least expect it, in a place beyond my reach, I hear Nina's child voice singing softly, like a lullaby: *Happy birthday to you, happy birthday to you, happy birthday to Mommy, happy birthday to you.*

I blow out a set of imaginary birthday candles into the empty woodland, one in which, as I stand here, no one looks on, or cares.

5

ELIZABETH

FOR A LONG TIME, I STAY IN THE WOODS, REEXAMINING THE VISUAL trails winding in and out of low trees, ferns, heathers, and ivy. My eyes chase patches of sunlight burning down on gnarled roots, broken trunks, moss, and twigs. In some ways, the woods are completely alien to me, my child stolen within them, yet I'm part of them, and I've earned the right to be here.

I've relived the afternoon Nina went missing many times, dissecting each millisecond of it, from the moments immediately before, during, and afterward. What if I hadn't allowed the girls to play that silly game? What if we hadn't gone to the woods? What if Alison hadn't chosen that place to hide? What if she'd listened when Nina warned her? What if the man was never there?

I'm crying now. You'd think after all this time, I wouldn't have any tears left, but that's the weird thing about grief, it travels its own path, and it, not you, is the one in charge.

Back at the car, I already know I'll revisit the woods again, hoping that by returning, a fresh piece of memory will come back, something hidden, stolen by the shock and disbelief of a lifetime ago, and how by being here, by coming back, I might finally unlock it.

When I reach Ellie's house, the little girl, April, is sitting at my front door, her face looking puzzled.

"You've been gone a long time," she says, her head tilted to the side.

I'm still reeling from my time in the woods, upset at this interruption, and not yet ready to assume the persona of someone who bothers with politeness.

"I didn't know you were keeping an eye on me," I snap.

Immediately, her face crumbles, picking up on my angry tone. It's not her fault. She's only a child. I attempt to take back my words, changing the subject. "How come you're not in school?" My voice gentler, putting my anger in check.

Silence.

She's still unsure of me, nervous after my angry outburst.

"It's a school day, isn't it?" I say, my words sounding more caring, curious.

"We've a day off," she finally replies, looking downward.

"Don't you have friends around here to play with?" The moment I ask this, I realise I'm being insensitive, as if in some way I'm expecting her to justify being alone.

If she takes offense, she hides it well, looking up and chirping, "I've a best friend called Jessica, and there's Jasmine too. She's the one with the rabbit. Both of them are from school, but they live far away."

"I see."

"Ellie was very friendly," she says, planking an exaggerated smile across her face.

I wonder if it's her turn to put me under the microscope, her opinion on Ellie's friendliness initiating a question mark over mine.

"Do you like school?"

"Oh yes," she says, her smile a little more relaxed, her eyes brighter. "I think I'm very popular, but I'm also the weirdest." She giggles at this, seemingly entertained by the contrasting notions.

"Why do you think you're the weirdest?"

"Because I'm different."

"Being different is good."

"That's what Mam says," she agrees, standing up. "Mam says being like everyone else can be boring."

She fixes her dress, which is crumpled around her legs, her dark untamed hair covering half her face. "Are you boring?" she asks.

I think about the question, before saying, "I don't know anyone quite like me." That knot in my chest tightens again.

"So, you're different too."

"I guess."

"You look sad," she says. "That's not good."

"I'm okay," I reply, despite it being a lie, remembering Ellie's words about April's absolute honesty, even if, at times, her words seem abrupt.

"You could try happy thoughts," she says. "That's another thing my mam says, but they don't work for me."

"No," I agree, "they don't work for me either."

I get closer to the front door. "Do you want to come inside?" I ask again, aware I need to keep my side of the accommodation bargain.

"Not yet."

I consider asking her why not, but instead I say, "Okay."

A second jumps forward.

"See you tomorrow then." She gleams, reconstructing that earlier exaggerated smile as she walks away.

"See you."

At the end of the laurel bushes, she pauses, turning around. "You have less wrinkles than Ellie."

"I'll take that as a compliment."

"It's not a compliment," she says, looking confused, "it's an observation."

"Right," I say.

"I'm glad you're back."

"I'm glad I'm back too."

I watch her walk away, seemingly content in the knowledge that I've returned, and that now, she knows exactly where I am.

Seconds later, as I'm closing the front door, I spot the car pulling up outside. I think about pretending I don't see it, or the driver. After all, I don't have to answer the door, but I already know, if I saw him, then he saw me too.

6

ELIZABETH

PART OF ME FREEZES WHEN HE RINGS THE DOORBELL, AS IF MY OLD life, the one I've just run away from, is invading far too soon. I don't rush. Instead, I linger in the hallway, steadying myself for the potential onslaught, because there will be one, that's one thing I'm sure of. The doorbell rings again. I tell myself that I'm no longer under his roof. I'm the one in charge here, but when it comes to my son-in-law, Ciaran, it's best to be on full alert.

When I open the door, I can tell he's fuming despite the stupid smile on his face. I'm a distraction from his day, and being Alison's errand boy isn't a title he wears well. I'd wager he wants to say something like, "Too busy to open the front door now, are we, Elizabeth?" but instead he asks, "Can I come in?"

"It's a free country," I say, smiling back at him.

He raises his eyebrows, a nonverbal but effective communication of being unimpressed.

"Did Alison send you?"

"Not exactly," he replies, standing opposite me in the hallway, his six foot two inches towering over my five-foot-four frame. You wouldn't think ten inches would make such a difference, but it does.

"Go through to the kitchen," I say, gathering myself, before following him.

He sits down without being asked. "So, what's it like, Elizabeth," he asks, "this newfound freedom?"

"More peaceful," I reply, sitting down opposite.

"You're not nervous?"

"No, why should I be?"

"Is there an alarm on this house?"

"It's a quiet street."

He raises his eyebrows again. "You can't be too careful, Elizabeth," he says, leaning in, his voice becoming a whisper. "Bad things happen all the time, and then there's your age to consider."

Right, I think, *this is the direction it's going in.* Undermine the subject. Inject fear. Point out the vulnerabilities.

"Only last week," he continues, "an old woman was found in the city beaten within an inch of her life."

"I'm careful," I say, keen to stop him in his tracks. "Would you like some tea, or coffee? Ellie has a cafetiere somewhere."

"Sure."

I stand up and open various cupboards underneath the kitchen counter. I'm sure that's where I saw the cafetiere. I spot it in the fourth cupboard.

"Why don't you sit down," he says then, standing up and again towering over me. "I'll look after things."

I don't want him taking over, but you have to pick your battles. Within seconds he's opening more cupboards looking for the coffee grounds.

"Alison wanted me to check you had enough food."

"I've already done the shopping," I say, feeling as if I'm being placed under a microscope.

"I can see that," he replies, picking up some chocolate cookies, followed by a packet of fairy cakes and a bumper bag of mixed jellies.

"The jellies were on *special offer*," I tell him.

He gives me a disapproving look. "What about your cholesterol? Alison won't be happy."

"Well, Alison won't be eating them," I snap back. "I'm not a child. I can manage my own eating regime."

"Let's keep it our little secret then," he says, "but remember to check the dates. The writing can be very small on these packets, and with your eyesight."

I'm able to see perfectly fine. I could argue the point with him, but the sooner he says what he has to say, the sooner he'll be gone. "Just as well," I mock, "I'm too old to die young."

"Indeed," he says, placing a cup with milk tea and a plate with three fairy cakes in front of me. The cakes feel like a form of entrapment. He pours his black coffee.

"If Alison didn't *exactly* send you, why are you here?"

"Because we care about you."

"Well, neither of you need to worry. I just want some space."

He eyes the fairy cakes. I already know he's going to tell Alison about the secret treats, which is another reason why I had to get out of there. The feeling that they're often conspiratorial about me, as if I'm a huge problem that needs to be constantly managed.

Plus, I also know what he's trying to do by being here. He wants to undermine me. I have his measure, because I've studied him a lot. He's different when Alison isn't around, and that coy and patronising thing he does is all part of his covert narcissism. I've read about it online. His type can be heavy on the fake charm, while sitting back, watching everything with a kind of quiet superiority. They smile sweetly, winning others over, charming their way into relationships to protect themselves, while being cruel to those they treat less favourably. It's a lot harder to convince someone that the so-called nice guy is an asshole when they've already won them over.

Alison was only a teenager when she met him, barely nineteen. Within a year, they were engaged, then married. I could see it all unfold right in front of me, and there wasn't a darn thing I could do about it. She wasn't going to listen to me, her desperation for "happily ever after" refusing to be knocked off its pedestal. Plus, I knew she needed to fill an emotional void, partly created by the loss of her sister, but also because of me. I pulled back from her, leaving her with no other option than to seek love and attention elsewhere. I think he recognised that too, her vulnerability. He's older than her, which she liked, but I've always been suspicious he recognised her desperation, that emptiness inside. An emptiness he was only too happy to fill, leaning into her willingness to be moulded. Sure, she's gone on to do great things in her career, now at senior management level in a multinational company, overseeing an entire department's budget. She's no longer a lovestruck teenager, but that doesn't fully change the relationship dynamics, even if, of late, I've heard her fighting back. Especially after that big promotion of hers. I bet he hated that, her being more successful than him, because that's the other thing I've come to realise. Mostly, as well as juggling her world of *endless responsibilities*, Alison is also avoiding her own set of eggshells, those between her and Ciaran.

He gives me another one of his patronising smiles, as I avoid eating the cakes sitting in front of me. I don't want him looking at me like I'm some kind of zoo animal. I'm not a spectacle, and I won't allow him to treat me like one.

"Not hungry?" he asks.

I shake my head, and wait. I'm sure the punch line, whatever it is, will be delivered soon.

"Don't you think it's time to stop this little rebellion of yours," he says, looking around the room, eyeing everything with a form of dismissive arrogance, including me.

It's my turn to raise my eyebrows. Part of me would like to take his superior attitude and shove a fairy cake right into it. I know his game, and he knows I know it. Which is another reason why his covert narcissism only comes out when it's just the two of us. The hair on the back of my neck stands up ever so slightly, but I keep my voice level, replying, "I don't want you, or Alison, to worry. I'm perfectly fine."

He jumps to his feet, pushing the chair back, his temper overflowing. I don't move. Best not to react.

He has his back to me now, standing at the kitchen window, before letting out a long sigh, as if I'm some kind of misbehaving child who has really pushed his patience.

"Alison won't be happy," he says. "This game of yours is hurting her."

Great, I think, *he's going for the emotional guilt card.* "It's not a game," I protest, "and I don't want to hurt anyone."

"No?" he says, turning around to face me.

"NO."

"Yet somehow, Elizabeth, you always seem to manage it."

"Manage what?"

"Hurting Alison."

The awkward silence that hangs in the air is there to intimidate me, but equally I know, he'll soon give up. He doesn't care enough to persist for long.

"Okay," he says then, as if resigned to the situation, "but after I leave, make sure you lock the windows and doors. At your age, you can't be too careful."

I want to say, I'm not living in a prison, only, I don't. Nor do I tell him that I make a point of always checking things are locked and secured. Either response would generate another, and I've no desire to extend this conversation.

"That old woman I was telling you about, Elizabeth, the one beaten within an inch of her life . . ."

"What about her?"

"She died yesterday. It was all over the news."

"Are you trying to scare me?"

"Nope, just making sure you're aware of the risks."

Again, I don't answer him. Let him be off with himself. He's already achieved what he came here for: (a) to unsettle me, (b) to be able to report back to Alison that he tried his best with the lunatic, although he won't use those exact words, (c) to ensure I realise that he'll call again if he, or Alison, think it's necessary, and (d) that any idea I might have had of being "away from it all" no longer exists.

"So, Elizabeth, you'll promise to lock the doors and windows after I'm gone."

"Yes," I say, wanting him to leave more than ever, my anxiety rising, but still trying to keep it in check—best not to poke the bear.

"Okay," he says then, leaning in, his large frame overshadowing me again, enhanced from all those multiple visits to the gym.

After he steps outside, I push the front door firmly shut, turning the double lock to secure it. I hear him walk away. Only for him, seconds later, to walk back toward the door again, turning the handle back and forth in fast, repetitive movements, causing the door and frame to rattle.

"Good girl," he says, sounding all smug.

In the past, I've tried to approach Alison about Ciaran's behaviour toward me, but I never got past first base. It wasn't that she dismissed me outright, but enough so I knew I probably wouldn't be believed. I'm used to not being listened to or believed. The police didn't want to listen to me either, especially with all my visits to the police station before moving in with Alison, when I thought someone was watching the house. The police never openly used the word "paranoia," but that's what they thought. In the beginning, they'd send a squad car around to appease my fears, but eventually someone suggested a dog. A dog didn't make any sense to me, because if there was someone watching the house, he wouldn't care about a dog. It wouldn't be a deterrent. Also, if the dog barked in warning, it would worry me even more, and it wasn't as if I could take the dog to the police station and ask it to give a statement. The word "nutcase" was never used either, but I'd wager it was thought too.

Once, after a particularly long session, as Alison led me toward the exit of the police station, in a glassed section, I spotted the reflection of the police officer I'd spoken to. He must have been having a particularly bad day, because he was making pretend gestures of strangling himself, his hands around his neck, his colleague laughing. They found it hilarious, but I didn't. Alison warned me I was in danger of becoming a nuisance. Logically, in my mind, the risk of becoming a nuisance was far more favourable than the risk of being in danger, but eventually, I stopped going altogether. I'm not sure the experience made me more resilient. I think it made me more stuck.

After I watch Ciaran's car drive away, I walk back toward the kitchen. I pause in the doorframe, looking into the room he just left, scanning it as if it's an empty stage set, checking that nothing is missing. I don't trust him, and objects going missing can be another warning sign. The first time, it was a cheap bracelet, a pink one with a silver edge, half a lifetime ago, but still, it was, and is, significant. Of late, other things have gone missing too. A gold pen, a set of stamps, and a letter opener. Alison thinks I lost them, but I know better.

Anyhow, once I'm positive nothing is awry in the kitchen, I sit down at the table again, staring at the fairy cakes, trying to decide between canary yellow, apple green, or the rose-pink icing. The canary yellow wins out. I pick up the cake, swallowing it in two large bites.

7

ISABELLA

(8 weeks earlier)

I LIE ON THE BEACH AS A LONE SEAGULL FLIES ABOVE ME. I CAN'T take my eyes off him or his circles of flight. He swoons downward toward the sea, before suddenly soaring. There's a kind of magnificence in his solitude, as I watch him go farther out, becoming smaller and smaller as he approaches the jagged coastline of Dalkey Island.

I sit up, my elbows digging deep into a mix of sand and grit. Today, the water is a deep shade of indigo blue, crawling toward the shore, the sun's reflection dazzling, its silver strands gliding with the ebb and flow. The bird, who is tiny now, reaches the island. I place a hand over my eyes, unwilling to lose sight of him, but then he's gone.

I stretch out, reconnecting with my body, thinking about the last few months of turmoil, while the easy sound of the ocean attempts to ground me. No doubt, a legacy from growing up by the sea. It's partly why I came here today, to reconnect, to seek calmness. I sink my fingers into the sand, which is hot to the touch, but as I dig deeper, I find a coolness free from the scorching sun.

A woman floats on her back in the water, the waves intermittently teasing her domed belly. Her skin is stretched, creating tiny white lines upward toward her belly button, her body surrendering to the weightlessness. The lightness a probable relief from the months of carrying an infant. A man shouts over, "Are you staying in there forever?" his tone impossible to determine.

"I might," she replies, laughing.

He's packing things up, sun mats, an umbrella, and a bright orange cooler bag. On his shoulder, there's another bag made of canvas, jammed with sun creams and towels.

"Don't forget my book," she roars.

His reflective sunglasses drop from his head onto his nose. I'm not sure if he's staring at me, but his eyes seem to linger. I take it as a sign to move on.

My baggage is less than theirs, sunglasses, lip balm, a lone bottle of sun cream, and a tiger-print wrap.

"Great weather, isn't it," he says as I tie the wrap around me.

"Terrific," I reply, already turning to walk away. An unexpected breeze touches my skin. A relief from the heat as trickles of sweat slide downward. I look at the woman again, oblivious to her partner's pleas to come out of the water, her swollen frame still bobbing, unwilling to leave the cherished buoyancy behind.

I check my watch. I'm due at work in an hour, but as I head toward the tunnel and the car park, I think again about the woman and her unborn child. I think about the undeniable connection between them, bonded by body and place. I think about the lone seagull too, gliding above the ocean, wings stretched, purposeful, and not for the first time over the last few weeks, that sense of foreboding I've been carrying raises its head. Perhaps that's why I quicken my steps as I notice the man has left his wife and is walking behind me toward the car park.

Near the tunnel, a young mother holds tight the hands of a little girl, a toddler, navigating their descent to the beach. The girl has wispy blonde hair. I notice her chunky arms and legs, along with her pink sequined sandals and matching swimsuit. The mother doesn't look out to sea. She only has eyes for the child, ensuring she reaches the beach without toppling over. As I get closer, I spot blobs of sun cream on the child's face, their whiteness battling the grassiness of her eyes. I step to the side, navigating my way past, thinking about the life I lost. The one I held inside me for eight weeks and four days. Initially unplanned, unwanted, but as time passed, how surprised I'd become that the idea had grown on me, before nature chose its own path and took that decision away.

I haven't spoken to anyone about the miscarriage, other than the staff at the hospital. Nor had I planned to tell my parents. I figured it would be better that way. A one-night stand, a pregnancy, and a miscarriage would have been a lot to deliver. Only, it didn't feel better, and certainly not after the car crash, the one that took both my parents from me.

The man's footsteps are closer now. I consider making a run for it, but instead I walk faster, telling myself I'm being stupid. Inside the car, I immediately lock the doors. He's at his car now, loading the boot. He isn't looking at me, but that doesn't remove the feeling, the one I keep having, especially of late, that someone is watching me.

I decide to make a phone call to work, telling them I'm unwell. Only, hanging up, I'm not sure what to do next. I already know I've changed from the woman I used to be. The woman before the miscarriage, and before, almost two weeks to the day later, that terrible car crash. My father was the one driving. He was killed outright, but my mother survived for another twenty-four hours, long enough to turn the already life-changing events into something more.

I message my aunt. She lives close by, and is probably the only one, right now, I can talk to. Because along with all the questions, there's another truth. The one that tells me, for most of my life, one way or another, I've seldom felt free. Rather, I've lived like a trapped insect inside a glass display.

I LEAVE THE CAR IN DALKEY VILLAGE, WANTING TO WALK THE REST of the way to Sorrento Park, where I'm due to meet my aunt. Making my way through the village, the vibe and energy of the place, with its art deco shopfronts and vibrant cafés, temporarily lifts my mood. I pass the bakery, with its intoxicating aroma of fresh bread and pastries, aware I'll need to avoid walking by the hotel where I'm helping out with the design work. They've been very understanding since my parents' deaths, but still, I pray no one sees me.

I'm still thinking about that man from the beach, the one who followed me to the car park, when I spot my aunt standing by a bench, unwilling to sit down until I arrive. She's my mother's sister, and the family resemblance is another trigger of my loss. Today, she's dressed in a peach cotton dress with white pumps. I'm in jeans and a loose T-shirt, having already changed in the car.

"Hi, Elaine," I say, exchanging hugs before sitting down.

"Are you unwell, Isabella? I was worried when I got your call."

"I rang in sick to work."

"Is it a stomach bug, because . . ."

"Nothing like that."

"What is it then?"

"Me, probably being sick in the head . . ."

"Don't be so hard on yourself. You've been through a lot."

"Maybe, but my head won't stop spinning."

"That's only natural, pet, considering everything."

"It's not just the car crash, losing both of them, it's . . ."

"What?"

I hesitate. Could I tell her about the miscarriage? Is there any point? I decide against it.

"Elaine, can I ask you something?"

"Of course."

"Did you ever get the feeling someone was watching you . . ."

"Like a stalker?"

"I guess."

"No. Jesus, Isabella, are you being followed?"

"I'm not sure."

"Have you gone to the police?"

"No . . ."

"Why not?"

"It's more an instinct than anything else."

"You can't be too careful."

"I could be overreacting, what with everything that's happened."

"Maybe it's shock. Grief can play tricks on you."

"Perhaps, but I've been feeling it for a while."

"Do you need to see someone?"

"A therapist?"

"It might help."

I shrug. "Look, that's not why I'm here. I wanted to ask you something about Mom and Dad."

"What about them?"

"It's something Mom said before she died."

"What?"

"She said the two of them always loved me . . ."

"Well, of course they did."

"No, let me finish. It was after she regained consciousness, with all those things attached to her, the drip, the heart monitor, her breathing so heavy, her constantly coming in and out of sleep, that she . . ."

"She what?"

"She told me, or rather, she warned me, not to look back."

"They say none of us should . . ."

"No, it was more than that. She said, 'Isabella, don't look back. There's danger there.'"

"Did she explain what she meant?"

"No, but it was then the nurse asked me to leave. Telling me Mom needed her rest. And then . . ."

My aunt puts her arms around me, already knowing what's coming next, that the following morning, my mother was gone. A massive stroke finishing off what the car crash began.

"She got out of bed," I say then. "That's what the doctors think brought on the stroke."

"Maybe she was delirious."

I shake my head. "No, she was trying to hide something."

"What?"

"A piece of paper with her handwriting on it."

"Was it a goodbye note?"

"No, but it must have been in her handbag for years. I found it in the wastebin after she died."

"Why do you think it was old?"

"It was folded and refolded over and over."

"What did it say?"

"That's the thing. It didn't say anything . . . it was an address."

"An address?"

"62 Charlesworth Avenue."

My aunt shakes her head. "It doesn't mean anything to me."

"No, but it meant something to my mother, along with her warning."

"Isabella, I'm not sure . . ."

"You don't understand. I can't stop repeating her words. She said, '*Isabella, don't look back. There's danger there*'—but what danger? And why was that address so damn important that she had to drag her sick body out of bed, risking her life, to get rid of it?"

8

HIM

She isn't at her usual spot, and he doesn't know why. He'd considered her reliable. It makes him angry that she's disappointed him, necessitating a change of plans. Which is partly the reason he goes into the bar.

Normally, he wouldn't visit a bar during the day, but the warm weather has brought a celebratory feel to the afternoon, with many already gearing up for the weekend.

Inside, the place is crowded, buzzing with loud voices and laughter, and an atmosphere that could easily shift up a notch. It doesn't take him long to spot the girl he followed. She's different from his current target, slightly younger and certainly looser with her tongue. He wonders if she knows he's studying her. She looks up on cue. He's confident she hadn't noticed him earlier, walking in behind her. If she had, he'd have noted the change in her demeanour—a faster walk, the tensing of her shoulders, ready to fight or take flight.

With him, it's all about removing any perception of threat, so the target is at ease, unaware. He's seen others play the opposite game, enjoying the tease, hollering after a passing female, making sexual gestures, all indicators of their sexual approval, despite the woman wanting none of it. Those predatory mind games aren't for him. He prefers to establish trust.

She's sitting with her friend. The friend's name is Jackie. From eavesdropping, he knows it's a colleague from work. Moments earlier, they'd made a private joke about it. People let lots of personal details slip when they think nobody is taking notice, and crowded places are the best, because it makes the target feel insular, invisible to the crowd, and to him.

Her friend is doing most of the talking, moaning about how her mother treats her like a child. She bores him, and for a second, he contemplates leaving, but then luck plays him a trump card. Two drunk guys start hitting on the women. They're younger than him, but that doesn't matter. He prides himself on keeping fit, regularly going to the gym, and being well able to hold his own.

Things are heating up. Jackie's looking around for help. Perhaps a member of security to come to their aid. The target is politely explaining they're out for a quiet drink, but the imbeciles are having none of it.

He walks toward them.

"Jackie," he says, as if she's an old friend.

She looks momentarily shocked, unsure why a stranger is calling her by name. He winks, forging a conspiratorial agreement.

"Any trouble here?" he asks.

"Fuck off," says the guy closest to Jackie.

This is his cue to grab the guy by the arm, twisting it hard behind his back. His drunken companion immediately registers disgust as he attempts to take a swing at the girls' new protector. The crowd pulls back, the spark of the unknown sending things spiralling. He figures it won't be long before the bouncers at the front door arrive, and seconds later, he's proven right. He can tell they're seasoned in the game of differentiating the good guys from the bad, placing him immediately in the former group. The drunks are given a swift exit, but both women still look nervous.

"Sorry, Jackie," he says, explaining how he'd passed their table earlier and registered the name, being the same as his sister's. They look relieved the crazy guys are gone—perfect.

"Can I buy you a drink? You look like you need one."

They mentally weigh up the pros and cons, but then Jackie says, "You've been too good already."

"No, I insist."

Politeness trumps, and they accept, unwilling to display rudeness to the guy who singlehandedly put himself forward as their protector.

It doesn't take long before he has them eating out of his hands. Spiking their drinks would have been easy, even if two targets are messy. They both asked about his career. He lied. An architect is his favourite, but today he opted for IT consultant, explaining he's project-managing a software app for the health industry. They seemed impressed.

After that, they freely gave information about their chosen careers, even if he suspected they were doing their own fair share of embellishing. It didn't matter. All he needed were details—location, work hours, start and finish times. After several rounds of drinks, the girls insisted on going home together. He wasn't sure if it was tiredness or reduced interest on his part, but both girls started to irritate him. Their nagging voices reminding him of his wife. Eventually they parted ways. Or, at least, that's what they thought.

Moments after they left the pub, he followed them, all the way to the potential target's house. If they'd reached Jackie's house first, and not the other way around, he might have struck, seizing the opportunity presented. But he's glad now he held back. Because his main target, the one he really cares about, is fully back in the frame, and soon, he'll make his move, and soon, like the others, she'll be his.

9

NICK

AFTER ANOTHER LONG SHIFT, IT'S PAST MIDNIGHT BY THE TIME NICK finally arrives home, the air in the apartment stale and clammy from the humidity of the day. He sets an air fan to top speed. If the previous nights are anything to go by, it'll be hours of twisting and turning in bed.

Until recently, after a tough day, he'd reach for a cool beer or a whiskey, but neither were an option. His "keep away from alcohol" plan didn't have room for exceptions. Instead, he takes a tub of "strawberry delight" ice cream from the freezer.

Waiting for it to defrost, he switches on Sky News, muting the volume, still thinking about Operation Shadow. Two victims mentioned they felt they were being watched, one having the sense they were also being followed. Another had an angry boyfriend, one fitting the psychological profile of a controlling partner, but who unfortunately had a rock-solid alibi. The last victim had an alarm system fitted weeks before her death. Perhaps her instincts warning her of danger. There were the missing items too, potential trinkets, which may or may not be relevant.

He takes his first scoop of ice cream before kicking off his shoes, remembering the times his father used to take him to Eddie Rocket's for knickerbocker glory ice cream as a child. On the side table is a photograph of his father in uniform. Both he and his dad trained in Templemore. Nick hears the voice of his captain at the training centre. "It's in your DNA, lad. Don't fight it. Go with it. Be like your dad." His father had gone with it all right, all the way to using his SIG Sauer service pistol several days after retirement to blow his brains out.

Had Nick forgiven him? No. How could he? He was still angry his father took the easy way out. That's what three months of therapy had cleared up for him. That, and the suspicion that if his father really loved him, he wouldn't have done it. His father's suicide, his therapist explained, felt like a betrayal. Someone he trusted, looked up to, had let him down, thereby altering Nick's worldview. He figured she was right about that too. It was another reason he'd decided to drop the booze for a while. The heavy drinking had sent his head to dark places. He wasn't willing to take the risk that the DNA inherited from his father went beyond the needs of a detective to solve a case but also included self-destruction.

Could he end up like his father, going to his grave desperately unhappy, haunted by an investigation he couldn't solve, that of the schoolgirl Nina Harte? Nick was only a teenager when she disappeared, but his father, the lead detective, had been obsessed with the case for years, and the questions surrounding her disappearance never left him. Culminating, some thought, years later, in him taking his own life.

10

ELIZABETH

IT'S DARK IN THE BEDROOM WHEN I AWAKE. MY MOUTH IS DRY, AND my heart is racing. It's not just because of Ciaran's house call yesterday; it's because I had that horrible dream again. I dreamt I was back in the woods. I was trying to find Nina, but each time I thought I was close to her, she'd drift away.

I throw the duvet aside and sit up in bed, a sort of physical acknowledgment to my brain that the dream isn't real, but the nightmare, the unknowing, is still my life.

Being here, in this house, on the road we used to live on when Nina disappeared, is triggering other stuff too. Yesterday, I thought I heard Nina and Alison playing outside, but when I reached the window, I realised it wasn't them. I was immediately upset. I'd wondered if I'd made the right decision to come here after all, a cloak of sadness taking hold, one I'm all too familiar with, including how it can suffocate. I didn't cry, but they say not crying is a sign of depression too, because when you're in a really dark place, crying is pointless. The depression quiz clarified lots of things for me, including how my lack of interest in daily life, feeling lost, unsure how I might find happiness again, are all clear red flags too. Tick, tick, and tick.

I get out of bed, wrapping myself in my dressing gown, feeling strange being away from the place I've called home for the last few years, even if it didn't really feel like home, even if I felt like a visitor.

Alison made huge efforts at the start, but I took her well-meaning words, turned them upside down, inside out, and shook them for all they were worth, before scattering the remnants. The remnants told me I was a burden, something that required fixing. Only, I didn't want to be fixed. The experts call this the "pre-contemplation stage," when you haven't yet admitted to yourself that you've an actual problem. It's at that point you try to avoid conversations with others for fear they might attempt to change you or intervene in some way. Alison gently suggested I might "talk to someone," someone other than herself, a professional who could help me.

"Help with what?" I shot back. I knew I was being unfair, but a cornered rat has limited options, and no matter how much you love someone, if you have to, you will attack.

I pick up my mobile phone, sending another short reply to her latest series of text messages. None of this is her fault. Except, when I think about the woods, and I relive that afternoon from years before, I remember how angry I was with her. Why did she have to run away to hide? Why did she go somewhere difficult for Nina to find her? Why didn't she tell the man to stop, to not take Nina?

When I think about my anger back then, I hate myself for it. No sane person would be angry with a child, yet I was, and if honesty is being dredged up and examined for all it's worth, I also know, even as a child, she sensed it too. Perhaps, back then, when neither of us had a name for it, or had properly acknowledged its existence, the divide between us, the wall growing brick by tiny brick, cemented itself into the ground, solidifying, until, when we finally recognised it for what it was, it was already too late. A part of me is still angry, but not with Alison, with myself.

I've grown to realise something else too. The love you bear for your child, the biological pact between you, even if you travel a complicated path, like the murky one I've travelled with Alison, that primal link is always there. Only, what also exists is another truth. One that is hard to admit, that when it comes to Nina, losing a child trumps all other cards. Something different happens when that primal link is severed, when your child, your firstborn, the one you carried for nine months and five days, the infant you watched over from her very first breath, smile, tooth, and her first attempts at crawling, taking those momentous steps toward independence, is stolen from you. The void left behind is not only dark and cavernous, and filled with unanswered questions, it also holds despair.

At the bedroom window, I stare out at the night sky. If I try hard enough, I know more stars will appear, because that's the other thing I've learnt. If you're not careful, the darkness can blind you from seeing things right in front of you.

It's only then I hear a noise from across the street and my attention is drawn to a young woman, probably in her late twenties, or early thirties, opening her upstairs bedroom window. She's sitting at her dressing table, the same room I'm standing in on the opposite side of the street. I immediately make comparisons between us. She's young. I'm old. She looks happy, while I'm sad. I'm standing in the dark, while she's sitting with the lights on, removing makeup from her face, a determination and eagerness about her. She should be aware I'm watching her, but she isn't. I guess that's the kind of knowledge that comes with age too. The understanding that there are things in life you cannot see, things you should be aware of, and if you're not careful, not only will you miss them, but the people lurking in the shadows will do you harm.

I check the time on my mobile phone—12:15 a.m. She was there at the same time last night too, removing the previous day's makeup. She reminds me of Nina, the way she might look if I'd witnessed her growing up. I envy this girl, this stranger living across the street. I envy her confidence, her free spirit, sitting there with the lights on and the window open, without fear, projecting herself to the world in the same way an actor would project themselves onto a movie screen, almost as if she wants people to see her. Unaware, others, those she cannot see, could do her harm.

I stay by the window until she turns off the lights, as if I'm some kind of gatekeeper watching over her. And then, like the previous night, when the room darkens, she doesn't close the window or draw the curtains. *She's taking a risk*, I think, but even so, she will fall easily into sleep, the trials and tribulations of her day forgotten or reimagined with a joy I no longer have.

I decide to take a sleeping pill to shut out all the negative thoughts. The water glass by the bed is empty, so I walk downstairs to refill it. In the hallway, I notice a folded sheet of white paper on the floor. Unsure how it arrived there, I'm nervous picking it up, but unfolding it, I see a child's handwriting.

The words on the piece of paper are surrounded by Pokémon stickers carefully crafted into a circle. There's a heart drawn with a bright red crayon too. I see April's name at the bottom, before reading aloud: "'*I'M GLAD YOU'RE DIFFERENT TOO.*'"

11

ELIZABETH

I DIDN'T RETURN TO THE WOODS TODAY, THE EFFECT OF LAST NIGHT'S sleeping pill having taken its toll. My mood is still shifting downward, and I'm not completely sure why. Maybe the thought of this adventure, if you can call it that, gave me a temporary purpose, and now I'm here, I realise the problem isn't where I am, but who I am.

This kind of thinking isn't good. I feel tired too, another warning sign, but I don't want to "take to the bed," so instead, I cover myself with a blanket on the couch.

It isn't long before I drift off, and it's in sleep that I hear the singing, along with the intermittent giggles. It must be Nina and Alison again. They're out in the garden. Why aren't they at school? I get mildly irritated. I need to tell them to come inside, only then, I remember, Nina isn't here. She's missing. The singing should stop, but it doesn't.

I sit up with a jolt, the blanket falling to the floor. My body is stiff, so I move slowly, another joy of getting older, and before long, I find myself at the kitchen window, staring into the garden. I can't see anything, and then, I understand why. The singing is coming from next door. Despite being awake now, I'm sure it's Nina. I'll need to hurry. I can't risk losing her again. I dart outside, not bothering to close the front door behind me, screaming "Nina!" at the top of my lungs, and soon, I'm at the side gate of the house next door, and moments later, I'm standing in the garden. I see a young girl, her expression startled, and then someone else, a woman. I'm already too late to retreat when I realise the young girl is April. She and the older woman, most likely her mother, are both staring at me.

A wave of sadness and shame hits me at once, part of me shrinking inside. They'll think I'm crazy, and maybe they're right. "I'm so sorry," I say, my face now hidden behind my hands. "I didn't mean to upset anyone."

When I finally take my hands away, the woman has her arms wrapped around April, protective, but April seems to be having none of it, instead shrugging her mother away, before walking toward me.

"Were you having a meltdown?" she asks, tilting her head as if examining my face for clues.

"Maybe," I say, trying to pull myself together. Shit, shit, and shit. I'm both embarrassed and ashamed, like I'm some kind of shoplifter who's just been caught stealing.

Now, the woman steps forward. "I'm Patricia, April's mom." She stops a couple of feet away from me. "I've been meaning to call over and officially introduce myself."

"Elizabeth," I say, relieved neither startled party seems to be holding a grudge.

"She's different," April explains.

"Oh?" her mom replies.

"I'm nothing special," I say, putting my hand out to shake hers like I'm a regular person and not some madwoman invading their back garden, searching for a daughter from a quarter of a century ago.

"Can she stay?" April pleads, as if I've now reached the elevated status of potential playmate.

"I guess," her mother replies.

I suspect it's not the most unusual question she's ever been asked by April.

"I'll be inside," her mother adds, "if you need me."

April sits on one of the two garden swings.

"This one is yours," she says, grabbing the other one and pushing it toward me.

She starts to swing, and I do too. I must look ridiculous, but I don't care. I spot her mother staring at us from the kitchen window.

"Why are you always sad?" April asks, her legs out straight, propelling herself forward into the air.

"I lost my daughter," I say, so matter-of-factly it takes me by surprise.

"How can you lose a person?"

I hear the *whish, whish* of the swings. "I'm not altogether sure, but it happened."

"Will you ever find her?"

"Probably, possibly."

Whish, whish.

"You need to decide which," she states, stopping her swing dead.

I stop mine too, staring back at her, somewhat shocked by what appears to be such absolute certainty and determination on her part, and a maturity that seems far in advance of her years. She takes my lack of a response as an invitation to fill in the gaps.

"Possibly isn't bad," she says, talking fast, "it doesn't mean you won't find her, but probably is better, as it's more likely that you will."

"I never thought of it that way."

"I think about choice all the time," she sighs, her eyes open wide.

"Why?" I ask, somewhat apprehensive about what she'll say next.

"I'm scared of regret."

"Scared?" I ask, thinking about all the stuff I regret too.

"Yes, once I spent a whole month deciding which Tamagotchi I wanted for my birthday, and every time I made up my mind, I'd start wondering about the one I didn't pick."

"I'll go with possibly."

"You're looking sad again," she says, her words no longer at breakneck speed. "I don't want you to be sad, Elizabeth."

I don't want to look or be sad either, as I wonder, not for the first time, if something fundamental changed in me all those years before, when evil visited, and if it's even possible it could ever change back.

I realise too late, she's crying.

"I'm sorry," I say then, fast, not wanting to upset her, as her face collapses and before I know it, the crying turns into a wail, wild and unexpected.

"ELIZABETH, I SO HOPE YOU FIND YOUR DAUGHTER. IT MUST BE SOOOOOO HARD FOR YOU."

"Please stop crying," I say, slightly panicked, "I don't want you to cry. I don't want anyone to cry."

This seems to settle her, as I realise she's breathing in and out, slow and deep, to calm herself.

"It's okay," she gasps. "I cry all the time."

I don't know what to say, so instead I stay quiet.

"I don't want to grow up either," she says then, as if this new direction is somehow connected.

"Why not?"

"My teacher says, because she's an adult, she doesn't get toy presents anymore. I wouldn't like that. I don't want people buying me curtains and things."

I stare back at her, still attempting to understand, having never met a child quite like her before. "Maybe," I say, offering comfort, "when you're an adult, you won't mind so much."

"I will," she replies, adamant, her face grimacing for dramatic effect. "I'll hate it."

"Right."

"Large crowds and noise bother me too."

"Okay."

"At parties I get overwhelmed," she says then, talking fast again. "Everything gets jumbled up, the people, the noise, the lights . . . attacking me like it's an *alien* invasion."

"Alien?"

"You don't understand, because you're not autistic."

I want to say there are lots of things I don't understand. I don't understand why Nina is missing, or why some men are so cruel, or even if I'm doing the right thing, placing myself and possibly others in danger. Because, by picking up the pieces, attempting to find Nina after all this time, I could draw attention to myself, and then, the man who took her, the man I hate more than anything else in this world, who is capable of enormous cruelty, could come back, putting myself, and anyone connected to me, at risk. But instead, I say, "I feel a bit like that at times. As if there are too many things attacking me all at once. Other people can't work out what's going on inside my head. It's not because they don't want to, they're just not able to."

"Like the aliens."

"Yes."

"I'm sorry about your daughter, Elizabeth," she whispers so sincerely, I nearly want to cry. "I do hope you find her."

"I hope so too."

We both resume swinging, a mutual understanding reached.

"I should probably go," I tell her. "I left the front door open."

"Okay," she replies, smiling, before again stopping her swing dead.

I stop mine too.

I see her mother approach. I wonder why she didn't intervene when her daughter was upset moments earlier, but then I see something in her expression, as I consider if, like her daughter, she too was putting me through some kind of test.

She's standing beside me now. "Thanks, Elizabeth," she says, her words low enough for only my ears. "Sometimes April feels things very deeply, but with patience, she finds her way."

"I didn't do anything special."

"You didn't rush her. That's important."

I nod, and as I walk away, I think maybe I'm a bit like April too, both of us navigating worlds we sometimes find overwhelming and hard to bear.

I've almost left the garden when April shouts after me. "Elizabeth, I think I really like you now."

"That's good," I say, "because I think I really like you too."

12

HIM

The target left a half hour ago. He slips into the busy street unnoticed, having perfected the ability to disappear within a crowd. Seconds later, he picks the lock.

His eyes scan the interior, kitchen, living room, bathroom, and finally, the bedroom. He's already decided on the basic locations for the cameras. One in the hall, kitchen, and living room, and two in the bedroom. Location is important, as he must be certain visuals aren't obscured by daylight or artificial lighting. The spy cameras are fitted with audio too, so he will need to be careful, ensuring nothing close by, like the sound of an oven fan, compromises the transmission. The last and most important factor is discretion—where will the cameras be hidden best.

When all the cameras are in place, he savours a few moments, picking up objects, books, running his gloved hands along tabletops, familiarising himself with her home—leaving the bedroom for last. It's here the real treasures lie. The strands of hair from the pillow, the fresh body smells from discarded clothes on a chair, the scents from her dressing table, as he imagines her wearing different fragrances, him moving in close, expectant.

He's not sure how much time he has, so despite wearing gloves and a mask, he quickly wipes down any surfaces that might betray him—door handles, countertops, light bulbs, aware you can now swab for DNA from a person's breath, even on glass.

He knows he shouldn't take a trinket, but it's too hard to resist. Like the placing of the cameras, he considers his choices, working out which items are easily forgotten, yet firmly part of the target's life.

Through the window, he checks the street below, making sure her car hasn't yet returned. Finally, he settles on something from the dressing table, so insignificant it's ideal—a piece of tissue previously placed to her lips, ensuring her lipstick is evenly distributed—as he mutters to himself, "Pucker and pout."

13

ISABELLA

(7 weeks earlier)

I ARRIVE AT THE ADDRESS IN THE MIDDLE OF RUSH HOUR TRAFFIC, driving through streets I'm unfamiliar with, searching for a parking spot. I find one less than a two-minute walk from the house. I'd hoped I'd be able to find a spot directly opposite, to study the house from the safety of the car, but in the end, I'm glad of the fresh air to ready myself.

Getting closer to 62 Charlesworth Avenue, something weird hits me. It feels strangely familiar in a way the online Google map image didn't, and there's no denying I've a clear sense of being here before, but when?

Opening the garden gate, I walk along the fractured gravel path to the front of the property, Georgian in design, with a half-circle of hand-painted glass above a black door. There's a doorbell to the right, but after a couple of silent pushes, I realise it's no longer working. I knock, even though, with the run-down condition of the house, I don't expect an answer. Still, I try it once more, and I'm about to step back into the garden, to peer into the ground floor bay window, when I hear someone call out hello. At first, I think it's coming from inside, but then I realise the voice, which is female, is from the house next door.

"Are you with the estate agents?" the woman asks.

"I . . ."

"I've the keys if you need them. He said someone might call to take photographs."

I raise my mobile phone. "That's me," I say as I take a quick photo of the house, "but I'll need some internal shots too."

"Right," she says, handing me the set of keys. "I'll be here for another hour, but if I'm gone, just pop them in the letterbox."

I wait for her to close her front door, still taking pretend photos of the external area, before turning the key with the label FRONT DOOR into the lock.

Inside, the hallway is devoid of any furniture, the walls covered in old and faded woodchip wallpaper and painted a deep shade of burgundy. I've the same sense of familiarity I felt outside, as I note that downstairs, there are four doors, with two on either side. I push open the first on the left, which leads into the front living room with the bay window. There's a '60s-style tiled fireplace in the centre, almost offensive to the original features of high ceilings, picture rails, and Georgian sash windows. The room, like the hallway, stinks of damp and rot. Under my feet, the exposed floorboards are painted a chipped black, and apart from the daylight coming in from outside, everything feels oppressive, as if, in this place, something horrible is seeping into me, a memory, a feeling, what?

I make my way in and out of the other ground-floor rooms. In them, I don't have that same sense of familiarity, but at the end of the hallway, near the staircase, that oppressive feeling returns. I snap more images, although I'm not sure why, as my lie about being an estate agent/photographer doesn't need to be proven here.

Standing at the end of the staircase, the one leading to the upper floor, I'm suddenly caught unawares again, an immediate sense of dread coming over me. There's something about this spot that scares me.

Even though I'd prefer not to, I close my eyes to work out why. Only, almost immediately, I open them again, because the voices, unknown and unfamiliar, are harsh and loud, invading the creaking silence of the house, and me.

None of this makes any sense. Why did my mother have this address? Why did she keep that piece of paper for so long, that the folds were almost threadbare? Before coming here, I'd thought this house would probably mean nothing. That there would be a perfectly logical reason why it's connected to my mother, except now, I feel there must be something more. It's not only the sense that I've been here before, or the knowledge that my mother, believing she was near death, desperately needed to get rid of that piece of paper. It's a weird feeling of history, of something possible, but yet unknown, and if my instincts are correct, whatever that something is feels both dark and ominous.

I take the first step onto the staircase, easing myself upward one step at a time. As I do this, I scan the different angles, with the ground floor becoming farther from view, all the time experiencing a sense of hot and cold, like that hide-and-seek game, when others roar "hotter," "colder," "lukewarm." But hotter and colder from what?

The second floor has more woodchip paper on the walls, each painted in a variety of dark reds, charcoal greys, and chocolate browns. In some areas, the wallpaper is peeling off with dampness, the sense of abandonment screaming out loud and clear. The property, I'd wager, was likely rented at some point, the location being so close to the city centre. If I were an actual estate agent, it could be described as a period property filled with potential—and no doubt, many would be interested.

Upstairs, I don't have that same sense of uneasiness or familiarity I felt downstairs. Could I have visited here as a child, and perhaps only stayed in the hallway, or in that living room?

After a few minutes, I descend the staircase again, and once more, that oppressive feeling returns. Did something happen here that frightened me? Is it somehow locked in my memory?

I stand on the edge of a dusty Persian hall runner, and again, I feel this particular spot is important. I take more images of the hallway with my phone, wondering if perhaps later, other bits about this place will make more sense. It's only as I'm about to leave that I notice the back door leading to the rear garden. I turn the handle, expecting it to open, but it's locked. I try each of the keys on the key ring, but none work. I'm considering asking the neighbour if there are any more, when I hear a knock on the front door. "Hello," calls a female voice through the letterbox, which I recognise immediately as the next-door neighbour.

I open the door. "Almost done," I say. "I just need some shots of the rear garden."

"Rear garden?" she quizzes.

"Yes," I say, pointing in the direction of the back door. "I don't seem to have a key for that one."

"Strange," she says, "let me try."

Like me, she puts each key in the lock, only for them to jam. "Maybe you could check back at your office," she says, "see if there's another set of keys."

"I'll do that," I say, deciding it's probably time to retreat in case she pushes the point, and suggests phoning my fake office.

Once outside, I breathe in deep, double-checking, as I've often done of late, that no one is following me. I take my time returning to the car, as if my physical and emotional self needs everything to slow down. I have to work out why this place felt the way it did. Could I have been here before? Could my mother have brought me here? And if so, why?

14

ELIZABETH

I SPREAD THE NEWSPAPER CLIPPINGS OF RACHEL MEADOWS'S MURDER investigation out on the living room floor. It took one of those *Unsolved Mysteries* on television for me to really sit up and take notice of Rachel's death. The poor girl had been raped too, but according to the television documentary, DNA was in its infancy back then. There wasn't even an Irish database, something about "personal rights and protections" or other such nonsense. I scan one of the articles, all the way down to the part about an item going missing before Rachel's disappearance, something the police weren't sure might be important. It could be nothing, but still, I know from all those true-crime series, it's good to keep an open mind.

The suitcase I brought to Ellie's house is open on the floor too. It has the VCR tapes in it, the ones with the recordings of the early police press conferences and other public appeals. Ellie's old VCR player still works. I'd checked that before packing the tapes. At Alison's, it's all high-tech apps and remote-controlled devices. If a VCR ever existed, it would have been put in the rubbish skip long ago.

I can't stop my hands from shaking as I place the tape into the VCR. Why am I so nervous? Isn't this why I'm here, to revisit, go back, remember, to attempt to find something I might have missed the first time around? It could be part of the post-traumatic stress, that feeling of intense distress at real or symbolic reminders of the trauma. Either way, the shaking won't stop.

FOCUS, I need to focus, and soon, the tape glides into the machine as if the past is still within easy reach. I press play, the curtains drawn, sitting back in a darkened room alone. I see myself from years before. I barely recognise myself. I look so young. After only a few seconds, I rewind the tape. I repeat this over and over, needing to take in every aspect, knowing this time, I can't afford to miss a thing.

The next time I press play, I turn the volume down. I watch the younger me enter the room, my head bent downward, my body stooped, as if there's an invisible weight on my back. There are flashing lights too, cameras clicking at speed. My late husband, Alison's father, sits beside me. He looks like a stranger, this man who became part of my life soon after Nina was born. He played a role, a pretence this younger, more stupid me thought could fix things, make them whole.

The police officer sitting to my left, DI Matthews, the one leading the investigation, clears his throat. There are more flashing lights. The reporters in the room now having a direct shot of the distraught mother—me. I look her in the eye, trying to remember what she was thinking, but I already know the answer.

She was thinking she didn't want to be there. That she should be out looking for Nina, but that the police, especially the lead detective, thought it important the family appeal to the public. And how, for a whole different set of reasons, ones she hadn't yet shared, she questioned whether the press conference, rather than helping Nina, would give her abductor an even greater sense of control. That despite him taking her daughter, this opportunity to watch her squirm, being brought out for public show, would give him pleasure.

I rewind the tape again, remembering how, back then, everything seemed to happen at such speed. How I barely heard things, barely saw what was going on, the grief cannibalising everything. This time, I put the sound back on. I listen as members of the police bring the public up to speed, emphasising how Nina may be still out there, a child who needs to be reunited with her family. She will be frightened, the senior investigating officer tells them, but with their help, they and the police can work together toward getting Nina home safe.

Did I believe him? Did this younger me still have hope?

I wait as the microphone is placed in front of me, the grieving mother, the crescendo of the press conference, my words the heart and soul of the appeal, as more cameras click. I'm transfixed watching this younger version of myself, her hands moving closer to the microphone, her breath, as if suddenly caught unawares, sounding too loud as she leans in. My late husband moves the microphone forward, reducing the volume, and then the younger me readies herself, thinking about what she's going to say. I already remember what she does next. She looks up, staring directly at the camera, as if she's talking straight to the man who took Nina, and says, "Give her back to me. She's mine, not yours." More camera lights click on and off as the younger me continues to speak, the rest of her words rehearsed, sentences agreed upon with the police, urging the public to help, expressing a mother's love, the devastation she and Alison's father are going through, and the need, the desperate plea, to get Nina back.

I pause the tape, temporarily trapped in time, as my mind drifts back again, thinking about the hours that slipped away, the hope everyone told me to hold on to, the drug-induced sleep, others telling me I needed rest, that I was no use to Nina without it. All their voices issuing instructions, including the police. It felt as if my world kept getting smaller, constantly being crushed from the outside in, and as time passed, it all became even more hopeless, because what I remember most, apart from the fear and loss, is my inability to change a single thing, regardless of how many press conferences took place, or words of comfort issued by the police, telling me they were doing everything they could, because deep in my gut, I knew, Nina wouldn't be coming home.

I press play again in time to see my late husband's hand touching my back, offering comfort. I'd forgotten about that, the love and support he once offered. I feel a heaviness in my chest. I stop the tape, suddenly overwhelmed.

I think about everything that has happened to me, all the aspects of my life that have made me the person I am today, including that latest visit from my son-in-law, Ciaran. I wish I could undo everything bad that has ever happened to me, only I can't. I know things I wish I didn't know. And I don't know things I should, in much the same way that Alison doesn't realise the type of man she's married to, but I do. He's not only cruel, manipulative, and controlling, he's also capable of physical harm.

I stare at the paused image on the VCR, my late husband still stalled in time. He hadn't known the truth back then, but over time, like everything else, it too would soon unravel. I guess I wasn't really surprised that soon after Nina's disappearance, he left me. Not when he discovered I'd lied to him. But mostly now, when I think of him, I feel a huge sadness, not only because our marriage ended, but because less than a year after Nina's disappearance, that awful cancer took hold of him, eating away at his body day by day, until finally, when the end came, it was a blessing, taking him, at the very least, out of his pain.

Only, the truth is, other pain remained, as it always does, for those left behind, especially Alison, losing her father, her sister, and in the end, being left with only me, a broken thing.

Looking down at my hands, I turn them palms up. I let out a low gasp, seeing the markings around my wrists, markings from being tied with rope.

15

NICK

NICK SPENT THE MORNING WITH RACHEL MEADOWS'S PARENTS, mainly because aspects of her case file held blanks. His visit proved useful, confirming Rachel, like two of the other victims, was missing for a prolonged period of time before her death, creating another potential link across the crimes. It also meant whoever took her likely kept her alive for a reason, and therefore needed a place to keep her hidden.

Staring at the evidence board in his office, outside of the victims' commonality of age, all of them had different careers. Their level of social standing was different too. And simple attractiveness alone was too broad a stroke to connect them. Slightness of frame and slim fingers could also fall within the realms of chance, but still, it couldn't be ignored.

Something else Rachel's parents told him was interesting too. They said before Rachel disappeared, her friends believed she was romantically connected to someone other than her ex-boyfriend. It was a fresh lead, as whoever this mystery man was hadn't been within the thrust of the initial investigation.

His mobile phone rings, and, recognising the assistant deputy commissioner's number, he answers.

"I'm assuming, boss, this isn't a call about my welfare."

"You assume right. Any progress?"

"Some early shoots."

"There's pressure on this one."

"I know."

"Some are questioning my choices."

"About choosing me?"

"Look, I know you're the right man, so to hell with them, but you have to understand, I'm heavily invested here. I'll need you to come back with answers."

"We're on the same page."

"Maybe, but I think a meetup is in order."

"When?"

"I'll call to your place this evening. Considering the sensitivity of this one, it would be best."

"Okay."

"Seven?"

"Fine."

Nick hangs up. Christopher Norris may be saying he has his back, but he'll need to give him something. The supposed "mystery man" was at too early a stage to be celebrating, so it'll have to be something else, and right now, everything pointed to the time lag between Rachel going missing and her ultimate death. And, if the killer had held her somewhere, identifying that location would be key.

NORRIS IS ALWAYS PUNCTUAL. AT 7 P.M. EXACTLY, NICK BUZZES HIM up, leaving the apartment door ajar as he waits for him to climb the stairs. Nick tidied the apartment earlier too, knowing that as well as punctuality, Norris likes order.

"A filthy night," Norris notes, strutting in as if the place is his.

Through the living room window, Nick sees a dark grey sky, murky with rain. "It's Ireland," he replies, aware they'll soon dispel with formalities.

"Let's get to it," Norris says, sitting down. "What do you have?"

Nick considers starting with a delaying tactic, so he begins with a reminder of the ground rules. "When I took this on, boss, I understood time wasn't an issue."

"I know."

"Cold cases have a time clock of their own."

"I know that too, Nick, but nothing lasts forever."

"I also understood the decision to keep this insular—a small team, initially myself, and then later, others, if need be, along with access to supports, including sensitive data—was because of the requirement for discretion."

"We don't want those media clowns dancing all over us, sniffing something's happening. When we're on solid ground, we'll broaden the team. Until then, we're keeping this close."

"Gotcha."

"Listen, Nick, you were picked because you think outside the box, seeing things others miss. So, let's cut to the chase. Where are we?"

"It's complicated."

Norris takes in the room. "Right then, what's a guy got to do around here to get a drink. It's been a stinker of a day."

"I've nothing alcoholic."

"It's not Lent, or is the bloody calendar as messed up as everything else?"

"I'm on the dry."

"Is this some kind of self-health kick, cleansing the system and all that crap?"

"Something like that."

"I hope you're not going soft on me. Next you'll be ordering Diet Coke with a dash of fucking lemon."

"I've water, or . . ."

"Don't bother. I'm already bored with your company. Tell me what you have."

Nick remains standing. "There are patterns," he says, "to multiple investigations, and this one is no exception. What's critical is determining which are false patterns and which are concrete ones."

"Go on."

"The timeline is key."

"Why?"

"Because the period between the confirmed disappearance of the victims, to the discovery of the remains, in three of the four cases, is now similar, meaning the killer held them somewhere prior to death."

"With what purpose?"

"As yet unknown."

"Hasn't this been hashed out before?"

"It was examined in two cases, but the time lag has now been extended to a third, meaning we're potentially looking at one killer in three of the investigations."

"Which one is newly in the frame?"

"Rachel Meadows. Initially, because of the hostile relationship with her parents, a precise timeline wasn't possible. Now, like the other two, it establishes another time lag. Two similar timelines could be dismissed as a coincidence, but a third is harder to ignore."

"Is it enough to conclusively link them?"

"We'll need more, but there's also another possibility."

"What?"

"A copycat killer."

"Are you serious?"

"Kimberly Campbell's body, the fourth victim, turned up exactly three years to the day from the time the third victim, Marie Byrne, went missing. It's possible someone is following a pattern."

"A fan of the killer?"

"Maybe."

Norris lets out a sigh, as Nick sits opposite, deciding it's time to change tack, bringing the discussion closer to home.

"I've been thinking about my father's death."

"Yeah?"

"You two were close."

"We joined the force at the same time."

"Why do *you* think he did it?"

"Who knows."

"Some say he missed the force."

"It's in our DNA."

"Others say it was that case, that missing schoolgirl Nina Harte."

"Look, Nick, people have all sorts of theories why folks do things, but the reality is this: only your father knows the truth, and right now, he isn't talking."

"What about the mother, Elizabeth Harte?"

"What about her?"

"Maybe I should talk to her."

"Jesus, Nick, are you even listening to yourself. Apart from anything else, she's a nutjob."

"I don't understand."

"I don't like speaking bad of the woman, but she isn't right in the head. Understandable, after everything she's been through. Losing her child hit her hard, and twenty-five years is a long time without answers, but for a while there, she was in and out of police stations spouting all sorts of nonsense, the other daughter being called to take her home."

"I'm sorry to hear that."

Norris shrugs as if to say, *Such is life.*

"There were rumours too," Nick says then, "about my father taking bribes . . ."

"Listen, do yourself a favour, Nick, now you're on this healthier than thou crusade . . ."

"It's not a crusade, it's—"

"I don't give a shit what you call it. Your father was a good man. He'd want me watching over you. Don't get me wrong, I'm not about to start holding your hand, but I'll keep you focused. Stop searching for ghosts. You've a job to do. Get on with it. I need to know I've chosen the right person for this one, so take my advice, and don't fuck it up."

16

ELIZABETH

LAST NIGHT I WATCHED THAT GIRL AGAIN, THE ONE ACROSS THE road sitting at her bedroom window. The more I looked at her, the more she reminded me of Nina, and for a split second, I considered phoning Ellie and asking her about her neighbour. But that would have been stupid. The girl might look like Nina, but that didn't mean it was her, aware, how often before, I've studied strangers in the street, or at the supermarket, always hoping that by some twist of fate, one day, Nina and I might stumble upon one another.

I know watching this girl isn't normal behaviour. I bet if I sent a letter into one of those women's magazines, or emailed a question, the respondent would tell me to stop doing it, or worse still, accuse me of stalking. They wouldn't understand that even though my gut tells me this isn't my daughter, it doesn't stop me imagining.

Now, with a morning cup of tea in hand, my focus shifts to the images of Nina shared with the world. How could she not have been recognised? How could she simply have vanished? Surely, someone must have seen her. Of course, there were plenty of false hopes raised. Once, she was supposedly spotted in the West, outside Galway city. Another time there was a suspected sighting in Paris, yet another in Sydney, Australia. Others were less far afield—a bus depot on the north side of Dublin, or outside a school in the city centre. Each time, hopes were raised. Each time, the police investigated. Each time, it led nowhere.

I take a sip of my tea, thinking about one of the early images of Nina shared with the media. It's a photograph of her with Alison, with Alison's face blurred out for protection. I guess one of the reasons I can't get it out of my mind is because I did a such good job of blurring Alison out myself.

Today, I plan to study in detail some of the news reports online, those from around the time Nina went missing. Back then, I couldn't, or wouldn't, read them. In fact, I was advised not to. It would be yet another hardship I was told, and best avoided, because often the media get things wrong, saying things that aren't true. But now, they too are part of the remnants left behind—other people's versions of events.

I scroll through the various headlines, finally stopping on one. "Police fear for young girl's life." I click on the link. "A young Dublin girl, Nina Harte, has been missing for ten days. The child was last seen in the woods with her mother and younger sister. Despite an emotional public appeal and extensive searches of the local area, there has been no confirmed sighting of the young girl since she disappeared from Massey Woods . . ."

My eyes are fixated on the screen, mainly because I want to go back there, to the days, minutes and seconds before I lost her, to somehow make time magically stand still, pause long enough for me to draw breath, to find a way to fix things and stop it from ever happening. Only, I can't, and not for the first time in my life, I consider how cruel it is. How your life can change in an instant, and everything that went before, and everything that follows, is both ravished and tarnished by it, because one single moment can do that.

It can change your life, and you, forever, until eventually, if you're not careful, you no longer recognise yourself.

I've suddenly lost interest in reading any more articles, feeling the need to retreat. I step back from the laptop, as if it's some kind of dark object that I must put a distance between.

Alison bought it for me for my sixtieth birthday, wanting me "to catch up with the twenty-first century." She said it as a joke of course, but both of us knew there was some truth in her words. I had retreated from real life, including advances in technology, other than my mobile phone. Initially, I viewed the thing with scepticism, only using it to hear RTÉ Radio 1, as the sound quality was better than the phone, but soon, tentatively, I branched further afield. It was then I began looking up "depression," "post-traumatic stress" and other stuff online, including how loss affects you.

Even after all this time, it's hard accepting I can't hear Nina's voice, or laugh, or touch her hair, or do any of the ordinary things I once took for granted. I consider writing my thoughts down, wondering if it would help, but decide against it.

When I hear a knock at the door, I don't want to answer it. I know it's not Ciaran, as I didn't hear his car, but still.

The knock repeats itself. I stay quiet, hoping whoever it is will go away, but after several more knocks, I hear my name being called and I realise it's April.

"I've been knocking for a very long time," she protests when I open the door, as if her mind is searching for a reason why an adult woman, obviously at home and capable of movement, wouldn't answer the door straightaway. She doesn't understand. She doesn't live with fear. She's lucky, and I intend to keep it that way.

"Sorry," I say.

"It's okay," she says; then, "sometimes I take a long time to do things too." She's talking fast again. "I'm usually worse in the mornings," she adds, stepping into the hall. "It's hard remembering everything, getting dressed, eating breakfast, brushing teeth, going to the toilet, washing my hands . . ."

I attempt to say something, but she keeps on going.

"Then there's the shoes, the tying of laces, brushing my hair, getting my schoolbag, my coat. It's exhausting." Finally, she draws breath, before dropping her head like she's a ragdoll.

I don't know whether to laugh or cry but considering her outburst in the garden the other day, I decide it's best not to react. Within seconds, she's in the living room standing in front of the laptop.

"Do you need help with this? I've read somewhere that offering older people help with computers is a good way to earn extra pocket money."

"I'm perfectly capable of using a computer," I say, indignant.

"Okay," she says, oblivious to my rebuke, pressing the return key as the page with the loaded newspaper articles reappears on the screen. "You really should have your screen password-protected," she says then, like she's a wise old soul, rather than a ten-year-old child.

"I didn't know I needed to until now," I reply, again indignant, again my remark going unnoticed.

"Is this your missing daughter?"

"Yes, that's Nina."

"She's very pretty."

"She is."

"It's terribly sad," she says then, her face doing that collapsing thing again, "and I know it's not the same, Elizabeth, but once, I lost a teddy on holiday. He fell off the balcony, and no matter how much we looked, we couldn't find him."

"He vanished?"

"Yes," she says, sorrowful, before her eyes brighten. "Oh, but what if Nina found him? That would be nice for them, wouldn't it?"

I stare back at her.

"I guess that wouldn't have happened," her voice sounding down again. "We were in a different country, but maybe Nina *could* be in a different country too."

"She could be anywhere," I say, "or nowhere." I switch the computer off, too much reality taking hold.

"Do you have a plan?"

"For what?"

"Finding her."

Again, I stare back at her, partly puzzled that I'm being interrogated by a child, before saying, "I thought I had one, but now I'm not so sure."

"We'll need paper and a pen."

"I . . ."

"Ellie keeps them in there," she says, pointing to a cupboard beneath the television, before dashing across the room, unwilling to wait for my brain to catch up with hers.

As she gives me the paper and pen, she says, "Hold these, while I walk. It helps me to think."

"Do I need to follow you?" I ask, unsure of the protocol involved.

"No, it's okay. You're old, you can sit."

"Right," I say, sitting down with the paper and pen in hand, again indignant about the age reference, again my mood going unnoticed, before I say, "But I don't know what to write."

"Start with Nina's name at the top," she instructs, "then consecutive numbers along the side for key points."

I do this, but once I've written Nina's name and the numbers, my mind is still blank.

"Nothing?" she asks.

"Nothing."

"Okay, let me think."

I wait, feeling both marginally irritated and inadequate.

"You could try sock skating."

"Sock skating?"

"Yes. You slide across the room in your socks. It can be really useful."

"I don't think . . ."

"I do it all the time. It definitely helps."

There's another knock at the door.

"Oh, that's my mam," she whispers conspiratorially. "I've got to go, but I promise I'll be back later."

"Okay," I reply, still partly panicked about the piece of paper in front of me, while another part of my brain, the one I'd almost forgotten about, the fun part, is imagining myself sock skating across Ellie's living room floor. The idea is sort of crazy, but not nearly as crazy as not knowing what to write.

Through the living room window, I watch April's mother help her with her seat belt in the car. I used to do the same thing for Nina. The memory creates yet another miniscule hole in my heart, but by the time the car pulls away, I'm not thinking about sock skating or old memories anymore, because I've written a name beneath Nina's on the piece of paper—*DI Frank Matthews*, the lead detective in Nina's investigation.

17

ELIZABETH

I'M SITTING IN THE POLICE STATION. I'VE BEEN TOLD TO WAIT. OTHER people are waiting too. No one is talking, and the only sounds from this otherwise silent crowd are the shifting of feet, or the odd cough, along with various reconfigurations of body positions, probably to get more comfortable on the hard seats. I consider if the hard chairs and benches are intentional. A ploy so no one gets too comfortable being here. I hear the crowd breathing too. In and out, deep and heavy, the way my parents used to breathe so deeply in sleep. It's been years since I thought about them or even gave any thought to when I was younger. I wonder what I'd tell my younger self, that carefree girl with all those notions about love and living happily ever after. I certainly wouldn't mock her enthusiasm. Instead, I'd probably hold her tight. Tell her it's okay to be naive, to have hopes and dreams. I'd tell her that I hope she's still inside me somewhere, deep down within my imperfect, sad, and sometimes scared older self.

Someone jingles a set of keys. I look up, but nothing has changed, and my mind drifts back, thinking about my parents again. I was lucky, having two people in my life who loved me. Even if being the only child of older parents made me feel different from my peers, a little bit like April. I smile, remembering our last proper holiday together. A camping trip to France, where we'd stayed just outside of Paris, and seeing those fields and fields of sunflowers, symbolising growth and strength, and also, I learned later, a way to find light, even in the dark.

It feels idyllic, looking back, me being innocent, happy, unaware of what lay ahead. I supposed it was a mercy; neither of my parents lived through my shame, and all the hurt and sadness that followed their only daughter. They died still having such high hopes for that bright young girl.

I open my handbag, taking out the image I brought with me to Ellie's of the house with the white rosebush in the front garden, my old family home. The rosebush was my mother's pride and joy. It's strange looking at an image, one that holds two completely different stories. The first, growing up with loving parents. The second, after they died, how months later, everything changed. I changed. I feel a mix of emotions looking at it now, because I know there are certain memories I would block out if I could. Only, that's not possible. It never was, and it never will be.

I look up again, my attention drawn to the desk sergeant rustling papers in front of him—more noise adding to the countdown music.

When I arrived, I'd asked to speak to DI Matthews. I'd assumed he'd still be here, like a ghost from my past, haunting his old stomping ground, but I've been told he isn't at the station anymore. That makes things awkward, the need to bring someone else up to speed.

A door opens, and a man who'd arrived before me is called from the waiting area. Perhaps I'm next. If I am, I'll need to prepare myself, work out where to start. That should be easy—start at the beginning: over twenty-five years ago my daughter Nina went missing. She has never been found. And now, I've a question, one I hoped DI Matthews could answer.

The door opens again. A male police officer in uniform calls my name. I stand up and follow him. He opens a door to another room.

The room is small, with slate-grey walls. There's a tiny window up high, and a square wooden table in the centre, with two red plastic chairs, as bright as red Smarties. I sit down. The police officer sits too. He takes out a notebook and pen from his top pocket. I think about little April, her youthful curiosity, talking about writing a plan. Unlike me, she'd be in her element here with this police officer. She'd certainly keep him on his toes.

"Elizabeth," the young police officer says, easing the muscles in his face, "is it okay to call you Elizabeth?"

I nod.

"Great," he says, smiling this time. "I'm Thomas."

"Hello, Thomas," I reply, before adding, "My late husband was called Tom."

"Right," he says, unsure if my last remark is a good or bad thing. "How can I help you?"

"I wanted to speak to DI Matthews."

"Yes, I heard that. He isn't here."

"I heard that too."

We stare at each other. Thomas is waiting for me to speak, his pen and paper at the ready. I attempt a delaying tactic, reluctant to ask the question I came here for, for fear I might be disappointed, as hoping is often far nicer than reality. "Is he at another station?" I ask then.

"No, he retired from the force a couple of years ago."

"I see," I say, still stalling. "Do you have a forwarding address?" It's a stupid question. This police officer isn't going to give me DI Matthews's home address. That would be considered personal information.

"I'm afraid—"

"It's okay," I say, interrupting. "I understand. You can't tell me."

"No, I can't, but maybe *I* can help you instead."

"Okay," I say, breathing inward, "it's about my daughter."

He flicks open the notebook, writing a time and date on top of the page. "What's her name?"

"I have two daughters, Alison and Nina, but it's Nina I'm here to talk about, Nina Harte."

"Go on."

"She went missing over twenty-five years ago."

He looks across at me, his body stiffening, readying himself for whatever else I'm about to say.

"She was never found," I say, deadpan. "It's a cold case now."

"I see." He scribbles something else in his notebook.

"I wanted to ask DI Matthews a question about it."

"Do you want to ask me?"

I pause again, counting backward from ten in my head, before saying, "I wish to enquire about any fresh leads," sounding more confident than I feel. "I realise you're unfamiliar with the case, but perhaps you could find out for me."

He scratches his head, frowning.

I keep on talking. "It's just, I understand these things are often reviewed around an anniversary, and twenty-five years is a long time. If it were a marriage"—I laugh—"it would be silver, not that anyone's celebrating."

The lines on his forehead deepen. "I'm sure if something important materialised, Elizabeth, someone would have been in touch."

"Oh no, that's not the way it works," I say, all knowledgeable, "the police don't usually keep the family up to speed. I know this from before—information is only shared with the family on a need-to-know basis."

"Well, yes, in part that's true, but when something significant happens—for example, a fresh piece of information, something you might be able to help us with—we would make contact."

"But . . ."

He raises his hand. "I'm not saying I won't check it out. I'll make enquiries, only, I'm not sure how long it will take."

"I have another name," I say then, "other than DI Matthews."

"Oh?"

"A female liaison officer, Lynda Keating. She was appointed a few years back, after the original liaison officer retired. She might know something."

"Hmm," he says. "I don't know the name, but I'll see what I can dig up."

"You'll need my phone number."

"Yes, and your current address."

I give him both pieces of information, first my mobile number, then Ellie's home address. He closes his notebook. I get the sense this means we've reached the end of the matter—meeting over.

"You said DI Matthews retired?"

"Yes," he says, looking slightly nervous.

"There's something else, isn't there?"

"Nothing for you to worry about, Elizabeth."

"What is it?" I ask, adamant. "I've become excellent at reading people's faces. In fact, I've had years of experience dealing with people saying one thing to me, when they mean the very opposite. Call it a benefit of getting older."

"I shouldn't even be talking to you about this . . ."

"About what?"

"DI Matthews is no longer with us."

"Yes," I say, impatient, "you've already said that."

"No, I mean he's gone." His eyes look upward, toward the heavens.

"Gone, as in, dead?"

"Yes."

"How?"

"How what?"

"How did he die?"

"I can't . . ."

"You've gone this far," I say, aware I'm taking advantage of this young officer's inexperience, "you might as well go all the way." I give him a reassuring look, as if to say, *It's okay, you can tell me, I'm not some mad person. I'm someone you can trust.*

"He committed suicide," he says then, "took his own life."

"Suicide?" I blurt out far too loud. "No, that can't be true. It doesn't make any sense, not for the man I knew. He was far too determined, too focused, too absorbed in his job, almost to a point of obsession, to do anything like that."

"I'm sorry, Elizabeth."

"No, no," I say, loud again, shaking my head, unwilling to accept the possibility that the man I remember so clearly could do such a thing.

"I'm sorry," the young officer repeats, attempting comfort, but it doesn't matter, I've already stopped listening.

He stands up. I stand up too, my body stiff, unyielding. "Right," I say, as if that's the end of the matter, even though it isn't.

Somehow, I make my way out of the room, back through the waiting area and finally out through the front door of the police station to the front steps. "No," I say again, muttering to myself, "it can't be true," as a group of teenagers pass by and stare. Reaching into my bag, I take out the list on the piece of paper I started with April. After DI Matthews's name, I write the word "SUICIDE," followed by two questions: (a) Did he take his own life? or (b) Did someone kill him?

18

HIM

He locks the door—eager for his time away from his wife, when it's just him and the target on camera. He doesn't hate his wife, but there are things he detests about her, including how lately she's started talking to him like she's the superior one, the one in charge. If only she knew the truth. If only she knew what he's capable of, or the thoughts going on inside his head.

He puts on earphones, firing up the computer and monitors with views of the target's home. She's oblivious to the cameras, thinking she's alone. Only, she isn't, not anymore, because he's with her, following her every move. This illicit intimacy pleases him, and will continue to please him, until the moment comes, when he wants her to know he exists, to realise he knows everything about her.

Turning up the audio, he hears her humming. It feels as if somehow, he's already walking in her shoes, possessing her. She'll undress soon, having pulled her pyjamas from the drawer a while earlier.

Her phone receives a message notification. She reads it, before placing the phone on the bed. She pulls off her jumper, revealing a camisole top underneath. There's a second ping. *Another message. Whoever it is, they're persistent. She keys in a response. Maybe he's made an error. Perhaps she isn't right after all. She could be a mistake. Some women are like that, giving the impression they're one thing, when they're the very opposite.*

He takes a sip of wine, a Haut-Médoc with a tar-tinged bouquet. He hopes his new target is deserving, but fears she may still disappoint, wriggling out of her jeans now, before heading to the kitchen for a late-night snack of toast and jam.

There's another text message. That's number three. What if there's someone else on the scene? Is it jealousy he feels, or something else? Either way, she'll pay for this.

Soon, she'll go to bed. She has an early start in the morning. Finally, after brushing her teeth, she heads toward the bedroom. He watches her curling up under the covers, foolishly thinking she's safe.

Only, she's not, because soon, it will be just the two of them, with him as the captor, while she'll be the opposite, weak, fearful, and needy.

19

NICK

NICK CLOSES THE DOOR OF HIS OFFICE AT TERENURE POLICE STATION as all hell is breaking loose. His colleagues are pumped up following a major incident involving an assault by several youths on a mixed-race teen. The boy is in critical condition, and the severities of his injuries necessitated the setting up of an Incident Room, with officers and other specialists scheduled to work around the clock, with the boy's life in the balance. It's over an hour since Nick started work, but the pent-up mix of adrenaline at the station is testing his concentration.

One of the officers roars, "The hospital says the boy didn't make it," quickly followed by raised voices and the shifting of furniture as chairs are pulled back, the key players making their way to the Incident Room, each under the leadership of the senior investigating officer. Last year, that SIO could have been Nick, but a mark on your record spirals you downward faster than success sends you up the ranks. He'd taken his eye off the ball. Too many hangovers got in the way. Missing key information a rookie officer would have picked up on straightaway. Meaning, he not only failed to do his job, but he'd failed others too, including the poor guy who took months to recover in hospital, after the assailant, the man Nick should have arrested, carried on unnoticed. It was a severe mark on his record, including the disciplinary hearing, but he doesn't want to dwell on that now. So, after a last attempt to keep his concentration in check, he abandons the station to resume his analysis at home.

Leaving his colleagues behind, the same feeling that's been troubling him for months, that of being an outsider, raises its head. Sure, he enjoys the challenges of the cold cases, but he still misses his old role, feeling part of a team. And he still has a lot to prove, his reputation tarnished due to sloppy errors. It would be easy to simply blame the booze, but Nick also knows the problem has deeper roots, including how, from an early age, his desire to please his father, to seek his approval and love, got torn apart after his father's suicide.

Nick's mind drifts to the first time he saw a dead body. He'd officially made detective that day—a milestone. It was early morning when the call came in. A seven-year-old boy was missing. The parents raised the alarm after they discovered he wasn't upstairs in his room. Nick assured them their son would be found. The young boy, Seamus, had ADHD. That morning, he'd failed to take his medication, and his disappearance was an immediate red alert. It was close to midday when a body was discovered floating in the canal. Within minutes, Nick was at the scene. He jumped into the bitter cold water, making his way toward the boy, knowing he was already too late. He'd never forget wrapping his arms around that lifeless frame, emerging with the boy from the freezing water. Nick changed that day, a fresh reality taking hold, but whatever pain he experienced, it paled in significance compared to how the boy's parents felt.

This cold case investigation into the murdered women felt the same way for him. The victims were all loved. And the families left behind lived a different life after their loss, and with that came a responsibility on his part, to find, and stop, their killer.

Arriving at his apartment, two things kept repeating themselves in his head: the missing items from the victims, and the absence of

DNA evidence. With a fifteen-year time span, lack of DNA wasn't surprising in the earlier victims, both deaths occurring when DNA was in its infancy, with no official Irish database. But with Marie Byrne, the third victim, only a partial DNA profile had been found; and the last victim, Kimberly Campbell, and possibly a copycat killing, had absolutely nothing.

The potential of trinkets mattered too, as they indicated a point in the killer's trajectory when he needed more. Two victims told friends jewellery had gone missing, while another mentioned perfume. Trinkets are the things of popular TV shows about serial killers, but many killers travel a similar path. Their need to have something of their victims becoming vital, so they can relive the experience, and their warped sense of intimacy.

What Nick was hoping for, after all this time, was that some witnesses might loosen their tongues. It wasn't uncommon, long after a crime was committed, for someone protecting a suspect to decide they weren't worth protecting after all. Allegiances could be fickle. Only, there's another reason people are reluctant to tell police the truth, and it's the most primal one of all: fear.

20

ELIZABETH

SOON AFTER I ARRIVE BACK FROM THE POLICE STATION, AS PROMISED, April returns. Now, she is sprawled like a starfish on the living room floor.

"How's your list?" she asks, moving her legs and arms like some kind of mystical water creature.

"I've made an addition."

She sits up, looking delighted.

"It's probably nothing."

"It must be important, Elizabeth, if you wrote it down. Is it a clue?"

"More a question than a clue."

"And?"

"And nothing, I'm still thinking about it," I snap back.

"Okay," she says then, eyeing me with suspicion, brushing off my irritation as if she's used to it by now. She doesn't ask me anything else. Probably because she's so engrossed writing something in that Harry Potter notebook of hers, as I wonder if this new note might be about me.

Staring at her, I can't help but think about being a young mother again, and this street too, where I used to live as a wife and mother, which was once filled with families, house-shares, and others living alone. It's only then I remember Mrs. Jordan, the widow up the street. She was probably in her sixties when Nina went missing, the same age I am now, but what if, after all this time, she still remembers something?

"Do you know Mrs. Jordan?" I ask April.

She glares back at me. "She *died* last year," she says, her bottom lip quivering, adding, "She was an octogenarian." Then, attempting to pull herself together, she says, "Eighty-eight years old."

I repeat the age in my head, my brain trying to get up to speed with the passing of time.

"Some kids called her the 'crazy woman.'"

"Why?"

She shrugs. "I thought she was nice."

"It was probably her age."

"What's wrong with being old?"

"Nothing, but old people can appear odd and different."

"Elizabeth, you look sad again."

"I'm just thinking, maybe Mrs. Jordan knew something about Nina going missing, and I left it too late."

"I'm going to cheer you up."

"How?"

"A game."

"What kind of game?"

"It's called Difficult Things."

"That's not going to cheer me up, thinking about difficult stuff."

"It will. I do it all the time with Sophie. It helps to get things out of my head."

"Sophie?"

"My cognitive behavioural therapist."

"Right," I say, reluctantly wondering if I might need one of those. "You go first."

"Night parties," she says, "particularly ones with fake smoke."

"Do you go to many night parties?"

"Just one, at Halloween. I didn't like it, or the noise, although I'm fond of police sirens."

"I'll bear that in mind," I say, smiling, realising of late, I've started smiling a lot with April.

"Your turn," she says.

"Food shopping."

She eyes me suspiciously.

"I mean it. Going around supermarkets, putting things in your trolley, going to the cash desk, loading your shopping on the conveyor belt, packing bags, bringing them to the car, filling the boot, driving home, carrying them in, then putting everything away, only to do it all over again a few days later."

"Wow, you're good at this."

I nod.

"My turn," she says. "Getting stressed, especially with too many thoughts jumping around inside my head."

"I hate that too, because I get stuck. So, I guess, getting stuck is another difficult thing."

"How?"

"I think about something, and even though I want to think about other things, the stuck thoughts won't go away."

"Do they upset you?"

"Yes."

"Then they're *intrusive thoughts*. Sophie told me all about them."

"Oh?"

"They're unwanted negative thoughts that pop into your head, and are often repetitive, as well as DISTURBING AND DISTRESSING." She says this as if she's learnt the words off by heart.

"How do you get rid of them?" I ask, somewhat surprised I'm expecting answers to serious life questions from a child.

"You need to think about something positive. It doesn't always work, because negative intrusive thoughts are *powerful*, and before you know it, they're multiplying all over the place."

"That's not good."

"It's terrible."

"Your turn," I say, deciding it's time to move the conversation on, because I'm already thinking about Nina, what happened to her, how it was my fault. How I failed her. I wasn't the mother she needed me to be, and ever since, I've been repeating even more mistakes with Alison, becoming a complete failure as a mother. Only, I don't know how to change any of it, even though I hate myself for it.

April gives me a weird look, almost as if she's picking up on the negative thoughts inside my head.

"Go ahead," I tell her, wanting to take the focus away from me.

"Okay," she says. "When the covers on my bed aren't straight and Mam has to fix them over and over." She looks at me with anticipation. "Your turn."

"Being invisible."

"Do you have a superpower?"

"No, it's like I'm here, only a lot of the time, I'm not noticed, which makes me invisible."

"People notice me *too* much, especially if I'm having a meltdown, or wailing uncontrollably, or talking too much, or I'm too loud, or when I can't stop talking, and even though I don't know what they're actually thinking, I know they're not thinking about anything good."

"Maybe being invisible isn't so bad," I sigh.

"Not if it makes you sad. You shouldn't feel sad, Elizabeth, you're a nice person."

"Thank you," I say, smiling again. It's been a while since I thought of myself as a nice person.

"You've a beautiful smile too. I prefer it when you smile."

"I don't mean to be sad."

"Is it because your daughter's missing?"

"Yes," I say, tightening my fists, "it makes me sad not knowing where she is, and that everything is affected by it. It makes me sad that I feel stuck, and sometimes lonely, and I don't even know who I am anymore."

"That's a lot of reasons to be sad."

"It is," I say, feeling wholly in the wrong, burdening April with my woes. "What about you?" I ask. "Anything else you want to add to the difficult list?"

"Loads," she says, readying herself. "Plans being changed. Worries too. People touching me, especially strangers. Not being able to colour coordinate my clothes. Food not being separated on my plate. Oh! and tags, the ones on clothes. Running too. Mam says I might have dyspraxia, a coordination thing. Her brother had it. He didn't ride a bicycle without stabilisers until he was twelve!"

"Right."

"Your turn," she fires back.

I pause, remembering my visit to the police station looking for DI Matthews, before saying, "When you want something to happen a certain way, but it doesn't."

"Like?"

"The thing I wrote on my list."

"The *How to Find Nina* list?"

"I didn't put that title on it, but yes."

"What did you write?"

"A name."

"Who?"

"You don't know him. He was a detective."

"It's good you're writing things down."

I think then about other stuff too, including the newspaper clippings of Rachel Meadows, and how the person who killed her could be known to me. I think about that photograph too, of my old family home, where I originally lived with my parents, the one from 1992, and the shadow across the side of the image, a photograph taken by a neighbour the year before Nina was born. I think about the missing items, especially that bracelet from years before, and how men can be so cruel, including my son-in-law, Ciaran, before I say, "I expected him to be at the police station, the detective, but like lots of my past, he's gone."

"Like Mrs. Jordan?"

"Exactly."

She gets up and begins walking around the room, as if she's promoted herself to person in charge. "You could try a séance, Elizabeth. I've seen that in movies. You need a table and candles and . . ."

"We're not doing that . . ."

"No . . . ," she agrees, slightly disappointed, sitting down again.

I want to reach out to touch her, to show her affection, before remembering she finds another person's touch *difficult*. I understand that, because, at times, even the slightest touch causes me to recoil. It doesn't matter if it's someone I feel safe with, like Alison, because my body can't help it, and I know why. He did this to me. He made me afraid, the man who took Nina, the same way Ciaran, my son-in-law, tries to frighten me too, sneaking up on me unexpectedly, causing me to jump, and taking pleasure from it. I think then about the fear I felt when Nina first went missing too. How it felt bigger than anything I'd ever experienced. It wasn't simply the pain of a mother whose child had disappeared. It was much more than that, because in my gut, where all the mixed-up thoughts about a person's life exist, I knew Nina going missing was partly my fault. I should have known. I should have been more careful. I should have trusted my instincts, just like that day a lifetime ago, in my old family home, with the white rosebush in the front garden. Because if I had paid more attention, if I had somehow changed things, when I sensed something wasn't right, I'd have realised that by doing nothing, all of it would eventually come to this.

I've almost forgotten April is in the room, when she says, "You don't know what to do next, Elizabeth, do you?"

"No," I say, "but I've the name of another person, a woman who might be able to help. Only, there's a problem."

"When I've a problem, like doing computer coding and stuff, I stick with it until it's sorted, even if I don't want to keep trying, because the thought of not fixing it is far worse than the thought of not trying to."

"Her name is Lynda Keating," I say, deciding she has a point. "She's a police family liaison officer."

"Great," she says, "we've a starting point."

"But, as I said, there's a problem."

"What?"

"I was told she'd contact me."

"When?"

"They said it could take a while."

She scrunches her face. "I hate when people say things like that. It could mean a week, a month, a year."

"It's annoying, yes."

"We need to find her," she says, grabbing her schoolbag by the couch and pulling out her smart tablet. "Elizabeth, you can't stay stuck forever."

"What are you doing?"

"I'm googling her," she says, giving me a slightly irritated look, annoyed I'm not keeping up with her, before adding, "I stuck a rubber band up my nose the other day, thinking it was funny, but then I thought it might be touching my brain, so I pulled it out. I mean it, Elizabeth, you can't stay stuck forever. You're hurting your brain."

I visualise my head being stuck in a giant lock.

"Right," she says, "here she is," now utterly engrossed in the screen. "She's based in Police Headquarters in the Phoenix Park. That's the place where deer run wild."

I peer into the screen, amazed, seeing the name, department address, and phone number.

"Do you want me to call her?" April asks. "I'm very good at making enquiries."

"No, no, I'll do it."

Seconds later, I get through, explaining to numerous people who I am, and why I need to contact the family liaison officer attached to the case of my missing daughter.

As I listen to orchestral music on the line, I see April writing furiously again in her red Harry Potter notebook. I already know Hermione Granger is her favourite character, and as I'm thinking this, a female voice says, "Elizabeth, is that you?"

"Yes," I say, a little startled.

"It's been a while."

I want to say "over twenty-five years," although I know she's a later addition to the case, so instead, I say, "It has."

"How can I help?"

"I wanted to know if there had been any fresh developments?"

April stops writing in her notebook, staring at me instead, and I'd wager a bomb could go off beside her and it wouldn't interrupt her concentration.

"I'm sorry," Lynda says, "nothing fresh has raised its head." I imagine myself in April's mind, thinking the way she sometimes thinks, literally, visualising a head rising from a body.

"Where are you, Elizabeth? Are you at home?"

"No," I say, "I'm taking a short break—staying somewhere different for a while, a friend's house."

"Give me the address. I can call over."

"It's 32 Serpent Drive."

The silence at the other end of the line tells me she's already made the connection. "The street you lived on when Nina went . . ."

"Yes, that's the one," I reply, attempting confidence.

"Elizabeth, I'm not sure if—"

I cut her off. "I've been told DI Matthews committed suicide."

April's eyes look as if they're about to pop out of her head. I probably shouldn't have used the word "suicide" in front of her, but I can't take it back now.

"Yes, that's right," Lynda replies, sounding unsure about what I'll ask or say next.

"I don't think," I say, clearing my throat, "he would have done something like *that*," not wanting to repeat the word "suicide."

"Why not?"

"Because he wouldn't."

"What makes you so positive?"

"He mightn't have found Nina, but over time, I got to know him, and taking the easy way out wasn't his way."

"People change."

"You're wrong, Lynda," I say, thinking about myself being stuck all these years, "some people stay exactly the same."

21

HIM

The adrenaline is like a tsunami, his heart pumping at twice its normal speed. He spots her circling the pathway surrounding the park, taking her familiar route, openly visible at first, before turning into the narrow pathway concealed by larger trees and dense undergrowth. His timing needs to be perfect. She'll do another two laps before slowing down and heading home. Once she starts to reduce her speed and is hidden by the larger trees, he'll only have seconds, so he'll need to get it absolutely right.

They've already exchanged pleasantries, him waving with a warm smile. She isn't aware of the chloroform-drenched cloth beneath his zip-up top. She doesn't know that sweet-smelling compound, used for centuries, will soon render her unconscious. The dose is key. Smaller doses will merely cause disorientation and fatigue. A higher dose causes loss of consciousness and temporary removal of pain. Go too high, and the victim might develop breathing issues with paralysis of the chest muscles, damage that could be discovered later, even after the chloroform leaves the body, during a postmortem. Nor does he want to lose the target before he's ready. The timing of her death is yet to be determined, because first, there has to be their time of intimacy.

His vehicle is parked nearby, and he's aware he'll need to guide her into it once the chloroform takes hold. The target won't immediately crumple to the ground the way it happens in movies. A short time will elapse where she'll initially be disorientated, and once he has her in the vehicle, she'll remain unconscious long enough to change location.

She's nearing the snatching point now. His feet pound the pathway as she does the same in the opposite direction. The adrenaline reaches fever pitch, nothing and no one can stop him. Metres away, again she smiles, and he waves back, her believing he'll continue in the opposite direction, until he turns, grabbing her from behind, the chloroform-soaked cloth over her mouth as her body limbers before giving way.

He's whispering in her ear, telling her everything's going to be okay, that she's weak and he'll help her. He knows she doesn't believe it, but it's how things need to be. By the time they reach the vehicle, her ability to put one foot in front of the other is gone, and his upper body strength compared to hers is enough to open the door and shove her in. It's only then, once she is safely inside and they face each other, that their eyes meet. He smiles back, in control, while the target, if she'd any time for regret, already knows it's too late. She's his now.

He slams the back door shut, aware within seconds she'll lose consciousness. He gets in the car and puts his foot on the accelerator, and soon, he's driving out the gate of the park, waiting for an opening in traffic. He waves thank-you to a woman who slows down to let him merge onto the main road before speeding away.

22

ISABELLA

(6 weeks earlier)

ARRIVING AT MY PARENTS' HOUSE IN KILLINEY, I PAUSE BEFORE OPENING the front door, the turmoil of the last few weeks still raw. Both of them should still be alive, but they're not. Nor is the life I recently carried inside me. Either loss on its own would be huge, but together, they feel seismic.

Finally, breathing in deep, I turn the key in the lock, stepping inside, the same way, last week, I stepped into that old Georgian house on the north side of Dublin, the one I'm sure I'm connected to. The feeling of someone watching me hasn't gone away either, but there's something else rattling in my brain as I close the front door behind me, a kind of sinking feeling, that perhaps, as far as my parents are concerned, soon I might unravel a whole set of lies.

In the living room, I pull a family album down from the bookcase, flicking through the images, hoping, as the past flashes before me, that something will jog my memory. I stop at photos of me from around age seven, my hair chopped short, wearing tomboy clothes, reminding me of how I used to wonder whether my father, in particular, had secretly wanted a boy, and that by being a girl, I'd disappointed him about that as well.

I flick forward, staring at images from a few years later, when I'm about ten. In these, I've changed, and not simply because I'm older, but because it's clear the "girly" me has finally appeared, and that tomboy look, the one I'd previously strutted, is gone. As well as longer hair, there are fancy headbands too. My clothes are prettier, even if they're somewhat over the top. Maybe my parents wanted to make up for the earlier years, or perhaps the pink girly me went into overdrive. Mostly, though, when I remember back then, I think about how lonely I felt. Later, others blamed my homeschooling, my father having very set ideas about a child's environment and its importance, especially when it came to education. Statistically, he'd say, girls will academically outperform boys, but they can slip back if biased societal pressures are allowed into play. Which is why, up to the start of secondary school, I was homeschooled. A decision, unlike many of my father's choices, that both my parents agreed with.

I flick through more photo albums, looking for younger images, but I can't find any. Perhaps they're somewhere upstairs, in an earlier album, but after another hour of searching, nothing turns up.

I check the time on my phone. It's past three o'clock. I still have time to reach the library before it closes. I've already confirmed they've copies of the Thom's Directory, although they only go up to 2011. Still, if the house on Charlesworth Avenue is listed, they may reveal the owner's identity.

A half hour later, I'm sitting upstairs in the library at the local studies section. I've several copies of Thom's Directory in front of me, all red volumes from 1990 to 2011. The address of 62 Charlesworth Avenue, North Strand, is there, as is the name James Lennox, beside the number 62. His name is repeated each year from 1990 until 2009, whereupon it's replaced by the word "vacant," but more importantly, I now have a name linked to the address.

Inspired by this small but not insignificant discovery, I use the library's internet service to search for "James Lennox." An American philanthropist from the 1800s appears as the top hit. I narrow the search to Ireland, and then further to Dublin. After some other historical references, there's a more up-to-date posting, a news article from twenty-four years earlier, with a James Lennox (no address given) being sentenced for two counts of fraud. The article also notes he had previous convictions, including physical assault and attempted rape. I scan farther down and see he was given a five-year prison term, with six months suspended. I check the date again. Assuming he didn't offend again, or perhaps, mightn't have been caught, he'd have been released from prison nearly twenty years ago. That's long enough to rebuild a life, to become someone else.

Is he still going by the same name, assuming he's still alive? And what, if anything, is his connection to me? I've no way of answering these questions. I'm not the police. Although, in theory, I could ask them, but what would I say? *I found an address written by my late mother. I've discovered a man, a criminal called James Lennox lived there, but he doesn't live there anymore.* They'd ask me why I needed the information, which again, I can't explain, other than a nagging feeling inside me that the address, and now this man's name, are important. Which is why, before leaving the library, I text my aunt Elaine to arrange a Zoom call.

AT HOME, WHILE I WAIT FOR ELAINE TO CONNECT ONLINE, I STUDY the images I took of 62 Charlesworth Avenue, enlarging them, searching for the smallest of details. At first, I don't see anything unusual, but then I see something I hadn't noticed before—a discarded cigarette butt near the end of the staircase. It looks fresh, so who does it belong to? The house is empty, although it's possible it could belong to the estate agent; only, would an estate agent leave a cigarette butt behind? The place isn't a pretty picture, but still. The other possibility is the place is still being used by someone, although I didn't get that impression from the neighbour. According to her, it's been abandoned for years.

I get an alert, telling me my aunt is waiting to be accepted into the meeting, and soon I see her face smiling back at me. For a second, I begin to doubt myself, wondering if this thing with the address is all nonsense, something I've fixated on because I don't want to think about either loss or grief, or whatever the hell else I should be thinking about right now, but then, after exchanging social pleasantries, I say, "I was looking at family photograph albums today."

"That must have been hard."

"I couldn't find any images of me as a baby."

"Maybe they're in another album."

"No, I looked."

She doesn't reply.

"Why, Elaine, did my parents dress me like a boy for years, with cropped hair, tomboy clothes, and then later, everything became more girly?"

"You probably wanted a change."

"It's extreme, don't you think?"

"You're overthinking things," she says a bit too fast, a tightness creeping into her voice.

"Am I?"

"Let it go, Isabella," she says then, but I detect a note of hesitancy.

"You know something, don't you?"

She swallows hard. She looks as if she's trying not to blink, as if caught in concentration, thinking about what she should say next.

"What about the name James Lennox, or that address I told you about?"

"I told you, Isabella, the address means nothing to me."

"But the name?"

"Why are you asking about this person?"

"It means something, doesn't it?"

"Isabella, I can't . . ." Her words trail off.

"You can't what?" I almost scream at her.

She closes her eyes.

"Elaine, whatever it is, you have to tell me."

"But I promised your mother."

"What did you promise?"

"That I'd keep their secret."

23

HIM

The target is exactly where she needs to be, but he doesn't plan to visit her just yet. It usually works best that way, keeping them isolated for a period of time.

His wife has left the house, and he's pleased to have the place to himself, allowing him time to reflect before the real games begin. He's often thought about being found out, and how others might study him, asking questions about his killer mindset. He's imagined TV documentaries, news headlines, or journalists interviewing people who know him, neighbours with hushed tones, telling reporters he seemed like such a charming guy.

The notoriety would bring female fans too. He's read stories the same as everyone else about how women become fascinated with killers, men they've never met, even writing to them in prison. Some would want to help him, guide him into seeing the error of his ways. Others might tell him it's not his fault, and that under different circumstances, he could have turned out okay. They might even blame the system, quoting whatever liberal bullshit is currently on trend, but he's already stopped thinking about "what if." He doesn't need a set of female saviours to tell him it's not his fault. He already knows that.

He's studied killers too. The foolish ones, hitting out in anger, seeking revenge. He couldn't learn from them, unless he wanted a lesson in stupidity. No, it was the smart ones, like him, who rarely acted in haste, or out of some rage or toxic-fuelled adrenaline rush. These were the kind to consider. Men who, before discovery, lived a normal life under the radar. They came in all shapes and sizes—the professor whose peers dismissed rumours of inappropriate behaviour as the wild notions of female adolescents; or the quiet guy everyone pitied, who used his lack of perceived worth to trick women into feeling sorry for him; or even the athlete who made it his life plan to charm everyone around him, including his prey. All of them stayed hidden for years.

He switches on the laptop, watching his fresh target, focusing on every little thing about her. He understands her far better than she realises, including that false bravado of hers, one born from a certain kind of privilege. A privilege that isn't governed by wealth or position, but rather her inaccurate belief that most people are basically good. And it's this privilege that's allowed someone like him to change her life forever.

24

ELIZABETH

THE GIRL WASN'T AT THE WINDOW TONIGHT. IT FELT STRANGE looking across at the emptiness, wondering about this person I know so little about, other than my wild observations from the vantage point of my opposite window. She seems to live an ordinary life, the kind, I guess, I'd treasure.

I think about Lynda Keating too, the family liaison officer. She's due to call in a few days, to check up on me. Everyone seems to have me under suspicion—Lynda, my daughter Alison, and even Ellie, who texted yesterday to enquire about my progress. The only person who isn't judging me is April.

None of them understand that since Nina vanished, an important thread was ripped away, and once that happened, soon everything had to unravel. If I'm being honest with myself, even before Nina's abduction, I was in a dark place. One I didn't manage well. They didn't have questionnaires back then about depression. It wasn't talked about, and it's not like there's a prize for people who do handle these things well, other than the obvious, that by not handling them, the end result, the fallout, isn't limited to one person. It affects everything and everyone connected to you—nothing is left untouched.

I used to sit in the dark after Nina went missing too. I felt nothing mattered outside of my little girl coming home, everything else paling into insignificance. It wasn't just the loss and guilt; it was the hopelessness, which now makes me angry. I wish I could take that young woman by the shoulders, the one I used to be after Nina disappeared, and shake her good and hard. Tell her to think wiser, sharper, and be goddamned less accepting. She was different from the woman I am now. She didn't fully understand that no one incident ever happens in isolation, and no matter how much you try to wrap your arms around a person, or how much you know, deep down, you need to protect them, if you don't understand the way an evil person thinks, they can and will destroy you. They will wait until your guard is down, for the moment you least expect it, and their wrath will be both swift and irreversible.

Frustrated, I tell myself I need to stop sitting here doing nothing. So, I pick up some laundry to put it away. As I place pairs of socks in the drawer, they remind me how April can suffer from sensory overload, including endless attempts at getting her socks to fit just right. A slight twist in them means she needs to rip them off. When I first heard this, I thought of that fairy tale about the princess and the pea, wondering if the princess in the story also had autism, because she could feel that tiny pea through all those mattresses, but mostly now, I'm thinking about all the other things I've recently realised, including the behaviour of my son-in-law, Ciaran. Alison is in denial about him, an affliction I'm very familiar with, but a lifetime of fear makes you more observant than most. I know he hides things from her, including receipts and money. I told her about this once, how I thought he might have a second bank account, but she dismissed it, saying she had her own account too, and it was all about trust. I wanted to tell her it was misguided trust, but it was pointless, because even if I could find absolute proof, and catch him out on his lies, he'd always find a fresh excuse. Which is why, for a while there, when I was still living with them, I decided to look for answers myself. It didn't take me long to find my missing gold pen hidden in his locker drawer, one of the items I'd told Alison about that she put down to forgetfulness, thinking I'd misplaced it. I'd been so tempted to create a fuss, to call him out on it, but then I realised that it would likely please him, as he'd simply find a way to blame me instead of himself. In the end, I left the pen there, hoping the less he knew about how much I was onto him, the better.

25

HIM

She's gained consciousness faster than he expected, disorientated at first, weak and violently ill too, but when the vomiting ceased, that's when the screams began. No one heard them, and once she worked that out for herself, her cries faded to little more than a whimper.

The cameras in her apartment have been removed too, but as he watches her in this new space, safely locked away, miles from his home, despite the noise his wife is making downstairs, clattering dishes and mildly irritating him, his mood is still buoyant.

This is his favourite part, the anticipation before their first proper face-to-face. Now, when they meet, it won't be like the days leading up to the abduction, the two of them as casual strangers, it will be the two of them together, with the rest of the world blocked out.

In the past, before he made his move, he used to get closer to other victims, unable to resist being a larger part of their lives, but over time, that aspect required adapting, him needing to be ahead of the police or anyone else who felt the necessity to interfere.

His latest target is currently searching for a means of escape—she won't find one. Like the screaming, she'll eventually realise it's useless. Ultimately, she'll reach a point where she'll sense there isn't anything she can do to regain her freedom, and with that comes the knowledge that her time, whatever's left of it, is fading fast.

Watching her brings back some old memories too, because it wasn't always like this. Things have changed over time. Abductions weren't even part of the earlier attacks. Nor were the killings. In the beginning, he simply watched the targets, telling himself it was an exercise in exploration, but soon curiosity alone wasn't enough. After that, he entered their homes. Initially when they weren't there, but then later, he used to watch them sleep, each of them unaware of his presence, knowing he could still cross another line. Finally, he did, the sexual assaults being the next step in his progression. He wonders if it was then he decided the killing was inevitable. Either way, each time he went a little further, each time he gained and lost a little more. Even if the first time for everything was always the most thrilling.

All of it pointed one way, toward ultimate control, because without that, he'd be at the mercy of others. Without that, he, not they, would be paying the highest price.

26

ISABELLA

(6 weeks earlier)

ENDING THE ZOOM CALL WITH MY AUNT, THE SUSPICIONS THAT have been hovering in the back of my mind since my mother's death ricochet now beyond my wildest dreams. I'd put my aunt under pressure for sure, but her confession, if that's the right word for it, wasn't only because of the pressure, it was because harbouring a secret she didn't want to be the owner of for years had taken its toll. And now, with both my parents gone, it freed her to talk.

I repeat our conversation in my head, trying to make sense of it. Had I ever wondered about adoption? Yes, of course I had, mainly because I wanted to imagine a different dad. Someone who was like the other fathers I'd gotten to know, even if I'd no way of knowing whether they were actually nice people. They could have been like my father, capable of being charming in public, while being different behind closed doors. Still, my aunt's words had felt like something out of a soap opera. One where the poor unsuspecting female, me, discovers her whole life, or what she thought was her life, is a lie. A lie, it seems, which also includes the falsification of birth records—my birth certificate, the document I'd used many times as key identification.

What did she mean, everything can be falsified given the right amount of money? How would my parents be able to do something like that? How do you even learn such skills, or did they, as my aunt had suggested, use their money to buy the help of an outsider, someone with the capability to forge documents, someone perhaps like James Lennox?

It feels too ludicrous, like some weird nightmare, or worse, that I'm jumping through so many loops ahead of time, I'm in danger of reaching all the wrong conclusions.

I think back to our conversation again, how we talked about the time my parents had gone away to England. They'd lost contact, as siblings do, but when my parents returned to Dublin, several years later, there were three of them, instead of two. A fact that surprised my aunt, not simply because they'd kept everyone in the dark about the pregnancy, but because my mother had secretly told her, before they went to England, conceiving a child was something medically beyond them. A reality my father, it seems, was unable to accept.

My aunt questioned my mother after they returned, my mother finally telling her the truth. That my father's lack of ability to conceive was something, he felt, reflected badly on his manhood. Which was why, when my mother suggested adoption, it was decided no one would ever know the child wasn't conceived naturally. My father looked at having an offspring as a status symbol, a positive reflection of his manly self. My mother was simply desperate to have a child. Later, she confided in Elaine how anxious and concerned she was that if I ever found out about the adoption, I might not love her the same way.

When I told my aunt the part about England didn't make any sense, because my place of birth was clearly stated as Dublin on my birth certificate, that's when she alluded to the possible falsification of records. After that, she became tight-lipped, saying all she was told was that the adoption happened elsewhere. She didn't want to ask too many questions, sensing, whenever she pushed either of my parents for more information, neither of them wanted to talk.

My mind is still whirling, wondering what part James Lennox played in all this. The name meant nothing to my aunt, who seems to have put two and two together over time and formed her own story. But he's attached to that house, and he's also a man capable of harming others. Did he falsify my adoption records? He was arrested for fraud, including other offences, so that part made sense.

But, unfortunately, that's not the only question hovering in my mind. A much bigger one is taking shape. Could this criminal, this man capable of violence and sexual assault, be my real father? Someone, perhaps, who was prepared to sell me to the highest bidder?

And where is my birth mother? Did she abandon me too?

27

ELIZABETH

I'M WATCHING THE BEDROOM WINDOW ACROSS THE ROAD AGAIN. There's still no sign of that girl, but then again, why should there be. It's the middle of the day. She's probably at work, although it was strange she wasn't there last night either.

I catch myself unawares. What the hell am I at? I should be doing something constructive to find Nina, instead of staring at an empty house. I should be adding to that list, the one April called *How to Find Nina*. A fresh rage rises inside me. I can't keep doing nothing.

Isn't that why I returned here, to revisit, to make a last attempt to do things I should have done the first time around? I won't be that lost woman anymore, the one who sinks into despair. I don't want to be her. I want to be someone else, someone who acts, who solves things, which is why I turn my back on the window, no longer searching for a stranger across the street.

April is right about starting points too, and the one growing in stature right now is DI Matthews's death. He didn't take his own life, I'm sure of it.

Grabbing my mobile phone, I go online. It doesn't take long to find the death notice I'm looking for, that of DI Frank Matthews on the RIP website. I also find the date, the name of the funeral home, the graveyard, along with an instruction for "no flowers," and a request that all donations go to a named charity. One I'm familiar with, which deals with suicide prevention. I guess that bit fits at least.

I scan through the list of bereaved family members. There's a son, Nicholas Matthews, with no mention of him being married or having any other siblings. Dolores, DI Frank Matthews's wife, is also deceased, and other than nieces and nephews, the only surviving close relative is the son, Nicholas.

I do another quick search on Google to see if I can find him, but as I'm doing this, I'm also wondering if Nina might be out there right now, doing the same thing. What if she's trying to find me, or at least attempting to put together the missing pieces of her life?

I like imagining things like this, because when I do, it feels more certain that my daughter is still alive.

The search for Nicholas Matthews brings up the RIP notice again, along with a link to DI Frank Matthews's appearance on *Crimecall*, repeating appeals to the public for more information about Nina Harte.

I click on Images in the tab bar, and it isn't long before I see the late detective again on-screen. Beside him are other official police images. I scroll farther down. Another image of DI Matthews appears. This time at an informal gathering with colleagues, and in this one, there's a young man who bears an uncanny resemblance to him. Could this be the son?

I change the search criteria to Nicky, Nic, or Nick Matthews. The last name pays dividends, as I find another photograph of the young man bearing that same uncanny resemblance to his father, and like his father, he's a member of the Irish police force, An Garda Síochána—the apple doesn't fall too far from the tree.

There are no address details, so I do a search on Facebook, taking a chance he might be a platform user. April would be proud of me, but that recent comment of hers, about helping older people navigate computers, hasn't yet been forgotten. She didn't mean any harm by it, but it's best not to encourage ageism in any form. Besides, why do people always want to categorise you, put you in a box and label it—it bugs the hell out of me, but I stop worrying about that when I see three hits.

The first, according to the profile, is a man with a wife and children. The second is too old, so also unlikely, but the third looks possible. I click the link. There isn't a proper profile picture, just an image of a large ice cream from Eddie Rocket's. If it's him, there are only a half dozen postings, but I know from Alison that if you're not a Facebook friend, you only get a restricted view. Importantly, though, you can still message the person. I decide to take a chance, trying to work out what I should write. It might not even be him. I decide to keep it short, not revealing too much information.

> My name is Elizabeth. I think I knew your father. I would like to meet with you about my daughter Nina.

I press Send before I change my mind. It's a long shot, but what have I got to lose. I look down at my wrists, the marks from the ropes reminding me again, I need to start taking action, and to stop behaving like a scared well-trained mouse. I think about Rachel Meadows too, and the other dead women. In that article about Rachel, the police said they were in a race against time, before the killer might strike again. I'm in a race against time too, because right now, I've no way of knowing if Nina is still alive, or if I've left it too late, the same way I left talking to Mrs. Jordan too late. She might have known something, but I simply sat back and let time slip by, feeling sorry for myself. That could happen with Nina too. You read about it all the time, how time runs out for people.

I check the message is gone, noting Nick Matthews isn't currently live on Facebook. He's probably like me, and rarely goes on to his account, but nevertheless, I could get lucky, because now I'm also thinking about that story April told me, about how, recently, she was running a race in school, and even though she knew she had no hope of winning it, and that she would most likely come last, she still had to try.

I realise I'm attempting something without any clear hope of succeeding, but at least, like April, I'll run that race. I can be proud of that at least.

28

NICK

NICK'S APARTMENT IS NOW TAKING ON THE APPEARANCE OF AN INCIdent room, a large evidence board with images of the victims and various headings taking up most of the living room wall. He underlines ATTENTION TO DETAIL before going back to the words SECRET LOCATION, a place most likely within the existing hunting ground of Dublin. A separate location also required additional planning, along with transport, most likely, a van or an SUV. Only right now, another aspect of the cases is troubling him. How Rachel Meadows and Lisa Cross were both sexually assaulted, but the latter two victims were not. Had the killer modified his behaviour with the onset of DNA? If he had, he'd be a killer with a high level of personal restraint, and if not sexual gratification, what was the killer getting out of keeping the women? Control, a sense of intimacy, or something else?

Again, Nick stares at ATTENTION TO DETAIL, aware the victims' homes didn't produce any significant forensic evidence. It's possible the killer didn't enter their primary residence, but Nick is sure, based on the profile, he did. The killer would have wanted to be there, perhaps even visiting several times, to be part of their lives, while also managing to control the crime scene. All indicating a killer who not only wanted to be close to his victims, including taking trinkets, but one who's familiar with the rudiments of DNA, possibly to the point of precision, even if it doesn't take a mastermind in forensic science to cover your tracks. An extensive Google search could tell a perpetrator a lot, but still, he had to know where to look, and what to look for, highlighting, if nothing else, an elevated intelligence, alongside a determination to go to great lengths to avoid detection.

Nick decides to concentrate on reaching out to all known associates of the first victim, Rachel Meadows, looking for anything, no matter how small, on the identity of Rachel's supposed other love interest. He makes a note to search the PULSE database too, for crimes outside of the four known victims, including those of sexual assault, where DNA profiling had proven impossible.

Either of the tasks could prove extensive, but Norris had promised him, if something solid materialised, extra resources would be applied. Right now, there was only one way to ensure things were done, and that was to take ownership of them.

He stares at his unshaven face in the mirror, the decision to work from home meaning he'd yet to shower. Working on a case like this demands a lot of an officer, sometimes infiltrating every waking moment, and sleep too. As a boy, he remembers his father doing the same, working long into the night. Nick would study him, watching from a distance, or through an opened slit in the door to his father's home office, as if it was a doorway into another world. One that, for a young boy's mind, offered intrigue. Being a police officer, a senior detective in the force, had elevated his father in Nick's eyes, making his role and his importance unquestionable. He was a man who made a difference in the world, and because of that, he regularly placed the need to track down the bad guys ahead of his family—ahead of Nick. "Other families," his father used to say, especially if a family trip was cancelled, or he couldn't attend a football match, or whatever other demands family life had made on him, "weren't as lucky as they were," causing Nick from a young age to imagine a great catastrophe befalling his family, one in which himself or his mother might come to harm, creating the need for his father to rescue them. He used to visualise it. Sometimes it was a car crash, or a burglar trying to break in, or Nick having an accident on his bike. The actual catastrophe didn't matter, the importance was the severity, sufficient to cause a shift in behaviour, his father rushing to their side to be a proper dad and husband who loved them more than anything, who would one day decide they were more important.

In the end, when something terrible did happen, it wasn't to Nick, or his mother, but to his father. When his father took his own life, it gave no dividends, especially not to Nick. The only thing his father's death achieved was a final act of deprivation, denying Nick the chance of more time with him. No childhood imaginings, no matter how heartfelt, could change that.

29

HIM

He stomps out his cigarette, another illicit activity his wife's unaware of. She doesn't know about the expensive bottles of wine either. Nor, in a million years, would she guess that right now he's watching a woman she'll never meet. A woman who will soon be dead.

He lights another cigarette, concentrating on the target, zooming in. He hears his wife start up the car outside. Sometimes, she feels like an unwanted layer of skin, relentlessly filling his head with her petty concerns. Which is why he relishes his precious time alone.

As her car pulls away, his body eases. His need is strong now, building by the hour, but only fools, he reminds himself, act in haste.

The target doesn't know he's watching, or anything about the decisions he's going to make around her future, or lack of it, but soon she will.

He turns off the camera feed, and when the screen goes black, he studies his reflection, thinking about the other women, those who for one reason or another eluded him. Sometimes, it was because of their imperfections, but not always. Some were special and still survived, before the killing, which came much later, causing him to wonder if one day he might revisit them again.

Lately, he's been thinking a lot about them, those women who are still out there, but mostly, if he's being honest, one woman in particular, who unlike the others, proved to be far more elusive, as well as complicated.

There was always something different about her, but then again, your first conquest is always special.

30

NICK

CHECKING THE FACEBOOK CONNECTIONS OF TWO OF THE VICTIMS, those who still had online accounts, Nick notices a series of messages in his inbox. He never usually uses the thing, an old account he set up before joining the force, but still, he clicks on the messages. Most are spam, random people wanting to connect, as he presses "delete" on all bar one, a message delivered a couple of days earlier.

The sender's name is Elizabeth Harte, the same name as the mother of that missing girl from years before. Is she the mother? If she is, why contact him, and why now?

He opens the message—*"My name is Elizabeth. I think I knew your father. I would like to meet with you about my daughter Nina."* Again, he wonders *why now,* while also considering if it's a hoax. People create fake names online all the time. There are enough crackpots out there, especially on social media, not to ignore the possibility. Anyone could have researched that old case online, the various press conferences, the public appeals via *Crimecall*, and the known association of his father to the investigation, including his death by suicide. Nick considers ignoring it, but finally decides to reply, asking for telephone details. If he gets an answer, he'll check the number is legit before doing anything more.

Before closing Facebook, he does his own share of snooping, clicking into Elizabeth Harte's account. She's about the right age to be the girl's mother. If it's her, there's a photograph with the other daughter, the younger girl, who was never publicly named. He remembers thinking about that other little girl, the younger one, the one left behind, as he learnt details of this high-profile case his father was working on. As a child, he looked at things simpler, wondering why this mother, whose missing daughter was taking up so much of his father's time, wasn't at least happy she still had a daughter. As an adult, things weren't that simple. He'd worked enough missing person cases to know, the questions never go away, the unknowing never ends, as everyone involved suffers the fallout, often lifelong, until that missing person returns home, dead or alive.

He's still thinking about Elizabeth Harte when his mobile rings out, and realising it's the assistant deputy commissioner, his mindset shifts fast.

"Nick, we've another missing woman."

He looks across at the evidence board, a feeling of *too little too late* staring back at him.

"When was she last seen?"

"Seventy-two hours ago, but she fits the age profile, so I thought I'd let you know."

"Do we have a name?"

"We're keeping it under wraps for now. No point running the risk of a leak before we're sure. As soon as we've a better grasp on things, I'll let you know."

"Okay."

"Any developments on Operation Shadow?"

"Right now, there are more questions than answers, but something is clear."

"What?"

"Normally, you'll find similarities, things you could call a killer's markings—location, cause of death, body found indoor or out, with clothing or without. Our killer went to great lengths to vary his MO, all four bodies found not only in different locations, but different types of locations, and despite the ligature marks, each had unique causes of death. Two by asphyxiation, another a knife wound, and finally, a drug overdose."

"So?"

"He likes to alternate."

"Maybe he wants to be one step ahead."

"I agree, but something else is at play."

"What?"

"His ego. He wants *us* to know how clever he is."

"Where's this going, Nick?"

"I'm not sure."

"What's your gut telling you?"

"They're all linked, but as yet, I can't prove it."

"And the prospect of a copycat?"

"It's possible with the latest victim, but again, either way, if it's one killer, or two, outside of being capable of murder, having a high I.Q., and being too fucking careful, his exaggerated sense of ego, alongside his need for control, is deep-rooted in his profile."

After Nick hangs up, he walks over to the evidence board, wondering what, if anything, he's still missing. The idea of the killer living a normal life has been around for a while, but the more Nick looks at it, the more convinced he is that not only are they dealing with a highly intelligent psychopath, and an extremely careful one, but a killer who likely prefers to act alone.

He stares at the word ACCOMPLICE? on the evidence board, considering the prospect that the killer didn't always act alone. It's possible at the start he had help, but then later, his desire to control would mean an accomplice would have been short-lived. This killer isn't likely to trust anyone other than himself. And if he's acting alone, somehow he gains the victims' trust, enough to disarm them or convince them to do something they shouldn't. None of the autopsy results indicated the use of a stun gun, meaning their abductor used another means once they became suspicious, and drugging them with something capable of leaving their system after a protracted time frame made the most sense.

Is that the reason he holds them? To use the extended time frame to hide evidence? Or does his need to be alone with them mean something more to him, enough to ensure they're held somewhere secluded, somewhere he wouldn't be disturbed? A place he's willing to revisit again, with whoever that next victim might be.

31

ELIZABETH

I'M PROCRASTINATING AGAIN, WATCHING A LONE BLACKBIRD IN the garden. It's brown, being female. Female birds usually have much duller plumage than their male counterparts, like the chaffinches arriving here in such large numbers of late. I'd looked it up once, discovering it's nature's way of ensuring females don't stand out, having to spend so much time in or near the nest. They need to be inconspicuous. I tried to be inconspicuous once, moving to this street over a quarter of a century ago, but I obviously didn't try hard enough. I allowed my child's abductor invade the nest, the perceived sanctuary of my young and fragile offspring.

Right now, the blackbird is happily hopping and skipping across the lawn, before suddenly taking flight. Someone is knocking hard on the front door. It coincides with a roar of thunder overhead, loud and ominous. Opening the door, I see April. She looks upset.

"Are you okay?" I ask, as the heavens open.

"No."

"Come in before you get soaked."

I wait while she positions herself on the kitchen floor, a thing she's started doing since her visits have become more regular. She looks even smaller down there with her legs tucked beneath her, holding her Harry Potter notebook tight.

A flash of lighting shoots across the kitchen window. She lets out a scream. I kneel down beside her, my body less agile, my bones, although not quite brittle, lacking the flexibility of years before. "Do you want to talk?"

"I don't think so," she says, breathing in and out, flapping her head and hands as if in warning.

"Okay," I say, "sometimes I find it hard to talk too."

"Really?"

"But they say it's good to talk."

"*They?*"

"It's just an expression."

"Oh," she says, sounding disappointed, "I thought you were talking about actual people."

"Sorry."

"I usually talk to Mam about stuff, but yesterday," she says, a glimmer of excitement taking hold, her flapping easing, "I talked to one of my Barbies."

"Was she supportive?" I ask, half-smiling at her innocence, talking to a doll replicated a million times over.

"She was a very good listener."

"Maybe you could talk to Barbie again. Listening is an important skill set, not everyone has it."

She reshuffles, lifting her body upward. "Oh, I'm getting a balloon foot."

"What?"

"I get them all the time if I sit for too long. My feet go numb, and they feel like a balloon."

"Right," I say, as she stands fully upright, and eventually, I do the same.

"When I get them," she continues, "I bounce on whichever foot isn't as balloony. It's fun . . ."

I've no choice but to watch her bounce around the kitchen, suffering from pins and needles in her foot, a.k.a. balloon-foot. I realise this is even more procrastination on my part, because I should be doing something more to find Nina, adding to that list of things to do.

"If the feeling starts to go away," she adds, breathless from bouncing, "you lift your foot up really high, and it gets balloony again."

I watch, mesmerised, until suddenly she stops. "You look so unhappy, Elizabeth. Is it the bouncing?"

"I . . ."

"It's okay. The balloon feeling is nearly gone now. You could try talking, but you're probably too old for a Barbie. A teddy might work, but it's unlikely you've one of those either."

"No," I say, "only it's not about who I can talk to, it's about the person I don't want to talk to."

"Who?"

"My daughter Alison. She messaged earlier."

"Don't you like her?"

"I love her."

"But talking to her is difficult?"

"Yes."

"Like a paradox."

"I guess."

"I don't like those. They're difficult to understand, containing two seemingly opposing facts."

"Indeed."

"Can I tell you something?"

"Of course," I reply, as I realise I may have now replaced Barbie as the selected listener.

"At school, or other places, especially when there's lots of people around, I feel as if others are inside of something, a kind of group, while I'm always on the outside."

"I think I understand."

"So, are you inside or outside, Elizabeth?"

"I don't know, except, when it comes to Alison, it's almost like we're both outside of something, and neither of us can find our way back in."

"You'll work it out. You're a very clever person," she says, before heading for the front door, as if there's an imaginary alarm clock going off in her head, reminding her it's time to leave. "I believe in you."

It's only then I realise she doesn't have her Harry Potter notebook, so I call after her, grabbing it from the floor. She's already at the front gate before she hears me.

"I didn't want you missing this," I say, catching up with her.

"Thanks." She smiles and I can't help smiling back.

"What do you use it for?" I ask, before I can stop myself.

"Observations."

"About what?"

"Everything," she says so flatly, I wonder if she's reappraising her earlier remark about my intelligence.

"Do you write about the neighbourhood?" I ask, my mind somersaulting to the missing girl from the window.

"Sometimes."

"The girl across the road," I say, pointing to the upstairs window, "she hasn't been home for days."

"She does that. She has family elsewhere."

"I see," I say, feeling stupid.

"What day is it?"

"Thursday."

"She'll be back tomorrow. Friday is her usual day to return."

"You sure?"

"Hold on." She flicks through her notebook, before saying. "Yes, here is it. Last time was a month ago. She came back on a Friday."

"Do you keep accounts of everyone's movements in there?"

"Not everyone."

And then she's gone, leaving a void where moments earlier I'd watched her bounce around the kitchen floor, and immediately my mood drops again. Is this what my life's become, a woman in her sixties gaining temporary reprieve from sadness with a ten-year-old child?

I let out a long sigh. One thing I do know. I need to stop avoiding Alison's latest text, the one insisting on meeting up. Only, it feels too soon. So instead, I switch on my laptop, considering more research. I hover over the keys, the Google search bar straight in front of me. But then, for some unknown reason, I think about my late mother again. Perhaps it was the blackbird. She always liked them, littering the lawn searching for worms. I think about how the dementia hit her hard, not long after my father died. In truth, she didn't last long after him. I guess losing both of them so close together was a necessary evil of being a child of older parents, but thinking about her now, I'm remembering how, during the last few months of her life, when she was in the nursing home, how she used to look out the window of her room at the beautiful landscaped gardens, constantly searching for the blackbirds as a reminder of home, her dementia and other medical complications dictating twenty-four-hour care.

I feel a tug at my heart, an ache, remembering my parents, especially my mother, with memories held so dear. Memories Nina hasn't had with me.

I start to think, what will it be like when it's my turn to need full-time care. I wasn't born into the IT age, but I've spent over half my life living in it. For all I know, when it is my time to go into full-time residential care, the place could be filled with all sort of technology, including Bluetooth earphones, audio books, smart tablets, or even customised high-definition 3D glasses, convincing the residents they are somewhere else, somewhere exotic. Or even, travelling back in time through memory. There'll be no need for window-views of the landscaped garden then, not if someone like Steve Jobs invents a new way for all of us to see the world.

I ignore the Google search bar. Instead, I click open my Facebook account. It's about the twentieth time I've done it since sending that message to Nick Matthews. I no longer expect a response, but this time, in the top right-hand corner, there's a reply. I double-click the message button, reading the contents. He's looking for my phone number. Has he already worked out who I am? Of course, it's typical of a police officer, answering your question with another question, but I've no interest in caring about things like that, not anymore, so I type my reply, giving him my mobile number. My fingers hover over the keys, trying to work out what else I should include in the response. I need to give him something solid to ensure he takes the bait. "Your father didn't commit suicide," I type, "and when we meet, I'll tell you why."

That should do it. I start typing again, telling him, I want to see him in a public place, one preferably this side of the city. I also want him to be alone, and not at a police station. If he's curious, none of these requests will bother him.

Again, I click Send before I can change my mind. If he takes the bait, soon I'll be sitting face-to-face with him, and soon after that, I'll be talking about things I haven't shared with anyone in years, including all the secrets I desperately tried to keep hidden, especially from those closest to me, including my late husband and both my daughters.

32

ISABELLA

(5 weeks earlier)

I RECHECK THE ADDRESS AGAIN, EYEING THE HOUSES ON EITHER SIDE of the street. When I reach the correct number, I stop at a small garden gate, taking in the exterior as if it might offer a clue as to whether this thing I'm about to do is a good idea after all.

I think about my parents' accident again, the shock of it, as imaginary flashes of the car crash form in my mind, the speed of the other car, the reported fatigue of the driver, the impact, and then my parents' mangled car, both of them being airlifted to hospital. I see the doctor's face too, before he told me that one of them had survived. Only for it to be short-lived, and somehow, because of all that, including the piece of paper with the address my mother tried to get rid of, my identity, something I thought was real, isn't real anymore.

I open the garden gate, because walking away is no longer an option, and soon I find myself on the path leading to the front door, and soon after that I'm buzzing the intercom. The top panel of the door is made of glass, my face and upper body reflected in it. I inadvertently fix my hair, as if my appearance, good or bad, might influence results. I realise I'm more nervous than I thought, but before I've time to dwell on it, the door opens. I expect to see a man, so I'm startled when a woman answers. She's small in stature, with Asian features, glasses, and dark hair. "Isabella?" she asks, her voice soft.

"Yes," I say, "that's me."

"Good, we're expecting you."

I follow her down a long hallway with a tiled black-and-white floor and doors on either side. She opens the last door on the right with the words "Waiting Room" near the top, indicating I should go inside. When she closes the door behind her, I take in the room. It's bright, painted in a soft white, with pictures of meadows and mountain peaks on the walls. In the centre there's a limestone fireplace, with scented sticks in small black jars. The fireplace is blocked up, but an ivy plant on the fire grate cascades in all directions. I hear voices. They're soft. One of them is male, the other female. I don't think it's the woman who opened the door, as her accent is different. I can't make out what they're saying.

I hear a door to another room close, followed by fast footsteps. They sound like the steps of a woman in high heels, clicking on the tiled floor. I hear the front door open. If I was in a room to the front, I might be able to gain a glimpse of the woman leaving. I'm not sure why I'm so curious. It's probably more nerves than anything else, wondering about the kind of person (other than myself) who visits a hypnotherapist. The idea of me being here, looking to hypnotherapy for answers, still feels odd.

After a few minutes, my mind shifts again to the night before my mother died. She was terrified speaking her words of warning. Was she terrified because of James Lennox, the convicted criminal who owned that house? Fear certainly dragged her out of bed that night, needing to get rid of that piece of paper. Why did she even keep it? Maybe she thought one day she'd tell me everything. She might even have imagined doing it, but that sort of unveiling of old truths requires time. Time she probably figured she didn't have after the crash, when her survival wasn't guaranteed.

Yesterday, I went back to my parents' house again too, searching for more clues, but I found nothing. I scanned the photo albums one more time, but still, I didn't find any baby or toddler images—only images of me from around the age of six or seven. It was then I thought about the night terrors, the ones I used to have. Is that why I can't remember my early childhood, because of some suppressed fear? People can do that, but equally, I tell myself, there could be a far simpler explanation. Apparently, it's not unusual to remember very little from the first years of your life, childhood amnesia being part of normal development, even though experts aren't entirely sure what causes it. Some believe it's lack of development in emotional memory in the early years, the theory being memories become stronger when they've a deep emotional component. Younger children don't have a fully developed range of emotions, and as a result, may not register the same emotional significance as those attached to the memories of an older child, adolescent, or adult—meaning early memories can disappear over time. Reading about it online, it was one of the final segments that piqued my interest, some experts believing these forgotten memories can be recalled, and how even a trigger in adulthood can unlock them. I'd felt something in that vacant house, and the way those feelings hit me, it felt like something sordid lingered.

The door to the waiting room opens, pulling me from my thoughts.

It's the woman who greeted me earlier. "Eoghan will see you now."

I take this as another instruction to follow her. Soon she opens a different door. Inside the room, a man is waiting for me, the person who's going to attempt to unravel my past and somehow unlock my lost memories.

"Isabella," he says with an accent I can't quite place, standing to greet me as he points to a chair for me to sit down on the opposite side of his desk. He looks as if he's in his mid-fifties, maybe older, but energetic, and a hint of something unexpected, probably because of his flaming red hair.

He's sitting down now, telling me about hypnosis, especially regression, and how recalling lost memories isn't as simple as it sounds. "The mind is complicated," he says. "It often has its own ideas about which memories to focus on. All we can do is explore whatever answers we find."

I'm nodding in agreement, still thinking about how much of my life has been a lie. And it's not simply because of the possible adoption—and likely, an illegal one; it's because, no matter which way I turn the information around, one way or another, I'm sure there's something dark about my past.

"Isabella, are you okay to go ahead?"

"It's just a lot to take in."

"I understand," he says, his voice calming, as is his demeanour. He stands up again, walking around the room. He's tall too, with a lean build.

"You're not Irish," I say. "I can't place your accent."

"I'm from Manchester, although I have Irish genes." He laughs, pointing to his red hair.

I sense he's being jovial to put me more at ease. He's probably done this a thousand times before.

"And yes," he adds, "it's normal to be nervous on your first visit."

I nod.

"You mentioned you'd recently visited a place that triggered a memory."

"Not a memory exactly, more a feeling, one of being afraid."

"It's good to have something concrete, although it doesn't always guarantee results."

"There's something else too."

"Oh?"

"The place where the trigger took place, I think it's somewhere connected to my past, and the previous owner has a criminal record, and he may have . . ."

He puts his hands up to stop me. "If it's okay with you, Isabella, we'll keep any risk of conjecture out of the frame. It's important to avoid influencing the hypnosis. As I said, the mind is tricky, and during regression, we're dealing with both the conscious and the subconscious mind, and as with normal everyday responses, the mind can be incorrectly influenced."

"I see."

"There's one other thing, Isabella, before we begin."

"What?"

"With hypnotic regression, when your mind returns to childhood, other factors are at play."

"Okay."

"The adult you, if we're successful with the regression, will be present, as will your child self."

"Both of us?"

"Yes, and with that, there's safety."

"What do you mean?"

"You'll be able to bring your adult experience to the memory. It will hopefully help you feel less afraid. I've worked with many clients who've found the very thing they'd blocked out, the thing they feared most, isn't quite as fearful as they remember, and the reason why is simple. A child will have anxieties that an adult won't have, mainly because the adult has a greater understanding of the trigger that caused the initial childhood distress and may determine it's not so fearful after all."

"I don't think that's the case here."

"Well, we'll see," he says reassuringly. "Let's begin."

He darkens the room by closing the blinds. He lights candles too. There is a smell of vanilla as he reclines my chair. When the chair is fully back, he says, "Isabella, I want you to visualise an iceberg."

"Okay."

"Your conscious mind is the part of the iceberg you see above the water."

The iceberg becomes clearer. The sky above it bright and cold.

"Your subconscious mind, Isabella, is the vast expanse beneath, beyond your initial vision."

The light in the room seems to dim even more.

"And remember, Isabella, when you regress, your adult self will be there at all times. Do you understand?"

"Yes."

"Good. Now, slowly breathe in and out, counting backward from twenty."

I begin counting.

"Breathe in," he says, "then out, relaxing the whole time."

I feel my body ease, my mind, although still conscious, already drifting.

"If you hear sounds, noises from outside, perhaps the sound of a car in the distance, your mind will not be disturbed."

"Okay."

"Soon, we'll be counting backward from two hundred. I want you to say the numbers in your head this time, still breathing in and out. When you reach the point where you can no longer keep track of the numbers, raise your hand."

It's harder to count this time. The numbers are slowing in my brain, although I can still hear Eoghan's voice guiding me, his tone soft, mixing with the potent scent of vanilla, as the next number becomes more difficult to remember, and I raise my right hand.

He's telling me to visualise a garden, somewhere I feel safe, and suddenly, I smell the lavender from my grandmother's garden. I'm touching the tips of the purple flowers, releasing their scent.

"There's lavender," I say, "in the garden."

"Isabella, I'm going to take you down deeper. This time, I want you to visualise a set of stairs that lead downward. As you descend, count backward from two hundred again, and once more, when the numbers get muddled, raise your hand."

As I go down the stairs, the sound of his voice is reassuring.

"Imagine, Isabella, your eyelids are now stuck down with glue, glue so strong, it's impossible to open them. Can you imagine that?"

"Yes."

The numbers are getting mixed up again. I raise my hand.

Eoghan eases my hand downward. "I want you to try to open your eyes."

He'd explained this to me before we began, that it would be his way to test the intensity of the relaxation.

"Can you open your eyes?"

I try hard, but I can't get my eyes to open.

"Good," he says. "I will count to three, and when I reach three, you'll be able to open your eyes. One, two, three . . ."

My eyes open. I feel unburdened, almost as if the many weeks of anxiety since my miscarriage, my parents' accident, and even that horrible feeling of being followed have vanished, and all the unanswered questions are suddenly silenced, because what matters now is breathing in and out and remaining calm.

"Isabella, can you hear me?"

"Yes."

"Where are you?"

"I'm in a hallway."

"What do you see?"

"Doors."

"What's on the doors?"

"Numbers."

"What numbers?"

"One to ten."

"I want you to open the door with the number six on it, and when you do, I want you to walk inside."

I do as he asks, and soon, I'm on the other side of the door. There are sounds, woodland noises amid the creaking of branches. The day is bright, warm, and my feet are bare. I smell moss, potent. It feels warm beneath my feet. My neck is hot too. And then, I see me, the little-girl me. I notice the start of sunburn on her skin, between her tightly cropped hair and the collar of her T-shirt. My father has arrived late, and my mother is arguing with him. I hate it when they argue.

"What do you see?" Eoghan asks.

"I'm in the woods. We're having a picnic. I don't want to be here."

"Why not?"

"Because my parents are shouting. Their voices are loud."

"Anything else?"

"She wants to hide in the woods."

"Who?"

"The little girl, me, only something's stopping her."

"What?"

"I don't know."

"How are you feeling?"

"Unsure. There's something about the woods that scares me." I feel my body grow more tense, frightened.

"Do you want me to take you back?"

"I don't know. Maybe I should comfort the little girl, help her."

"You're able to see her, Isabella, but she can't see you. She's part of your memory. You can't help her."

I feel my body tighten even more, my eyes searching the woods, before looking back at the picnic blanket, seeing a half-eaten sandwich beside a large grey flask, and bright red strawberries piled up high in a bowl, so real I can almost taste them, and then my eyes are drawn upward again, seeing my father's face. It's angry.

"Are you still scared, Isabella?"

"Yes."

"Then for now, I think I'll take you back."

"No," I say, "I need to stay. I need to help her, the little girl."

"Isabella," he says, "it's time."

"Okay," I say, still unsure.

"Close your eyes again, and this time, Isabella, I want you to start counting forward to twenty. When you reach that number, you'll find the door you entered through, the one with the number six on it. Are you counting?"

"Yes."

"Good."

I reach the number twenty. I tell Eoghan, "I'm at the door."

"Open it and walk through to the other side."

Soon I'm back in the hallway.

"Look down the hallway," he says. "Can you see the staircase?"

"Yes."

"Start walking toward it."

"Okay."

"Think about your breathing, Isabella. Concentrate as you breathe in and out."

"I'm at the staircase."

"Take the steps one at a time. Soon, you should see the garden."

"I see it."

"Remember, this is where you felt safe, the one with the lavender."

With each step, the smells from the garden become stronger, the scent of the lavender increasing. Soon, my fingertips touch the flowerheads again.

"Are you in the garden?" Eoghan asks.

"Yes."

"Now, close your eyes, counting forward to twenty, breathing in and out. When you reach the number twenty, Isabella, you'll be back in this room."

I count again, all the time breathing in and out.

"As the numbers get closer to twenty," Eoghan says, "you'll hear the sounds from this room, the distant noise of traffic, easing you back to the present."

"Okay," I say, as the count continues inside my head.

"At the number twenty," he instructs, "you'll be able to open your eyes again. Isabella, have you reached twenty?"

"Yes."

"Open your eyes."

They open with ease. I see Eoghan beside me, aware I'm back in the room.

"Stay in the chair for a while," he says. "There's no need to rush."

I take in my surroundings, the flames of the burning candles, the smell of vanilla, the darkened room, as gradually, the sound of the traffic from outside grows louder.

"Whenever you feel comfortable, Isabella," he says, "you can sit up."

I hear the sound of a light breeze outside, teasing the window-panes, as Eoghan lets the light back into the room.

"Are you okay?" he asks.

"I think so."

"You did well, Isabella."

"Did I?"

"Yes."

I sit up.

"What can you remember?"

I try to visualise myself back into the memory, back to the place I'd been only moments before. "I remember my parents were arguing. We were having a picnic in the woods."

"Anything else?"

"I saw myself as a little girl. My hair was cropped, and the day was hot. My neck was sunburnt too, but I didn't care about that. I hated my parents fighting. I wanted them to stop."

"You felt afraid?"

"Yes, which was why I wanted to run into the woods, only I couldn't."

"Why not?"

"I don't know. I just couldn't. The woods scared me too."

"Isabella, it's okay."

"But the regression hasn't given me any answers."

"These things take time. What's important today is that it worked."

"But what if I'm imagining it, creating a false memory, taking all the pieces I can remember to create something that isn't real?"

"I can't answer that, Isabella, but if you want, we can try again."

Part of me is still questioning what I just experienced, but another part of me is remembering that frightened little girl. She wanted to run away, to hide in the woods, only she couldn't. Something was stopping her, something I'm unable to remember, which is why I finally say to Eoghan, "Okay, let's give it another try."

33

HIM

Her strength is weakened from the lack of food, although the meagre water supply keeps her hydrated. Her resolve is at its lowest point, having tried frantically for days to escape, to scream herself free. She's lost track of time too, the lack of daylight important, as within the darkness, there's always terror, leading her mind to all sorts of assumptions. All of it weakens her physical and mental ability to rationalise, to maintain a sense of self, because ultimately, the captor, not the captive, is the one in charge.

The key turns in the first lock. He waits, listening to see if it registers a response—nothing. It's only a few steps to the next door. This time, she'll definitely hear the key turn, her mind a mix of possibilities. She might even think she's being saved. This thought will soon be followed by the other less attractive one, that the person she's about to confront means her harm.

He hears a gasp as he turns the handle. Soon, he's pointing the torchlight at her, the light stark after the days of darkness. She retreats, instinctive, afraid.

"What do you want?" she wails, her back pressed tight against the wall, as if he repulses her.

"You don't need to know that," he says, "not yet. But I know things about you."

Her eyes aren't yet accustomed to the light, but soon they'll adjust, and when they do, she'll recognise him. She'll be startled at first, unable to comprehend that the nice guy in the park, the one who'd been interested in her fitness regime, may be the very person who'll end her life.

"Would you like me to tell you what I know?"

She doesn't respond. Perhaps she's trying to work out a strategy, but it won't do her any good.

"Your name is Charlotte Marry. You're thirty-five years old. Your birthday is May eighth. You're the eldest in your family, with one sibling, a brother named Luke. He was in town recently. You met him for dinner, and insisted on paying, being the older sibling. Work has been a trial of late. That new boss of yours is applying extra pressure, which is why, two weeks ago, you booked a holiday to Italy, a chance to explore Italian cuisine. You're very fond of certain recipes, including carbonara, your favourite. I've watched you order it time and time again, licking your lips, adoring its creamy texture. Your latest fitness regime is an attempt to get your body back in check."

She breathes in deep.

"I also know what's in your fridge, and every item in your wash cycle that's been sitting in your washing machine for days. I've read your little notes written to yourself as reminders of things to do, the yellow Post-its stuck all over your apartment. I also know what you're thinking right now. Your logical brain, despite everything, is trying to sort it into shape. Part of you already knows I will kill you. You've seen enough crime programmes on television to know the killer can never reveal his or her identity unless their victim ends up dead."

He hears another gasp, the realisation hitting home, before instructing her to sit on the wooden crate closest to her. Perhaps she'd wondered why there were two crates, and if she had, now she knows the answer, as he sits on the second, opposite her.

"That's right," he says, "it's time for us."

She nods, compliant.

"The first time I killed someone, Charlotte, I thought I'd feel a sense of remorse, guilt even, but it was nothing like that, it was rage."

She whimpers—her terror gaining momentum.

"Have you ever felt like that, Charlotte, full of rage?"

She shakes her head in denial.

"No?"

"No," she whimpers.

"It's good to share things, though, isn't it?"

This time she nods in agreement.

"Great. I like that you're already starting to understand me."

She nods again.

"You probably think I'm some kind of weirdo."

She shakes her head in denial, trying to appease the captor.

"I've tried to live a normal life, Charlotte, and, to an extent, I've succeeded. Others, outside of these four walls, view me as normal, but appearances can be deceptive. Only, you already know that."

Her body seems to shrink in size, as she crouches inward, unsure.

"But once you've killed someone, Charlotte, you realise it's the ultimate power. You become almost godlike, deciding who'll carry on living, and who won't."

"Are you going to kill me?"

"Yes," he says, "but the real question is how."

34

ELIZABETH

I WISH I HAD A NOTEBOOK LIKE APRIL'S, WHERE I'D WRITTEN EVERY-thing down, things from months ago, or years ago. It would help me when I meet Nick Matthews. If I had written everything down, I'd be able to recall the exact details of the days and weeks leading up to Nina going missing. How I felt someone was watching me again, and how I'd dismissed it as paranoia, too stupid then to understand the *real* reason he might have returned. Instead, putting it down to delayed trauma. If I hadn't been so stupid, then maybe . . .

"Oh, stop it, Elizabeth," I say aloud, "stop all the *if only this, if only that* . . . they're not going to help anyone." My eyes dart around the kitchen, making sure I'm alone, in case talking to myself gives someone else another reason to dismiss me, or call me crazy.

What I still recall is how I had a sense of him, even if I was in denial. The same way I know when my son-in-law, Ciaran, is lurking around, a kind of crawling feeling, clingy and instinctively insidious. I'd tried to explain that crawling sensation to the police once, and Alison too, but neither of them got it. Later, I'm sure Alison shared my fears with Ciaran, because afterward, it became a new habit of his, appearing unexpectedly, creeping around corners, suddenly staring at me, or moving things, like my purse or my keys. At first, the missing items would turn up, usually somewhere different, somewhere I hadn't put them. It was useless trying to tell Alison I hadn't misplaced them, or that I wasn't being forgetful or stupid. In part, I think Ciaran wanted me to openly unravel, to become hysterical, and outright blame him. That way, I'd fall into another one of his little traps, so he could undermine me even more. And I know exactly when it all started, Ciaran's efforts to undermine me. It was after I found that receipt for a hotel stay in Galway, when he was supposedly in Wexford for work. I'd put it aside, planning on telling Alison about it, but then, like the other items that would disappear for no reason, it too was gone. I'd challenged him over it. He denied it of course, suggesting I'd been overdoing things. Perhaps I'd watched too many crime dramas on television, laughing at me. He even goaded me to tell Alison, saying he'd already suggested to her that I was losing it. It could have been a lie, him warning Alison that I was losing it, as making things up on the spot is a talent of his, but either way, I decided to hold my tongue until I had more proof. But by then, the damage was done, Ciaran having invested so much time and effort in undermining me with my daughter at every turn that unless I had something concrete, other than my word against his, it was a losing battle.

I guess I should have written all of that down too. I read once that diary entries and journal notes can be used as evidence in court. Still, no point in thinking about that now. Instead, I need to plan my prospective meeting with Nick Matthews.

He'll be keen to know why I'm so convinced his father didn't commit suicide, and that's understandable. I realise people often have their reasons for doing something like that; heaven knows, I'd considered it in the past. I'll explain this to Nick too, as well as telling him the person I'd spoken to all those years before, about wanting to take my own life, was his father. I told DI Matthews a great many things. Things I hope his son is prepared to hear now.

I spread out the newspaper clippings again, the ones about Rachel Meadows. I had the same dark, sinking feeling when I found out about her, that the man who abducted and killed her is known to me. I look again at the markings on my wrists, a physical reminder of his cruelty. I wish I could have spoken to Alison about this, but that was impossible, and now, I feel like a bit of a traitor, being prepared to tell a stranger all the sordid details, instead of her.

I suppose there are things in life everyone wants to hide. I heard once how humankind can only bear so much reality, and it's true, because I've been running away from reality for a very long time. Only now, I can't do that anymore.

It's getting late, so I pull the living room curtains over, a part of me still wanting to retreat, even for a short while. Sitting down, I allow my mind to ease, the room now darkened, as my exhaustion takes hold. As on previous evenings, I curl up on the couch with a blanket over me, my mind searching for oblivion, needing everything to slow down, or stop. Only, closing my eyes, my head seems to have other ideas, bringing back into focus another afternoon, one from years before. An afternoon I did my utmost to eradicate from my mind.

I hadn't heard him enter the house. I had no knowledge he was even there, until it was too late. I realise now he must have been biding his time, waiting, ensuring when he entered I'd be alone, defenceless, and not for the first time in my life, I wonder about human cruelty, and how, just because some people can't comprehend it, doesn't mean it doesn't exist, and once you've been exposed to it, it changes you, like an imperfection on a piece of fruit that needs to be severed or it will rot the fruit to its core.

35

ISABELLA

(4 weeks earlier)

TODAY, VISITING EOGHAN AGAIN, I UNDERSTAND MORE ABOUT hypnotic regression, realising you can't force your mind to behave in a certain way. Eoghan is aware of my disappointment, that although the regression has worked, it hasn't given me anything concrete. Which is why, before we attempt any further regression, we're discussing options.

"I think I've blocked out huge chunks of my early memories," I say. "I can't remember a time before any of the photographs in my parents' house."

"As you said yourself, Isabella, it's not unusual for this to happen. Early childhood memories don't hold the same level of emotional intensity as later ones."

"But something feels wrong."

"It's also possible your mind is preventing you from remembering, blocking your subconscious, the part that holds all your memories intact. Indeed, even if you try to momentarily gain access to those locked memories, your mind will respond so fast, it shuts them down before you even realise it's doing it."

"I know we can't instruct the mind to go back to a particular memory, but you mentioned there were other options."

"Yes, we could *try* to guide it. Regression via hypnosis enables the mind to travel more easily across the dimension of time. We might suggest a certain age for you, ask your mind to travel back to it, and see what happens."

"What age?"

"What age do the photographs in your parents' house begin?"

"Probably age six."

"Okay then. We'll try an age before that."

"That simple?"

"No, Isabella, it's not that simple, but possible."

Just like before, during my first regression session, Eoghan asks me to count backward, and soon, I'm standing in the same garden, the one with the lavender bushes. This time, I feel the ground soft beneath my feet, like a cushioned carpet, and the light is dazzling too, sunspots forming in front of my eyes.

Again, Eoghan asks me to find the staircase that leads ultimately to the same hallway, this time asking me to look for the door with the number four on it. The numbers are all mixed up, so it takes me a while to find it.

"Isabella, when you open this door, you'll be brought back to age four, are you okay with that?"

"Yes."

"Then, if you're sure, turn the handle."

As my hand reaches down, I feel the brass knob, shiny with a tiny bump on it. It's cold in my hand, but I turn it, and soon I'm on the other side.

"What do you see, Isabella?"

At first, I can't see anything, as if I'm wearing a blindfold. All I hear are sounds. I hear a woman's voice, and then that of a young child, a girl. It's summertime again, I can tell by the heat of the sun on my face, and then I say, "I'm standing outside."

"Where are you?" Eoghan asks.

"I'm in a garden. My vision is clearing. There's red fuchsia bushes and blue and white lobelia." I reach down and pick up a fuchsia bud. It feels velvety, and when I look up, my vision becomes even clearer. I see the shape of a woman. She isn't alone. There are two young girls on a set of garden swings. They're swinging back and forth, laughing. The older girl has dark hair, and the younger one is blonde, bleached from the sun.

"Are you alone?" Eoghan asks.

"No, there's a woman here. She has her back to me, but there are two young girls with her. They're on a set of swings."

"Describe what you see."

"The swings have a wooden frame, with green seats. The two girls seem to be in some sort of competition with each other. The older girl is four or five, and the younger girl might be three, or younger. I think the older girl could go faster, but she wants to encourage the younger girl, telling her she's doing great."

"Do they call each other by name?"

"No."

"Do you know them?"

"I can't be sure, but there's something about the older girl . . ."

"What?"

"I don't know. I can't risk getting too close. I don't want to frighten her."

"Does she look afraid?"

"I'm not sure. She was laughing before, but now, it's as if she's concentrating hard."

"What do you want to do, Isabella?"

"I want to walk closer."

"Take five steps forward."

I do as Eoghan instructs.

"What can you see now?"

"The same thing, only . . ."

"What?"

"The woman, she doesn't want to turn around, and the little girls . . ."

"What about them?"

"They're calling her Mom."

"See if you can walk even closer, so you can make out the woman's face."

"Okay." Again, I do as Eoghan asks, only when I do, the sun is so dazzling, it blocks my vision again. "I can't see it," I say. "The sun is blurring everything, but there's something . . ."

"What?"

"A feeling."

"What kind of feeling?"

"It's hard to explain."

"Take your time."

I try to find the words, but it's like I'm stuck in a dream, unable to work things out. I step back from the woman and the young girls, studying them from a distance. They look so happy, all three of them, which is why the feeling I have inside seems totally wrong, disjointed.

"They're happy," I tell Eoghan, "and I'm sad."

"Why do you feel sad?"

"Because I want to be part of them, but I don't think that's possible."

"Why not?"

"I don't know. I want the woman to turn around, to see me, but she can't."

"Are you feeling distressed?"

"Yes. I want to cry."

"Then it's time to take you back, Isabella."

"No, not yet," I say, realising I'm already crying.

"I'm taking you back," Eoghan repeats.

And like before, I count as he guides me through the doorway, out into the hall with the staircase coming back into view, before finally, I reach the garden with the lavender bushes, and I feel safe again.

The same as the last time, he doesn't rush me, but eventually, as the sights and sounds of the room return, and the light in the room is no longer dark, I sit upright, a part of me more confused than ever.

"What do you think?" I ask him.

"About which part?"

"All of it."

"Well, the initial regression definitely brought you back to a place you didn't feel safe, in those woods."

"Yes, but this felt different."

"Why did it feel different?"

"Because it's something I've no real memory of. How could I? I don't know that woman, but maybe it's part of my suppressed memory. I mean, why did I see a woman and two children? There's nothing in my past, or at least that I know of, to explain them."

"You said you felt sad in the garden, but yet, they seemed happy."

"I wanted to be part of them, even though I didn't know why. It's really difficult to explain."

"Take your time."

I try to make sense of it, the emotions I felt, and after a few moments, I realise something. "I think I understand the feeling now," I say, "the one I had with the woman and the two little girls."

"What?"

"It was a feeling of loss."

"For what?"

"Seeing them happy, being a family, a unit, something I no longer have. Something, perhaps, I never had, not really."

He nods.

"Do you think that scene, Eoghan, might be a lost slice of memory, or perhaps something I've made up in my head because I want to be part of a family again?"

"It's too early to tell, but it's a beginning."

"Okay," I reply, unsure what else to say.

"When you go home, Isabella, I want you to take care of yourself. You'll feel extremely tired. There's a lot of emotions involved here."

"Okay," I say again.

"Do you want to schedule another session?"

"Yes," I reply.

"It's a process, Isabella, but perhaps soon, we might try another approach."

"What?"

"Let's take it one step at a time."

Leaving Eoghan's office, the word "time" circles around in my head. I think about the regression again, the potential elements of my unknown past being rediscovered, or worse, that this could be a complete waste of time, my mind tricking me into all sorts of imaginings. Only, I know I can't stop now.

I'm halfway home when another thought strikes me. *What if I don't have enough time?* I've heard so many stories about adults seeking out their natural birth parents, only for them to find out who they were when it was too late. I think about my parents in that car crash again. My father didn't expect his life to be cut short, and even though my mother might have worried death was near, she couldn't have known for sure. None of us know how much time we have left, and if my suspicions about my birth details are correct, and I was potentially illegally adopted, I've no guarantee either of my biological parents are still alive, even if one of them could be a criminal.

36

HIM

Charlotte didn't last long. After that first conversation, he could tell she was going to be a disappointment. A pity, because she'd showed so much promise at the start.

At home, in the bathroom, as his wife busies herself downstairs, he rinses his face and hands, staring at his reflection, wondering if there's something about a killer's face that could, once identified, give the game away.

He splashes more water. It's not like him to dwell on things, but it's probably tiredness from the night before. Despite his physical fitness, each time he kills, it takes a little more out of him.

"Breakfast," his wife calls from below. She doesn't know anything about what he did last night. She thinks he was seeing old friends, and in part, that was true, even if the "old friends" part was singular.

In the end, the way he killed Charlotte was born out of both necessity and desire. The pressures of the last couple of days had taken their toll. He needed silence more than anything, and time to think too. Which was why the killing had to be fast. One swift cut to the neck, tearing the inner wall of the carotid artery, causing internal bleeding and blood flow problems. The desired result, an immediate stroke. Strange as it seems, many wounds inflicted by a knife are relatively clean, with the demise of the victim so rapid, there isn't enough time for a body to bleed out.

The killing part was easy, but the burial took more effort, needing to be done somewhere both dark and secluded. Hiding the body was important, because he needed to buy himself more time. That phone call yesterday changed everything, completely shifting his area of focus.

"Coming," he shouts downstairs, after his wife calls him a second time.

He considers how fortune often favours the bold, because at long last, the woman now at the centre of his attention is exactly where he wants her to be.

37

NICK

AT DAWN, NICK AWAKES, HAVING SLEPT FULLY CLOTHED AGAIN ON the couch. His body aches, stretching upward, the nightmare still hovering. He'd been dreaming about the killer, searching for the place he kept the women—an abandoned farmhouse, a warehouse by the quays, somewhere underground? There was something about a vehicle too, an SUV or a van, because the killer needed something large, a means of transporting victims without being detected.

He's frustrated his searches on PULSE; searching for crimes where DNA profiling failed resulted in a ridiculously large list, meaning another cross-reference point was required. He walks over to the evidence board and writes: "Reports of victims being stalked." His mind shifts to the profile again, a killer who is intelligent, orderly, living a life under the radar, a normal existence, but someone who along with his ability to stalk victims holds a sufficient grasp of DNA to alter MO, always keeping him one step ahead. The location where he keeps his victims is likely isolated, or soundproofed, or both. Right now, he's riding high, believing no one is going to stop him, and his need to kill again is absolutely guaranteed, potentially via a trigger, pressure from a wife or partner, or something else.

Odds are, he's socially skilled too, someone the victims find socially acceptable, possibly disarming, meaning he'll likely communicate with them before any violence occurs, but then after the abduction, what then? Is he reconstructing something from his past?

Pacing the floor, he also wonders if there are answers in earlier parts of the killer's trajectory, but how far back should he look? The pre-killing stage, certainly, perhaps when sexual assault gave this guy all the control he needed. It's another potential haystack, but perhaps one easier to explore. After all, only 1 percent of sexual assaults ends up in a conviction. Could he get lucky? Could this killer have appeared in the courts before?

He stares at the word "EGO" on the board, because it's ego that's usually their undoing. They start to feel invincible, and when they do, even the most careful killer makes a mistake. When that happens, Nick wants to be the one to nail him.

His mobile phone rings out, and grabbing it from the couch, he realises it's Norris again. If he's phoning this early, it's important.

"That missing woman hasn't turned up," Norris says, "and more elements are matching the victim profile."

"Go on."

"As I said before, her age for one; plus, it's completely out of character for her to fall off the radar like this. And according to friends and family, she recently took up jogging. This new hobby means she's been running alone in the local park, one that doesn't have a lot of CCTV coverage other than the car park, and even that's limited."

"The perfect opportunity for someone with bad intentions."

"Yep."

"Any talk of her being watched? Did she mention being nervous, or anything like that to family or friends?"

"No, but it's been viewed as high priority because of the profile of the victim and her disappearance being out of character."

"What about her work?"

"She had time off, so her going missing hadn't immediately registered on their radar."

"Our guy would have known that. He makes it his business to know these things."

"Either way, I thought I'd fill you in."

"If she's another victim, Norris, he's taken his time—four years."

"He's waited that long before. Besides, I'm not sure psychopaths follow the same timelines as the rest of us."

"This guy is different. He likes his details, but still, all it takes is a trigger. What's the missing woman's name?"

"Charlotte Marry."

Nick doesn't want to write another potential victim's name on the board, but he does, and after hanging up on Norris, he notices an alert on his phone. It tells him he has a new Facebook message. Opening it, he sees it's from Elizabeth Harte, giving her phone number and some broad instructions about meeting up, but what grabs his attention most are her words. *Your father didn't commit suicide, and when we meet, I'll tell you why.*

38

ELIZABETH

I'M DUE TO MEET NICK MATTHEWS TODAY. I NEED TO BE BRAVE, because no matter how many years have passed, the thought of going back in time, remembering, recalling, reliving it, makes it all real again. I've never considered myself particularly brave, and in truth, a lot of us avoid having to be. Mostly, bravery happens by accident or is forced on a person. The second kind I'm familiar with, the forced kind. Does that make me brave? I'm not sure. All I know is that for a time, for me, survival had to be enough. But today it's different, because today, meeting Nick Matthews, I want more. I want answers.

The agreed meeting point is the Black Sheep restaurant in Terenure. He's kept to his side of the bargain, following each of my requests—public place, not a police station, meeting alone, and on this side of the city. I'm due to see him in less than ten minutes, which is why I'm so tense. I really shouldn't be. I've delivered two babies, survived a broken marriage, lost a child, buried an ex-husband, and lived through a fair amount of cruelty. Nick Matthews should be a piece of cake. Except meeting him opens up old wounds. Ones that are still fragile, and therefore emotionally risky.

When I arrive at the restaurant, it's extremely busy, the demand for tables brisk. I feel unsure again, but when a young waitress dressed in black, wearing a white name tag that says ELEANOR on it, smiles in my direction, I feel a bit more at ease.

"Table for one?" she asks.

"For two, please," I say, "and at the back, if possible."

If I were younger, she might think I'm having an illicit affair, needing discretion and a certain level of privacy, but either way, she doesn't comment, grabbing two menus and indicating I should follow her.

"Thanks, Eleanor," I say once seated. "I'll wait for my companion before I order, if that's okay."

Waiting makes me anxious again, and the sunlight streaming in from the large front window causes the restaurant entrance to become less clear, placing me on high alert. Maybe I *should* order some tea, to calm me, give myself something to do, rather than just sit here. I mean, I don't know how long Nick Matthews might be. He could be one of those people who never arrives on time.

Eleanor catches my eye. "A large pot of tea, Eleanor, please."

"Sure."

A few moments later, taking an initial gulp from the white mug with a funny black sheep on the front, I feel more grounded. I wonder if Nick Matthews intends to interview me the way you'd interview a suspect or a witness to a crime. Does he operate that good cop/bad cop routine, the one you often see on television, and being alone, which one will he be?

He's no doubt thought about our meeting. Even if he hasn't questioned his father's suicide before this, he'll likely be questioning it now. His father was a high-ranking detective. You don't get to a position like that without accumulating your fair share of enemies but getting Nick Matthews to accept the possibility of foul play is another thing entirely. Killing a high-ranking police officer, even a retired one, wouldn't be an attractive proposition for the average criminal, but unfortunately, if my suspicions are right, and DI

Matthews did discover something about Nina, and therefore needed to be silenced, there's absolutely nothing average about the person who might have killed him. Men like that are capable of almost anything, if the stakes are high enough.

Then there are the rumours to consider. I've spent enough time hanging around police stations in the past to learn a few things about how the police operate. It was all innuendo, whispers, but I bet Nick Matthews must have heard them too, the talk of bribes and suspect police behaviour.

The door to the restaurant opens, and even though he's blurry initially, I know it's him, looking so much like his father, for a second I have to do a double take. He waves in my direction, obviously having checked out what I look like too, armed with a visual of the potential suspect/witness.

"Elizabeth," he says, "may I join you?"

"Of course."

He orders a large Americano, maybe figuring he'll be here for a while. I brace myself.

"Your message was intriguing," he says.

I decide honesty is the best policy. "I wanted to ensure you'd turn up."

"Well, I'm here. So, you succeeded."

"You look like your father."

"I know."

"Are you like him?"

"Probably more than I want to admit."

"He was the senior investigating officer on my daughter's missing persons case."

"Yes, I know. Although I was only a teenager at the time."

"Was your father still working on the case before he retired?"

"No, but he kept a keen interest. Others looked after the case reviews."

"I think the police gave up on finding Nina a long time ago."

He repositions himself in the chair. "I'm not going to lie to you, Elizabeth. With the passing of time, leads become stale, but that doesn't mean the police give up. It's our job to find answers, to solve things, and cold cases like your daughter's are challenging, but you never know when a fresh lead will turn up."

"Or not."

"Indeed, or not."

I take another sip of tea.

"I know it's hard for you, Elizabeth."

"Nina's been missing over twenty-five years."

He leans forward, his voice low. "Look, Elizabeth, I'm sorry about Nina, I truly am, but if you've information about my father's death, which I assume you have, then I want to hear it."

"Now I'm here," I say, looking away, "it feels more difficult."

"Take your time."

I scan the restaurant; the habit of checking that no one is watching or listening is hard to shake. "Over time," I say, "I came to understand certain things about your father."

"Which are?"

"He was a man of secrets. He only ever told you what you needed to know."

"Lots of detectives are like that, Elizabeth. They keep their cards close to their chest."

His words sound confident, but his right eyebrow is twitching, and I'd wager he's placing that reference to "secrets" firmly inside his head.

"I became close to your father during those early days of Nina's disappearance, a forced relationship of sorts."

"It was a 24-7 investigation."

"It was. And your father liked to give out advice too."

He nods in agreement.

"When I say we became close, I don't mean in an intimate way, but yet, over time, he managed to find out a lot of intimate details about me."

"That's the job, finding out information."

"I guess," I say, breathing in deep, placing my hands flat on the table. He looks down at my long, slim fingers and I already know why. His detective brain is taking note of them. He might already be wondering if his current cold case enquiries are anything to do with me, the ones investigating the murders of those four women. A piece of information I discovered only yesterday, but information I'm happy to know about before meeting up with him.

"I told your father certain things," I say, "things I never told anyone else—private things."

"Private?"

"Yes, because once Nina went missing, nothing was private anymore. Even my late husband was placed under suspicion."

"That's not unusual. Sadly, Elizabeth, perpetrators are often far closer to home than we realise."

"Your father said that too."

He nods. "Go on."

"So, I had to tell him . . ."

"What?"

"About my assault, my rape." I clench my fists. There, I tell myself, I've done it. I've opened the windows to my past. I've said it aloud, and now that I have, there's no taking it back.

He looks startled, this last piece of information surprising him.

"It happened before Nina was born," I say, suddenly, as if a part of me wants to blurt the whole thing out.

"How long before?"

I look away again, stalling, biting my lip to gain courage.

He repeats the question. "How long?"

"Nine months."

His facial muscles tighten, his brain moving fast now, acknowledging the obvious implication that Nina's birth was likely the result of my assault.

"And you told my father this?"

"Yes."

"So, I assume the biological father, your attacker, must have entered the frame."

"He became another suspect, yes."

"And?"

"And nothing. There were never any worthwhile leads to help your father identify him, or to find Nina."

"So, you didn't know him? Your attacker?"

"Only in the way you'd know a passing stranger."

"Were you able to give a description, create a sketch?"

"Yes, but it was difficult. I mean, before the assault, I really hadn't registered him as important. I didn't have a clear recollection of his face, and during the attack, all I could see were his eyes. I'll never forget those."

"I know this is difficult for you, Elizabeth, but what does any of it have to do with my father's death? You said you had proof it wasn't suicide."

"I know it wasn't suicide."

"Because?"

"Your father was complicated."

"I know that too."

"He had regular bouts of arrogance, frustration even, but yet, I felt I could open up to him."

"He had a way of getting information out of people."

"Which is why, when I finally spoke to him about the assault, I told him absolutely everything, all the sordid details, including how, during it, my attacker tied me up."

There's another movement of his eyebrow.

"Go on."

"At the time, I thought the assault was the worst part, but I was wrong. I learned the aftermath was far worse. You don't realise, in the beginning, that so much is taken from you. Or how your vulnerability, in all its terrifying forms, is laid completely bare. Someone else, you realise, can decide your fate, and that's a scary place to be, because *they*, not *you*, have all the power."

I think about my son-in-law, Ciaran, and how I see the same need for power in him. When you've met someone capable of the worst of crimes, others like them are often far too easily recognisable.

"Even if I couldn't identify my attacker," I say, "I know he's still out there, because men like him don't stop. If anything, they get worse. They do even more heinous things." I consider mentioning the articles I've read about the murdered women, including Rachel Meadows, but I've shared too much with the police before, and often, too soon, so I hold back.

"I'm sorry to hear about your assault," he says.

"I'm sorry too."

"Sadly, Elizabeth, I've heard stories like yours before, and assaults like the one you experienced are life-changing."

"I told your father that afterward, I tried to rebuild my life, start afresh, and even though I could never go back to the 'before,' despite everything, after Nina was born, I *did* rebuild my life. She was the prize, you see, the gift for all the horror. The only thing I could tell myself, that made any sense of it."

"Go on."

"And then she was gone, and all the fears I'd managed to bury came right back to the surface. Only, this time, it was worse, because along with the fear there was the loss of something more precious than me. There was the loss of Nina. And it was then, in those dark days of despair, that the prospect of taking my own life felt like the only way forward. I'd no more fight left in me."

"You wanted it all to go away."

"Yes."

"Only, you didn't take your own life, Elizabeth, did you?" He takes my hands in his. It immediately feels too intimate. I pull them back, recoiling. I tell myself to calm down. I can't go losing it now. He's not going to do me any harm. He's not my attacker, or even Ciaran. He's just a man, a person, who for a moment wanted to ease my pain.

"I'm sorry," I say.

"It's okay."

I breathe in deep again. "I told your father about the suicide, Nick, how I'd planned to do it."

"And?"

"He told me it was the coward's way out. And, at first, I was angry. I mean, what right did he have to judge me? But then later, when the prospect of Nina being found diminished, I thought about it some more, and I knew he was right. I couldn't take the easy way out, because to do that would have meant abandoning Nina, and my other daughter too, to give up on them, and no matter how dark and horrible life became, I couldn't do that."

"And this is why you think my father didn't kill himself?" he asks, his entire body tense now. "Because he told *you* not to do it?"

"Yes."

"People aren't always good at following their own advice."

"Maybe not, but the way your father said it, it didn't feel like he was just talking about me. It felt like he was talking about himself, as if it was something he'd previously considered and decided against. Your father, as I said, was complicated, but once he forged a belief, it became embedded."

"You can't be sure."

"No, but I felt it. The same way I'm positive someone else played a role in his death."

He looks at me as if he's trying to square things up in his own mind, finally wondering if I could be a nutjob. I'm sure he's probably heard things about me too. He hasn't arrived here unprepared.

"Do you have a theory, Elizabeth, as to who that *someone* might be?"

"It could be the person who attacked me, the guy who took Nina."

"You've no proof all three are connected. I mean, even if you're right, why wait all this time?"

"Perhaps before his retirement, your father figured something out. It's possible, isn't it? You said yourself, Nick, he always kept a keen interest in the case."

"In theory anything's possible, but, Elizabeth, honestly, it's a long shot."

"Maybe so, but all I know is this: the moment I heard about your father's suicide, I thought it, and that idea hasn't gone away. The same way I cling to the hope of finding my missing daughter. The same reason I contacted you, because with your father gone, you're one of the few links I have left."

"Elizabeth, I can't bring your daughter back. I'm not even assigned to the case. In fact—"

"That doesn't matter."

"No?"

"No," I say, adamant. "Part of the reason I came back here was because I needed to at least try one more time to find her. It doesn't matter how many needles in haystacks exist, because one of them might have the answer."

He leans back in the chair, taking it all in, before saying, "I used to think about you, Elizabeth, when I was younger."

"Why?"

"Because my father was so obsessed with the investigation. For months, we barely saw him. I guess some cases are like that, they get into the core of you, so much so that even as a young teenager, I knew this investigation was different from the others."

"I've spent over twenty-five years placing my life on hold."

He nods in acknowledgment.

"I've even sabotaged a relationship with my other daughter. It was one of the reasons why my marriage failed too, and yes, before you ask, it was only after Nina went missing that my husband found out about the assault. I foolishly thought for a time, I could pretend, put it behind me, but the investigation changed all that. There wasn't anywhere to hide. But, do you know, one of the hardest things about all of it?"

"What?"

"Even if a miracle happened, and Nina is found alive, I can never get my five-year-old daughter back. The best I can hope for is a thirty-year-old stranger."

"So why now, Elizabeth?"

"Why not now?"

"Look," he says, still staring at my long, slim fingers, "I'll do what I can, and if I find out anything, I'll be in touch."

"That's all I can ask."

As the lunchtime crowd disperses, it feels as if everything has been said. I wait, watching him walk away. Aware I've at least struck a chord with him, a sprig of curiosity. It even might be enough for him to start digging into old police files, because all it takes is one needle, in one haystack.

39

ELIZABETH

ALL THE WAY HOME, I CAN'T GET THE CONVERSATION WITH NICK Matthews out of my head. I know I've changed, and I'm not sure if it's April and her unfailing unorthodox spirit, being different to everyone else, or if the change goes deeper, something coming from the inside out. But at least now I'm actively trying to find Nina, instead of living in Alison's house as if I'm some aged figure from a Dickens novel, with the hours of my life falling like snow, making me more invisible day by day, not only to others, but to myself.

The other me, the woman, and the life I lived before running away, wouldn't have taken a leaf out of April's book and tracked Nick Matthews down. Nor would she have found out where he was stationed. But that's exactly what I did yesterday. I stalked his place of work. I sat in Terenure police station for hours on end, even though I'd no guarantee I'd find out anything about him.

At first, I was anxious sitting there with no official reason for it, but then I told myself, *Nobody's noticing me.* Most people are caught up in their own lives, including whatever reason brought them to the police station in the first place. My insignificance allowed me to go unnoticed. I don't have the allure or attractiveness of a younger woman. I'm not male, with the potential for anger and therefore a threat, nor am I a child either who might pique a person's interest. Nobody really notices older people, making it the perfect camouflage. They certainly wouldn't think me a spy, even though I was listening intently.

I'd been there for over an hour when the two plainclothes detectives struck up a conversation. Initially it was about the Premier League, then the age of their police cars, which I assumed weren't the latest models, much to their irritation. I was already losing interest when one of them asked, "What do you think about Nick Matthews?"

I looked up immediately, listening hard.

"He breezes in and out of here like he's bloody God Almighty, but Norris likes him, so watch your back."

I couldn't hear the next part of their conversation, so I stood up to get closer, on the ruse that I was checking something out on the notice board.

"He's looking into those four dead women."

"Nobody has been able to connect those."

"Well, Norris must have high hopes."

"Delusional."

"For sure."

"How do you know about it?"

"Because Nick Matthews went to the Meadows's house last week."

"Really?"

"It was on his expense sheet, and Norris cleared it."

They both smirked, delighted with their elevated detective skills. Either way, that's when I discovered Nick Matthews was investigating the murders. Which is why I also knew what he was thinking when he looked at my long, slim fingers. The fingers were mentioned in the last documentary about the dead women, talking about Rachel Meadows, and another woman, Kimberly Campbell, having had additional locks fitted at her home.

In the car, I stare down at my hands. I don't think Nick noticed the markings, but then again, I did tell him I was tied up—another connection to his cold cases.

After our conversation, I didn't drive off straightaway. Instead, I allowed my mind to wander, revisiting the time before Nina was born, in the early stages of my pregnancy, when I'd wondered how I could even carry this child, conceived by the man who stole so much from me, who caused me to live in fear, to become someone who didn't have any idea how to crawl her way back. That crawl back began with the child inside me. The one I'd do anything now to hold in my arms.

Nina was, and is, part of me. It was me, not him, who carried her to full term, protecting her, right down to her tiny unique fingerprints. I nurtured her when she couldn't sustain herself, and it was her dependence on me that saved me, because her need meant we were in this fight together. And after she was born, it was my job to continue to protect her, and my failure to do that defines me too.

In my mind's eye, I visualise the house in the photograph, the home I lived in with my parents before they died, and then afterward alone. I see the white rosebush in the front garden. The roses large, fully in bloom. I visualise the pebbled pathway behind the small, black wrought iron gate with low concrete pillars on either side. Beyond them is the front door, which, like the window frames, boasts a shade of royal blue. I imagine the rooms behind the windows. I can't help but shiver, because the younger, innocent me was waiting upstairs in that house, unaware her life was about to be turned upside down. He had been so quiet in the house before he entered the bedroom. I had no knowledge of his existence, not until it was too late, but somewhere within me, even before it happened, even before I'd fully acknowledged it to myself, I'd the sense that someone had been watching.

Again, I think about the assault, how he'd waited until he was sure I was alone, defenceless, my friends having left an hour before, and how, when I finally realised he was there, how hard I screamed, but it was as if my screams were silenced long before he covered my mouth. I knew he would take whatever he wanted from me. It wasn't just the physical act of defiling me. He wanted me to understand fear too, alongside his need to destroy, and for me to accept that he had all the power.

Afterward, when I acted as a form of compulsory listener, I learned to understand him more. Which is why I know, when he found out about Nina, he had to take her from me, because allowing me to keep her would mean that instead of destroying me, I'd taken something from him.

That was why I moved all those years before, after marrying Tom, to the house up the road from Ellie's. Only, he tracked me down there too, and when he did, and he found out about Nina, once he saw her, all bets were off.

I'm nearly home now, and as I turn into the street, the one I used to live on with Nina, Alison, and my late husband, I spot a lone jogger in dark clothing running at a steady pace. I'd seen him yesterday too, but like yesterday, he has his back to me. After parking the car and stepping out, I look around to see if I can still spot him, but he's already gone. I stand at the front door for a few seconds before I turn the key in the lock, as if there's something I should take note of, or remember, but it has already slipped away.

40

HIM

*The street is dark apart from two amber streetlamps as he stands in the shadows. He did the same thing the night before, noting how little has changed, with the same road markings painted in white on the tarmac—*DRIVE SLOW. BEWARE OF CHILDREN*—along with the familiar mix of suburbia, front gardens of similar size, some more attractive than others. There are the cherry blossoms too, larger now, but well past flowering, and all of it brings him back to the first time he came here, over twenty-five years before.*

Back then, he wasn't sure what he'd find, and just like now, the reason he was able to locate Elizabeth so easily was an accidental conversation with another, someone unsuspecting, who told him where she'd be, and uncannily, history has a strange habit of repeating itself.

She's unaware of his presence, which is exactly how he wants it. She's no longer living in the same house, but he knew that even before his recognisance. She lives in her friend Ellie's house, as a temporary arrangement. He remembers the friend too, but now there's the additional complication of that young girl next door. Children are unpredictable, and a variable best avoided. Except the last time he was here, it was the child, not the woman, who was the ultimate target.

His anger had been difficult to control. Elizabeth had humiliated him, becoming pregnant, and even worse, hiding the truth from him, creating a new life for herself, thinking she could leave him behind. She was both naive and wrong to believe the child could remain with her. That's not how the game is played. He's the only one in charge. And tonight, the person in his focus is once again Elizabeth, because no matter which way he looks at it, she's unfinished business.

He won't strike yet. He'll savour the chase a little longer, thinking about his earlier visit today, and the day before, when that young girl, April, was with her, aware this time there can be no mistakes.

Elizabeth was special, and not because of the child she bore. The child was never part of the plan, but because there was always something about her, something that decades later still remained. None of the others had it, and even though she likely despises him, she also understands him. He could see it in those eyes of hers, when the shock was replaced by something else, fear, sorrow, and even acknowledgment, along with a hint of regret, that really, she should have known, she should have trusted her instincts. But then again, most people, when it comes to suspected danger, tend to dismiss it, thinking they're overreacting, or perhaps the harsh reality of it is something they don't really want to believe.

41

NICK

AFTER PARTING WAYS WITH ELIZABETH HARTE, NICK ISN'T CONVINCED his father's death is anything other than suicide. She's one of those ghosts from his past Norris warned him about, those that are hard to ignore, but he's glad now they've met.

At Terenure police station, he puts a call into Head Office, requesting access to the Nina Harte case files, currently archived in the Santry depot. It's a long shot he'll find anything new, but ghosts like Elizabeth don't go away easily, nor do the nagging questions about his father.

He thinks about Elizabeth's long, slim fingers too, and the use of ropes, although victims being tied up during a sexual assault isn't unusual, but still. Is it a step too far? What if there's a connection, and her theory is right, that the man who attacked her is not only the same person who took Nina, but someone who could have gone on to carry out more heinous crimes? It would place the killer in his late fifties, or early sixties, and it's obviously a stretch, but men of that age can remain fit, and the desire to kill never goes away.

He'd already wondered if the killer had crossed paths with police and the courts before, especially in the early stages of his trajectory before killing was part of his MO, and moments later, he's back checking PULSE for rape convictions spanning fifteen to thirty years before the first killing, narrowing the search down to Dublin on the basis it's the killer's preferred hunting ground. As he digs deeper, he rules out names because of age, men now in their seventies, or others, now dead. Lack of intellectual ability, as well as being socially challenged, are other disqualifying factors. As the list narrows, Nick decides to rule out sexual assaults with a strong personal connection to the victim, leaving him with a list of twenty names. Based on a conviction rate for sexual assaults of less than 1 percent, the names didn't offer any guarantees, but still.

So far, the only thing he'd gotten back on the unknown romantic connection of Rachel Meadows was the initial *J*, a sort of nickname she used when referring to a man her friends hadn't yet met. Scanning the list of twenty names, only three begin with the letter *J*: Josh Kennedy, James Lennox, and Jack Lyons. They could mean nothing, but all three names are now firmly within his focus, as he requests the full case files on each.

Still in analytical mode, he considers again his conversation with Elizabeth Harte, including his father being a man of secrets. Nick didn't need a date with a stranger to tell him his father wasn't someone to take at face value. A lifetime of knowing the man had told him his father was often different with other people around. He only had to recall the many arguments with his mother, his father's angry words, and how he'd instantly change when someone called to the house. He'd become friendlier, of lighter mood, as if there were several personas he could call upon. Meaning, it was difficult to determine which of the personas were real, and which were fake.

He thinks about the rumours about bribes too. Was his father involved with something shady? If he was, was it covered up, the Garda Síochána family looking after their own? Risk of contamination could have played a role too, his father's suicide going beyond tainting his record, but potentially that of the force as well. All Nick is sure of is that the rumours about his father started around the same time Nina Harte went missing. It had to have been a pressurised investigation, a missing child, with few enough answers, alongside numerous lines of enquiry leading nowhere. Was that why people started to ask questions? Because with all the resources at his father's disposal, there was still no trace of the child? Only, very few things happen in isolation. Usually, things are more complicated, including his father's money worries, when his gambling got out of hand.

Nick had let sleeping dogs lie for long enough, but after talking to Elizabeth, if nothing else, he's convinced something doesn't add up, which is why, after he gets the email giving him the all clear to visit Santry depot, he knows digging into that old case file of Nina Harte's is now inevitable.

ARRIVING AT SANTRY, HE'S AWARE SOME OF THE EVIDENCE, INCLUDING forensics and other computerised records, is stored elsewhere on PULSE, and access to it requires a higher authorisation than his current pay grade. Only, he's not about to ask Norris for permission just yet. Norris wouldn't be pleased he's back chasing "ghosts" as he called them, digging into his father's suicide, meeting Elizabeth Harte, and now, searching Nina Harte's missing person files.

With several evidence boxes to wade through, he's assigned a desk in a secluded corner. In the background, a printer comes to life, but soon, even the voices from the front desk are muted, because his concentration is elsewhere, on the contents of the first box. He hadn't pushed Eizabeth on the full details of her assault, but here, within these records from over twenty-five years earlier, when Elizabeth admitted to his father that the missing child, Nina, was the result of sexual assault, he'll find the details he needs.

It doesn't take him long to locate the hard copies of the original witness statements, including those from Elizabeth. It's strange, he thinks, as he scans her words, how a person's voice doesn't alter all that much over time. He notices something else too, how every time his father took a statement, it was as if Elizabeth was revealing more. Did his father develop a bond with her, or was her willingness to provide information the result of police pressure, and perhaps clarity too, that as each day passed without finding her daughter, a fresh reality set in? One in which holding back the truth wasn't helping anyone, least of all her missing child.

It's only within the final statement held in Santry that Elizabeth talks about the assault. This time, her words seem different, as if she's reliving it at a distance. She states she was alone in the house. She hadn't heard her assailant enter, but she was positive the front door was locked. She said her attacker knew a lot about her, including the time she went to work, came home, visited friends. He knew her favourite meal, the kind of books she liked to read, the addresses of work colleagues, and any other location she'd recently visited. He'd told her he'd watched and studied her for some time, as if she should be pleased with this, him paying her so much attention. He'd used ropes too, to restrain her. She remembered screaming but not believing anyone could hear her. He'd kept her tied up for hours, while he shared more information, including how she'd been chosen, and because of that, they'd a special bond.

Farther down the page, she talks about how six years is a long time to forget things, to block them out. She mentions the pregnancy too, and how it wasn't fear of another attack that caused her to move away, but rather, once she decided to keep the baby, she had more than one life to protect.

At the end of her statement, the sound of the printer churning paper returns. Nick considers the final section again, convinced his father must have made a solid link between Elizabeth's attacker and the abductor of the child, because to ignore the possibility would have been insane. Assuming he's right, his father must have reexamined Elizabeth's original assault records too, either to rule it in or out. Yet, having scanned all the evidence boxes in front of him, there were no records of the original assault, or any follow-up.

He examines Elizabeth's last statement again, searching for the precise date of the assault. There isn't one. All he has, working backward, is the year 1992 and the name Elizabeth Conway, her maiden name. It shouldn't be hard to track down the original records, but why weren't these details in the evidence boxes? Was it a leap to conclude someone didn't want them readily available or included in the boxes of evidence relating to the child's abduction?

It's in the final evidence box he finds the list of suspect vehicles examined at the time of Nina's abduction. All were parked in or near Massey Woods, but only two of them were transit vans. In truth, the child could have been taken in any one of the cars parked in the area, and with each examined at the time of the abduction, more than likely it would be another dead end, but still, Nick writes down the registration plates of the two larger vehicles.

42

ISABELLA

(3 weeks earlier)

LIKE THE FIRST TIME I CAME HERE, THERE'S SOMEONE WITH EOGHAN when I arrive. I'm early, so that's understandable, but the waiting spins my mind back to the last regression session, and those two little girls with the woman. Who are they, and why are they part of my memory?

It's possible, I tell myself again, it could be a false memory, something imagined. Eoghan has explained this to me, but if that's true, and I imagined it instead of remembering it, what does that scene in the garden really mean? Is it really some kind of fabricated desire to have a family, one without a father who wanted to mould me into his idea of perfection, and a mother, who, despite everything, lived a life where her true self only appeared when he wasn't around?

I hear footsteps in the corridor. Eoghan's last appointment must be leaving, which means, soon, he'll call me, and soon, I'll be back in that chair, regressing, or reimagining, something I don't yet understand.

Almost on cue, Eoghan opens the door. "Isabella," he says, before turning, expecting me to follow. I know the routine by now, so it isn't long before the lights in the room are dimmed, and all I hear is his soft voice directing me.

This time, when I'm in the hallway with the doors, Eoghan asks which number I want to choose. I tell him I want to go to number five.

"Okay," he says, "when you're ready, open the door."

I do as he asks, and soon, my senses are hit by an abundance of aromas, woodland smells, moss and trees and dried leaves. Like before, initially my vision isn't clear, but then more parts of the image come into focus.

"Where are you, Isabella?"

"I'm in the woods again."

"What age are you?"

"I'm five."

"Are you alone?"

"No."

"Who else is there?"

"They can't see me."

"Who?"

"Someone is looking for me," I say. "I can hear them."

"Listen carefully."

"I hear a woman's voice. She's calling out. She wants to know where I am."

"Anything else?"

"Yes."

"What?"

"I hear something else. There's a little girl hiding with me. She's giggling, so I tell her to shush. We're playing a game—hide-and-seek."

"Is it one of the little girls from the swings?"

"Yes, the younger one, only now, she's moving farther away from me. The woman's voice is becoming more distant too. I don't like how I feel."

"How do you feel?"

"As if something bad is about to happen."

"Why do you think that?"

"I don't know," I say, concentrating hard, trying to work out why I feel so scared, but then I realise, it's the smell, not of the woods, but something else, something I've smelt before. "I smell something," I tell Eoghan.

"What?"

"Nicotine—someone's lighting a cigarette."

"Could it be the woman?"

"No, it's definitely not her. I can't see or hear her anymore."

"Can you hear the other little girl?"

Again, I concentrate. "I'm not sure. She could be close by, but now, I'm hearing something else."

"What?"

"Footsteps. They're moving slowly at first, barely making a sound, but then, as they become faster and closer, I hear the snapping of twigs and crushed moss."

"Are you still afraid, Isabella?"

"Yes, but I need to stay here."

"Why?"

"Because my body is stuck. I want to move, but I can't."

"Remember, Isabella, I can bring you back at any time."

"Wait," I say, my voice high-pitched, alarmed, "they're even closer now."

"Do you know who the footsteps belong to?"

"No."

"Look around you, Isabella, tell me what you see and who you see."

I can't answer him. I'm more terrified than I've ever been in my whole life, as the sound of the footsteps gain pace, as if suddenly, whoever it is knows they need to move faster. The younger little girl is nearby again. She looks at me, and then upward, a dark shadow looming over us. She wants to warn me, but no words come out, and then, I'm being pulled away.

Eoghan must sense my distress, because he asks again, "Isabella, what's happening?"

And again, I can't answer him, because I'm more scared than I ever thought possible.

I hear Eoghan's voice telling me to leave the room, asking me to count backward. I say the numbers aloud, and with each one, gradually they bring me back, as if I'm being awakened from a dream, only it doesn't feel like a dream, it feels real, and soon, as Eoghan instructs, I open the door to the hallway, the one leading to the staircase and the garden where I'll feel safe.

My senses begin to return to the room. My body feels cold, so cold I'm shivering. Eoghan places a blanket over me.

"What was that?" I ask, unsure about what's just happened.

"I'm not sure, but something has changed."

"In what way?"

"This time, Isabella, when you went back, somehow you became that little girl, the older one on the swing."

"So, she is me?"

"Perhaps."

"But why couldn't I move?"

"Fear."

"Fear of what?"

"Something you're not yet ready to face."

43

ELIZABETH

I CAN'T SLEEP, WALKING BACK AND FORTH ACROSS THE BEDROOM floor, as if I'm trapped between looking into the past and moving forward. It's only then the sound of movement from outside draws me to the window. The girl, the one missing for the last few nights, just as April had predicted, has returned. Why did I get myself into such a frenzy about it? I need to stop this wild paranoia, unless I want to add "insane" to my already long list of suspected mental challenges.

I'm still staring out the window when I see something from the corner of my eye, a movement in the shadows. My immediate instinct is fear, but then I tell myself I've felt this way a million times before, and the reason why is simple. It's because I know he can always return and finish what he began thirty-one years ago.

I also know now, it'll be impossible to sleep, so instead, I spend the rest of the night listening for sounds, the slightest movement of floorboards, or rattle of windows, normal house creaks, because once the paranoia grabs you, it's hard to let it go.

I've been thinking about that questionnaire again too, the one covering depression, wondering if I'd do any better if I were to re-answer the questions a second time. I consider trying some mindfulness, an attempt to switch off the conflicting thoughts inside my head, but I've never been very good at switching off, or developing an awareness of the here and now. It feels like a lost battle, because right now, no matter what I do, my negativity won't shift.

They, the experts, say it's okay to have strong thoughts about present dangers. We need that instinct to survive, but repetitive negative thoughts, especially concerning the future and the past, aren't a good thing. Our imagination usually makes things seem ten times worse. This form of repetitive thinking is called "rumination," leading to chronic stress, and if severe enough, anxiety and depression—bingo.

They also say being proactive helps, and I've at least done that, but the flashbacks, or "intrusive thoughts," as April calls them, haven't gone away. I think about Nick Matthews's father again. Was I being cruel insinuating he didn't take his own life, setting myself up as some sort of elevated authority, casting opinions on the dead? Maybe. Only, the nagging doubt is there, still wondering if his death is somehow connected to Nina.

I tell myself these negative thoughts, like thinking something ominous had happened to that young woman across the road, are the thoughts of a crazy person, a woman, at least according to the questionnaire, who is living with depression, and an extra caveat of post-traumatic stress too. But now, I'm also thinking about the other parts of my conversation with Nick Matthews, around the assault. While not revealing all the details to him, still, I know, the man who raped me is capable of almost anything, including the abduction of my daughter and ultimately, if he wanted to, killing me.

At some point I must fall asleep, because hours later, I awake to the sound of my mobile phone ringing out. It feels jarring, as if it belongs to somewhere else, the real world outside my head.

I recognise the number as Alison's. I should answer her, but I hesitate. The phone keeps ringing, the sound feeling as if it's getting louder all the time. I can't resist it anymore, so I pick up and say, "Hello."

"Mom, we need to talk," Alison says, her words more like a command than a request. The quiver in her voice tells me she's really hurt by my absence, cloaking it in anger, but she's also attempting to control the situation, that of me, the misbehaving parent.

"Alison, I need more time."

At first, she doesn't reply, but then she asks, "Time away from me?" Her voice is softer, broken. "Is that it?"

There's no denying the hurt in her voice. Perhaps regretting her earlier harshness, born out of frustration, having a mother who does things like running away, things a normal sixty-something wouldn't do. At first, I don't know what to say, but then I say, "We can meet, if you want."

Another silence. She's thinking about what to say next.

"I would like that," she finally replies.

I want to tell her, I understand she's hurt, that I know Nina's loss affected both of us, but instead, I say nothing.

I hear her suck in air.

I hold the phone tight.

"Why, Mom?" she asks. "Why do you need to stay stuck in the past?"

I pause before answering, thinking, *It's not just about being stuck in the past, it's also about how I allowed this distance to grow between us.* I think of April's words then, when she spoke about choices, saying she thinks about them all the time, even when choosing a Tamagotchi, because she's so fearful of regret, and how every time she decided, she was sad for the Tamagotchi she didn't pick. Did I do that, when I chose Nina's loss over Alison?

"I don't know, Alison," I say, "but I'm trying to work it out."

After I hang up, I think about another afternoon, shortly after Nina went missing. I'd left the house on the guise of going food shopping, despite being incapable of something as mundane as even that back then. I sat in the supermarket car park for hours, trying to decide whether I should go in and buy food, or stay in the car park watching the seagulls pick up leftover scraps. The way the birds swooned fascinated me, their flight so assured, so full of precision. I didn't want to take my eyes off them, so I waited and waited. I waited until the supermarket closed, and all the other cars had left the car park. Until it was just me, sitting in the dark. And as I'm thinking this, I'm also thinking that I've been doing the same thing for years, not knowing what I should do next. So instead, I do nothing. And doing nothing isn't living.

44

ISABELLA

(3 weeks earlier)

AFTER LEAVING EOGHAN'S, I GO BACK TO MY APARTMENT, FEELING A strange combination of loss, and a fear of the unknown about my past, and even my future. There seem to be so many missing pieces, and because of that, I keep finding myself going down rabbit holes, hoping one of them will give me the answers I need.

Now, I'm searching "Illegal Adoptions in Ireland," and just like the articles on memory, there are a huge amount of hits. All say more or less the same thing, that potentially thousands of Irish children have had their births falsified. Sometimes, in collusion with religious orders, and sometimes, other arms of the state are involved, including those with the knowledge and power to authorise fake documentation as legitimate. It's one thing to falsify a document, but it's another thing to have it recognised as "real." That requires the services of others, including a stamp of approval from the police.

My late father was powerful, and if my birth records involved anything illegal, something connected to James Lennox, he would have known who to contact to ensure all the nasty details were buried, and whether it involved a religious order, or someone else, they'd have been paid a hefty price.

I shut down the laptop. I've done enough internet searches to know James Lennox has fallen off the radar. He might have changed his identity, but if he is my real father, I need to accept he's someone capable of doing bad things, as I remember my mother's words: "Don't look back, Isabella, there's danger there."

I know, after this latest session with Eoghan, I won't be able to stop thinking about the woods, reliving the sound of those footsteps approaching, over and over. I've called in sick to work again. I know I shouldn't, and I know I'm not the first person dealing with grief, but a miscarriage, losing two parents at once, and all of this, still feels seismic.

My world has been thrown into disarray, and added to the grief is the enormous sense of unknowing. Who am I, if not my parents' child? Is Isabella even my proper name, or is there another name on my real birth certificate? I don't even know if my birth date is correct, which on its own shouldn't matter all that much, but it adds to the sense of ignorance. Who was that woman with the two little girls? Could she have been a kind of foster parent? I can't even be sure if I've imagined her, but all I know is this, the regression felt real.

After another hour of trying to find answers, I feel as if the walls are closing in on me. I need to do something, and soon I find myself in the car driving to Rathmichael Woods.

It's mid-afternoon, so it's too early for families with schoolchildren to be about, and others are likely still at work. I already know the pathway I want to take. It's off the beaten track, where the likelihood of seeing anyone is remote. I need to be alone. I need to think long and hard about Eoghan's words, especially when he said he wasn't sure if I was ready to face my fear.

As I reach a narrow pathway with high trees on either side, the woods suddenly feel alive with movement. I imagine tiny animals scurrying about in the undergrowth as birds fly back and forth, fluttering their wings. I hear insects humming too, as other sounds make their way through, that of swaying woodland branches, or the faint sound of people talking, now safely in the distance, their words echoing through the dense rows of trees, as the sun shimmers through gaps in the woodland canopy.

I'm thinking about something else too, not just my late parents, or the regression, but the life I lost. It's nearly as if I haven't had time to grieve the person once growing inside of me, the person who is no longer there.

Nearing a small clearing, I pause. It's not dissimilar to the wooded area my regression brought me back to, and I wonder if my subconscious mind may have played a part in choosing this particular route. Either way, I stop now, reimagining myself as a child, a young girl hiding in the woods, my body crouching, trying to bring myself physically back there. I think about the night terrors again, the ones I experienced as a child, being terrified of the dark. Were my fears connected to what happened in the woods, if it happened at all?

I hear more voices, people calling after one another. They're far away; the sound reminds me of the regression too, and it's then I hear the footsteps, the same as those during the last session. As before, they seem to be getting closer, gaining pace. The other little girl appears; she wants to warn me, only her words won't come out. But it doesn't matter, because I already know whoever those footsteps belong to means to do me harm.

45

ELIZABETH

IT ISN'T LONG AFTER I HANG UP THE PHONE WITH ALISON THAT I SEE April heading toward the front door. Seeing her lifts my spirits, and it's not because I'm trying to relive some sort of lost connection with Nina, or even Alison. It's because this ten-year-old has somehow moved the needle of the broken record of my life.

Opening the door, again today she has her prized Harry Potter notebook positioned safely under her arm.

"You were right about that girl across the road returning," I say, "she came back on time, exactly as you said she would."

"Good," she says, breezing past me toward the kitchen, "timing's important."

I follow behind her, arriving as she pulls out a kitchen chair, which up to a few days ago I hadn't realised was "her chair." A notion put in her head by Ellie, which I'd no intention of dislodging.

"You were saying," I say, sitting opposite, "how timing is important."

"Yes," she says, staring at me, "would you like an example?"

"Please."

She opens her Harry Potter notebook as if searching for a particular page. "Here it is. Yesterday, my mam went to the hairdressers, leaving at precisely 3:35 p.m."

"Okay."

"I calculated it would take ten minutes to reach her destination. That meant she likely had an appointment for 3:45, and my mam is never late. That last point, Elizabeth, is important."

"I'll bear that in mind," I reply, thinking again about how timing has influenced so much in my life. My attacker timed it to ensure I was alone when he broke into the house. If I'm right, and he also took Nina, then he waited his time then too, until both girls were a distance from me, vulnerable, beyond my reach.

"Elizabeth, are you listening?"

"Yes," I say, bringing my mind back to the here and now.

"Okay then. My mam said she'd be back in an hour and a half. I noted this as accurate based on the maths, allowing ten minutes to reach the hairdressers, one hour to get her hair done, an additional ten minutes factored in for any potential delays, and then finally, ten minutes to return home. In total an hour and a half. Estimating her return at 5:05 p.m."

"Right," I say, "timing and details are certainly important to you."

"Precisely, Elizabeth, because they influence outcomes."

"So, what happened?"

"When it reached an hour and a half, and my mam wasn't home, I was concerned. Later, I panicked. I spoke to my dad. He told me not to worry, which was crazy, how could I not worry."

"What time did you start panicking?"

"Precisely fifteen minutes after Mam was due home—5:20 p.m."

"So, what did you do?"

"I called the hairdressers, but the line was engaged, so I dialled 999."

"Did your father know about this?"

"Eventually, yes, but by then my mam was home."

"A little drastic, April, don't you think?"

She shakes her head. "Not if my mam was actually missing. If she was, those fifteen minutes could have been vital."

She's right of course, every minute and second counts, which is another reason why I've so many regrets. What if, when Nina vanished, I'd handled things differently? What if I'd asked Alison to take me to the spot where Nina had been, instead of wasting valuable seconds and minutes interrogating her? What if I hadn't panicked? Maybe I'd have been able to see them running through the forest, because when I did go searching, I saw nothing.

April is looking at me, expectant. I quickly form a question in my mind. "Did you get into trouble for calling the police?"

"Not really"—she smiles—"and I got to hear police sirens. I told you I like them, didn't I?"

"Yes, you did."

She goes back to writing a fresh entry in her notebook, and I wonder again if it's an observation about me, or a plan for future 999 calls.

"I spoke to my daughter today," I say. "Alison, the one who isn't missing."

"Good."

"I'm glad you approve," I say, realising she's drawing, not writing. "What's that?" I ask.

"It's an alien. I draw them to get them out of my head."

I could tell her again, aliens don't exist, but it wouldn't matter. They exist to her. The same way all those flashbacks exist within me, and as I watch April frantically creating whatever creature is caught up inside her head, my mind flips, remembering how afterward, after the assault, when he spoke for hours, initially about choosing me, telling me about all my movements, my life, including the smallest of details, he eventually turned the tables and spoke about himself. It was then I realised, for him, the assault was only part of it, because along with his need for control, he needed something else too, a captive audience, someone with no choice but to listen attentively, to him, to his life beliefs, no matter how damaged they were, as if his voice had previously been smothered, and the only means he had of being heard was through creating an ardent listener, even if that meant using violence.

46

HIM

In his attic room, he reexamines his thoughts. Elizabeth is a deviation from the plan, but sometimes deviating from the plan is exactly the right thing to do.

Despite the passing of years, or the lines of age visible on her face, watching her again over the last few days has brought back strong memories, and what he remembers most is her earlier innocence, so unsophisticated, giddy, and pure, her searching for a new life with her parents gone, full of hope and vulnerability too. She was the start of his journey, and he can still hear her whimpers, his hand tight across her mouth, blocking out the screams. He can taste her terror too, the rise of adrenaline within him, that feeling of dominance, and the delight within the darkness.

She's changed over time, becoming more life weary, the early brightness partly faded, but the younger him still remembers how everything shifted the first time he saw her, the image still vivid in his mind: her perfect frame, those long, slim fingers, her hair shoulder-length, delicate, warmed by the evening sun.

He'd watched her for hours, long before he approached, and when he did, he made her laugh. He smiles at that, alongside remembering her vulnerability. It was one of the many things that drew him to her, why she was chosen—her need to appear strong, when deep down, all she ever wanted was for others to like her.

Like him, she had been an only child, and he could tell, after her parents' passing, along with her sadness, there was a vacuum created, one that was as yet unfilled. The need to feel loved, to have other people in your life, someone special to care for you, can be enormous. He saw that in her, that desperation, that need for more. It was her "need" that made her unique, her susceptibility within the desire. A susceptibility he understood, because within human fragility, feelings of loss always bring with them a certain depth and understanding, and a realisation too. That there are things in life you cannot change, no matter how much you want them to.

Even though she's older now, he'd wager much of that early fragility still exists, and like a strange aphrodisiac, it still calls him.

47

NICK

IT DIDN'T TAKE LONG FOR THE REGISTRATION DETAILS ON THE TWO larger vehicles from the car park near where Nina Harte disappeared to come through, and one of them jumps out—James Lennox, matching a name on the narrowed list of sexual assault convictions. Could this be their guy? He potentially fits the profile, his criminal history starting with breaking and entering, indecent assault, physical assault, and then finally, aggravated sexual assault and rape. There were other charges too, including fraud and money laundering, indicating a high level of intelligence, again, matching the profile. But, where the hell was James Lennox now? And was he capable of child abduction? If it had been Nick's investigation all those years before, James Lennox would have been absolutely in the frame, especially when Elizabeth's original assault came to light.

But right now, Nick is more intrigued by his disappearance, as there's no mention of him on PULSE since his earlier conviction a quarter of a century earlier. Men like James Lennox don't get rehabilitated. So again, where is he? Or, perhaps, who is he?

Could the abduction of Nina Harte, receiving such enormous coverage in the media, and therefore bringing huge pressure on the police, have initiated James Lennox seeking a new identity, a need to start over? And if he found James Lennox so easily, why didn't his father look deeper into this potential lead?

Could there have been errors in the investigation, things overlooked, or worse, did someone tamper with evidence? Could that someone be his father? And if it was his father, were all those rumours about police bribes true? His father had let him down once, taking the easy way out, but this?

Nick can't get Elizabeth Harte's conversation out of his head either—the use of ropes, age profile, the long slim fingers, or even the potential stalking. Elizabeth had said her assailant knew everything about her, fitting the profile of the killer in Operation Shadow. Could it be the same person? Could he have kept himself physically fit over the intervening years?

Then, there's the missing details from the files regarding Elizabeth's original assault, including the precise date it happened. It took him working backward through the files to establish the year, and even more digging to get her maiden name, Elizabeth Conroy. Why didn't the assault get higher prominence in the investigation?

All of it questioned his father's professionalism, pointing either of two ways—sloppy police work or the deliberate oversight of evidence.

He'd worked enough sexual assault cases to know how difficult they are to resolve. Alcohol or drugs are often involved, causing blurring of facts, and rarely to the advantage of the victim. However, in Elizabeth's case, there was no mention of drugs or alcohol during the assault. But yet, as Nick combs the list of sexual assault cases recorded on PULSE, scanning in excess of nine months before Nina's birth, no record exists. The question now is, why?

Was Elizabeth too ashamed, and failed to report the crime after the assault? It's not unusual for victims to harbour blame, criticising themselves for not being careful enough, or for placing themselves in situations best avoided. But the lack of an official record spikes

Nick's curiosity, and surely, twenty-five years ago, his father's curiosity would have been spiked the same way.

Nick doesn't have a magic mirror to look back in time. Perhaps his father hit a brick wall? Or James Lennox had an alibi, and was later ruled out of having any connection to Elizabeth's assault? Or those rumours circulating at the time of the girl's disappearance, whispers about bribes and other dodgy dealings, are part of all this.

Charlotte Marry is still missing too, and the risk that she'll end up as another addition to Operation Shadow isn't lost on him. If the case moves from missing person to murder, being part of the Cold Case Unit, he won't be directly involved, but he'll do the same thing with Charlotte as he's done with the others. He'll try to piece together a detailed picture of her life.

Thinking this, he wonders if his father formed a detailed picture of Nina Harte. Was she a cautious child, or someone who did things without thinking? Was she inquisitive, susceptible to someone or something luring her from the woodlands where she was last seen? His father must have done that, the same way he'd have formed a detailed picture of everyone in Nina's life, including Elizabeth and her husband. The husband was probably the first person under the microscope, but soon after that, Elizabeth would have been looked at too. From the boxes of evidence, he's sure Elizabeth was dismissed as a suspect early on, but her attacker, the one she finally spoke about in her witness statements describing her rape, should have been foremost in his father's mind.

Since first visiting Santry, Nick has examined other evidence boxes too, those from the various case reviews. Within them, he found records out of sequence, perhaps the result of others searching, but that wasn't the only thing bothering him. There were file references to the sketch drawing of the attacker, re-created with Elizabeth's help, but the actual sketch was missing. It wouldn't be the first time Nick encountered messy police work regarding the safeguarding of evidence, and probably not the last. However, the file references confirm what Elizabeth told him, that other than her attacker's eyes, she was unsure about other facial details. The eyes alone wouldn't have been enough for the sketch to be publicly shared, as attempting partial facial recognition could cause more problems than it solved, but either way, the sketch was missing, and along with all the other questions, Nick still wanted to know why.

48

ELIZABETH

I PICK UP THE FOLDED PIECE OF PAPER ON THE BEDSIDE LOCKER, THE one from April, telling me she likes that I'm different. At times, I wish I wasn't different. I wish I was ordinary, and that none of this had ever happened to me. Only, sadly, attempting to change the past never works. Like all the other dark thoughts, it doesn't change a darn thing.

April is unlike anyone else, and partly because of that, she brings out a different side of me. Is it because, with her, I'm a clean slate, or is it because she accepts me the way I am? Sure, she doesn't like me being sad or irritable, but still, she accepts it as part of *me* being *me.*

I'm still apprehensive about meeting Alison. She isn't like April. She'll want to fix me. She thinks by fixing me, things will turn out better, but I doubt it.

It's dark now, and as the faint lights from the neighbouring houses drift in, I try, as I've done several times before, to work out what I can say to Alison to make our relationship better. It should be easy, only, it isn't. There's been too many years in between for that, and this thought drags me out of bed.

Soon, I find myself staring into the night sky, the way I used to as a child, in the hope of seeing a falling star, gaining a wish, even if it might never come true.

Tonight, the sky is clear, and the longer I stare at it, the more stars appear. They give me comfort, the sky being full of so many possibilities, but then, after a few moments, my eyes are drawn downward. I see that lone jogger again, as a light from one of the neighbouring windows goes dark, and soon after that, another window follows. It feels as if everyone else is going to sleep, everyone except for the madwoman in the window.

I should go back to bed. Being overtired will only make things worse when I see Alison tomorrow, but then, out of the corner of my eye, in the street below, as far away from the stars as it could possibly be, there's another movement in the shadows. I tell myself it's probably nothing, perhaps a stray animal, or something else, but as I focus hard, somewhere in the core of me, my instincts are again warning me to be careful.

49

ELIZABETH

THIS MORNING MY MIND'S IN OVERDRIVE. FIRSTLY, BECAUSE ALISON is calling today, and secondly, because of that weird sensation I got last night, as if there was someone hiding in the dark, watching me.

An item has gone missing too, a top from a perfume bottle in the shape of a pink bow. I've looked everywhere for it, but I can't find it. If I was still in Alison's house, I'd suspect Ciaran, who was always searching for new ways to undermine me, but I need to push that thought out of my mind, mainly because I don't want it getting in the way when I talk to my daughter.

It was inevitable that returning to this street would dredge up old fears, and if I want to stay sane, I also need to be careful not to let those fears take over. Fear immobilises you. It stops you cold, and I've done enough of that for two lifetimes, never mind one.

AT LUNCHTIME, AS EXPECTED, THE DOORBELL RINGS. I SUCK IN AIR. I know it's Alison. She's a little early, but that's not unusual for her, her life a constant juggling act, keeping all the balls in the air—being a mother, wife, career woman, meeting up with friends, choosing the right interior designer, decisions on schools, cars, clothing, where to go on holidays, with all the usual haunts already visited, and the children not yet old enough to go somewhere off the beaten track. I must be such an additional torment, the "misbehaving mother" now at the top of her "to do" list.

I open the door. She looks beautiful, her hair in a perfect long blonde bob, her clothes the right side of casual-formal, and her makeup suitably understated.

"Hello, Mom," she says.

"Hello."

For a second, we stare at one another, like we're about to play a new board game, one in which neither of us are familiar with the rules. "Come in," I say, standing back in the hallway so she can enter.

She follows me to the kitchen, and I wonder if, like me, being in Ellie's house causes her to pause, the layout almost identical to her childhood home.

"Is Ellie away for long?" she asks, her question delivered in an understated tone, wanting to avoid alarming the crazy mother by placing too much emphasis on establishing a solid timeline.

"A while."

She sits down. "The children are upset."

Like Ciaran, she's going straight for the guilt card, although his motives are far more menacing. Needing to constantly undermine me in front of Alison, so I don't pose a threat, become someone my daughter might actually listen to.

"That wasn't my intention."

"No?"

"No."

"Why, Mom?"

"Why did I run away from home?"

"Don't be so dramatic, you're not some bloody teenager."

"I'm not being dramatic. It's the truth. I needed to get away. I didn't feel like *me* anymore."

"We could have talked about it, before you . . ."

I hear the hurt in her voice again, that vulnerability she normally does such a good job of hiding now unintentionally creeping to the surface. I understand that vulnerability, because at times I feel it too.

"I was afraid you'd try to change my mind."

She removes her coat, as if only now she's decided to stay.

"I didn't mean to hurt anyone," I say then.

"Well, you did."

"I'm sorry. As I said, that wasn't my intention."

She sits up straighter, physically establishing a stronger presence. "I'm assuming you being here, on this street, is all about Nina?"

I'm surprised at the mention of her sister's name, neither of us having used it for years, avoiding all references to it in case it might finally bring our relationship, that delicately structured house of cards, tumbling down.

"It's about me too."

"Do you think you're some kind of amateur detective or something?"

This was a bad idea. Us being together brings out the worst in both of us. "I'm not exactly sure what I thought," I say, "but I've worked something out."

"What?"

"Since leaving, I've realised, mentally and emotionally, I've been running away for a very long time."

"I don't understand."

"There are things, Alison, about my past you don't know about, and I'm not sure if I ever want you to know about them."

"You're shutting me out again."

"I don't mean to." I move in closer, wanting to take her hand in mine, but not daring. "What I'll say is this, long before your sister disappeared, when you were an infant in my arms, I tried to be a person I couldn't be. I tried to act normal, to pretend everything was okay."

"Was it postnatal depression? Was that it?"

"No, it wasn't that. As I said, it was something from my past, something I couldn't move on from."

"And you think you'll be able to move on by coming back here?"

"I don't know," I say. "All I know is I have to try."

She bites her bottom lip, a childhood habit of hers, and something she does when nervous, or hurt. I see the early indicators of tears in her eyes, and immediately I feel like the worst mother in the world.

"None of this is about you, Alison. It's all about me."

"No," she says, a fresh bitterness taking hold, "it's never about me. It's always about Nina, and now, *you*."

"That's not true."

"Isn't it?"

"No."

"Just remember, Mom, whenever you *find yourself*, by doing this crazy thing, or work out all those unanswered questions about Nina, I'm the one who's always been here." A tiny bead of blood seeps from her bottom lip.

"I know that, Alison, about you being here, and I also know I've failed you as a mother. If I could change things, if I could turn back time, I swear, I'd do a whole lot of things differently."

"Then stop this crusade or whatever you think it is and come home."

I want to say yes. I want to tell her that I'll run upstairs right now and pack a bag. I want to tell her I'll do whatever she wants, but I can't. "I'm sorry, Alison," I say, "but if I came home now, very quickly, we'd be back to where we were before I left. I need more time."

"Time for what?"

"To find out who I am, or maybe, who I want to be."

"And what about Nina?"

"I don't know, but she's part of this, only . . ."

"What?"

"I've also realised of late, whatever it is I'm searching for isn't only about your sister, or being back here, or even trying to remember, it's also about something deep inside of me, and until I know what that something is, coming back home wouldn't achieve anything."

"It would make me happy," she says, biting her bottom lip again.

I want to tell her a million things. I want to tell her she doesn't need to be the parent in our relationship, that I'm parent enough for both of us. I want to tell her to leave that damn husband of hers, that he's not worth the dirt on the soles of her shoes, that he can't be trusted, that he lies to her all the time, and if he could, he'd have me gone for good, because all he cares about is himself.

"Jesus, Mom, don't you see, I need you now. I need you more than ever."

It's only then I notice the dark lines under her eyes.

"Is it Ciaran?" I ask, a fresh anger rising inside me.

"You never liked him," she shoots back, but too fast to hide the quiver in her voice.

"You're right," I say, "I never did, but my feelings don't matter, Alison. What matters is how you feel."

"Look," she says, looking downward, "I know I've probably taken you for granted, and I'm sorry for that, but since you've left, Ciaran is also acting bloody weird. He keeps shutting me out, being too damn secretive, and is constantly on edge."

"You need to listen to me, Alison," I say, more determined than I've felt in a very long time. "By being here, by doing this crazy thing as you call it, I've taken a risk. A risk, which I don't know all the answers to, not yet, but *you* can change too. You don't have to stay with him, living a life you're no longer happy in. It isn't healthy for you."

She looks at me as if I've two heads, but I can tell my words have hit home, even if she's not yet ready to admit it.

"Perhaps, Alison, both of us have some learning to do."

"What do you mean?" The sting in her voice from earlier, slightly abated.

"I never thought I'd be brave enough to do what I'm doing now, to step out of my comfort zone."

"But you said yourself, you still don't know exactly why you're here."

"Maybe not, but I knew enough to realise, things needed to change."

The tears well up in her eyes again. I want to tell her she's an amazing person, and a great mother, and a wonderful daughter, even if at times I was too stupid or blind to see it, but in the end, I say, "I love you, Alison. I really mean that."

"I love you too."

My hand tentatively touches her arm, stalling, not wanting to let go, because even though, as her mother, I foolishly allowed this wall to grow between us, I've always loved her. I still want to cry and smile, remembering how she used to drag that poor doll of hers by the hair, remembering her baby smell too, and how close we once were, and perhaps, somehow within all of this, we can still grasp that bond we once had. I let my hand ease away. "Give me time," I say, "and I promise you, Alison, I'll try to work things out."

There's another silence, and I'd wager, like me, she's thinking hard, both of us at a crossroads, with neither of us wanting to smash the eggshells of our relationship completely.

"Okay," she says then, as if temporarily beaten down, even though that wasn't my intention.

"Thank you," I say. It feels like a truce of sorts. "I'll call you," I say then, as she stands up, retrieving her coat, another indicator that whatever just happened, for the moment, has been temporarily placed on hold.

After she leaves, I feel worse than before her impending visit, which is why, as her car pulls out of the drive, and I see April making her way toward the front door, my mood isn't good.

"Hello," she says.

"Hello," I reply, my eyes tracking Alison's car as it goes farther out of view.

"Are you angry with me?" April asks.

"No. I'm just a little on edge."

Alison's car turns the corner. She's gone.

"A little what? What edge?"

"Sorry?" I look at her, confused.

"You said you were little, and on an edge."

"I see," I say, opening the door wider as she walks inside.

"Was it one of those things people say, Elizabeth, things they don't mean. Like, it's a piece of cake, when there's no cake, or, I'm all ears, when they clearly have only two."

"I guess, yes."

"My dad's especially fond of saying things he doesn't mean, like when my mam tells him my grandmother's coming to stay, and he says "great," when really, he doesn't like her all that much."

"Some things are confusing."

"They're called idioms, and everyday expressions, including those with double meanings."

"Yes, I know."

"I looked the word up once."

"Idiom?"

"Yes. It comes from the Greek word *idioma*, which means 'peculiarity.'"

"I'll bear that in mind."

She sits on the same chair Alison just vacated.

"Some people think I'm stupid when I can't understand them, especially Marcus at school, but in my opinion, it's a bad choice of words. He teases me all the time about being stupid, even though I'm way better than him at maths. We did an IQ test in school once, and I scored twice as much as him, so I guess he can't be a real expert, but still, it upsets me."

"How come you knew his score?"

"I sneaked a look at it over the teacher's shoulder," she says, without an ounce of guilt, as if it's the most normal thing in the world, taking a peek at someone else's test results.

"Is it your daughter, Alison?" she asks then. "Has she put you on edge?"

"No, April, it's me."

"Why? What's wrong with you?"

I must look downhearted, because straightaway she says, "I should probably stop asking questions. I'm always asking too many questions, but they keep coming into my head, and there are so many of them, if I don't get them out, it hurts."

"It's okay."

"I wish I wasn't like this," she says then, almost pleading, "I wish I was like neurotypical people," pausing to draw breath, "only, not all the time, just when I hate being different."

"I'm glad you're not like everyone else."

"Are you?" she asks, her voice immediately cheering up.

"Yep," I say, "and you've helped me."

"How?"

"You've taught me it's okay to be different."

"Really?" Her eyes widen.

"One hundred percent."

"Tell me more," she says, like this is a whole new adventure to explore.

"You made me realise being stuck isn't a good thing either. And that, as I said, being different is totally okay too, and something else."

"What?"

"Like with you and Marcus, I need to acknowledge that some things make me sad, but equally, I need to work out how to be happy too."

"Really?"

"It's tricky to explain, but it's like, sad things happen to all of us, like Marcus teasing you at school, or bigger things, like me not knowing where my daughter Nina is, but you've taught me that somehow, like when you ran that race in school, even though you thought you might come last, that you needed to keep on trying. You needed to strive for something good, because if you don't, you'll get stuck again, and being stuck isn't good for anyone."

"Are you trying, Elizabeth?"

"I am," I say, "I'm trying hard. And not just for me, but for my family too." But as I'm saying this, I realise she's already distracted, as now she's staring intensely at the kitchen window.

"What are you looking at?"

"Your window, it isn't closed properly."

"What do you mean?"

"You usually have the latch completely over. I've watched you check it all the time."

Both of us are staring now, because she's right. Maybe I forgot to pull over the latch. Maybe, by being obsessed with Alison's prospective visit, it caused me to forget, but still, I'm usually so careful.

I walk toward the window. I pull the latch over to lock it, before double-checking for a second time that it's definitely locked. I think about the movements in the shadows from last night, and how they unsettled me. "Stop it," I say aloud, thinking outside my head, trying to prevent myself from getting spooked when it's probably nothing.

"Stop what?" April asks, opening her notebook, as if this fresh sequence of Q & A might be worth writing down.

"Letting my head run away with things that probably mean nothing."

Her facial expression changes as I realise she's likely visualising my head physically making a run for it.

"It's okay," I say, needing to change the subject, at least until I work out exactly what's going on, "it's just another one of those stupid things people say."

"A bad choice of words?"

"Exactly."

50

ISABELLA

(2 weeks earlier)

"ARE YOU SURE ABOUT THIS?" EOGHAN ASKS.

"Absolutely," I say, noting the concerned look on his face. "I'm prepared to do whatever it takes."

"That may be so, but still, we need to be careful."

"I know."

"And as a trained hypnotherapist, if at all possible, the aim is always to avoid heightened negativity, unless it's absolutely necessary to help a person move forward."

"I know that too."

"And whether it's a phobia, or something else, safety within regression is key."

"I understand your concerns, Eoghan, believe me I do, but in my case, taking a risk is unavoidable. As I said earlier, after our last session, when I went walking in the woods, my memory was triggered again. I heard those footsteps, as if they were getting closer, gaining pace. And I knew whoever those footsteps belonged to meant to do me harm."

"Okay," he says then, "if you're really sure."

I let out a sigh of relief. Which seems ridiculous seeing as how I should be feeling the opposite. But I'm willing to do whatever it takes to get answers.

Eoghan is talking again. "As I said before, Isabella, at times, in order to overcome supressed memories, facilitating the release of hidden or squashed negative emotions, the only way forward is to alternate the means of regression, and this in turn requires the use of additional safety measures."

"What do you have in mind?"

"Separation or dissociation during regression is an approach we can look at. This ensures you're able to partly protect your conscious mind from any potentially disturbing memories, mainly by creating cues to act as barriers. Hopefully, then, you can relive those memories from a more distant perspective. During the session, I may ask you to step out of the memory, and indeed for you to watch it from a third-person perspective."

"I'm not quite sure what you mean."

"The simplest way to explain it is this. In our earlier sessions, the 'adult you' was present, even though during the regression, you were returning to a suppressed, or forgotten, childhood memory."

"Okay."

"So, there was the safety of the adult-self being there. That will still be the case, but this time, we're going to distance the 'adult you' even more."

"How?"

"When you regress, instead of you being within the actual memory, you will see the memory playing on a TV screen."

"Is that possible?"

"Oh yes. I've used this technique before. This time, when you open the door and walk inside, the screen will act as a partial barrier, or disassociation, between you and the memory."

"Can I still feel fear?"

"Yes, only this time, you won't be in the actual memory, but rather, you will be a spectator, separated."

"I see."

"Are you still happy to try?"

"Yes, but I've another question."

"Go on."

"Can we attempt to go back to a time directly before the night terrors?"

"It's possible, although it's hard to guarantee, but we could use suggestion to guide you."

"What kind of suggestion?"

"You previously mentioned a house you visited recently, one that you've no conscious memory of, but yet somehow, you're convinced you're connected to it."

"The house on Charlesworth Avenue in the North Strand?"

"Yes."

"We could start there, by placing your mind in the same spot where you think you reexperienced some kind of past fear."

"At the bottom of the staircase in the hallway."

"Yes. Are you prepared to try?"

"I'm nervous."

"That's understandable, but I promise you, Isabella, I'll pull you back if need be. And remember, you'll be more distant this time. You'll still be the adult spectator, only this time, you won't be inside the memory, but outside of it."

"Okay."

I sit back in the chair, and like before, Eoghan closes the blinds, restricting the sunlight coming in. Soon, the counting begins, and soon after that, I find myself back in the garden with the lavender. I follow Eoghan's instructions, as moments later, I take that same staircase leading to the hallway with the various doors and numbers.

"This time, Isabella, seek out the door with the question mark on it. It's the one that will bring you back to that house."

Again, I do as he instructs.

"Are you at the door?"

"Yes."

"Are you ready to go inside?"

"Yes," I reply again.

"Before you enter, Isabella, you need to realise, it will be different this time. This time, when you enter the room, whatever memory you see will be illuminated on a large television screen."

"Okay."

"You will be brought back to that house as a young child, but Isabella, you will be outside of the memory. It will be on the screen, separate from you."

"I understand."

"When you enter the room, concentrate on your senses—sight, hearing, touch, taste, and smell. Can you do that?"

"Yes."

"Now, as you turn the knob on the door, imagine you're back in that house, the one your adult-self visited some time ago, the one on Charlesworth Avenue."

"Okay," I reply.

"Now, walk into the room."

Even before the door fully opens, I see darkness.

"Are you on the other side of the door, Isabella?"

"Yes."

"What do you see?"

"Nothing. It's pitch black."

"Keep moving forward."

"Okay."

"Your eyes will be drawn to a light."

I do as he asks, and soon, I see a large screen on the back wall of a room. The screen is on, but there's no image on it, only interference, the sound loud, jarring, the screen covered in snow-like dots. Soon, zig-zag lines appear. I wait. The lines are far too bright. I consider looking away, but then it changes again, and an image of a dark hallway comes into focus.

"What are your senses telling you, Isabella?"

"I feel a chill. It's cold, so cold."

"Anything else?"

I stare at the television screen. "I see a Persian carpet in the hallway, the same as the one in that house in Charlesworth Avenue."

"Good, Isabella. Now, slowly, breathe in and out. Remember at all times, you're separated from the memory."

I steady my breathing.

"I want you to absorb as many details as possible."

"I see the bottom of the staircase. I can . . ."

"What?"

"I can smell something. Nicotine, I think."

"Are you sure?"

"Yes. It's very strong."

"Keep looking at the screen—take in every detail."

My eyes stare at the television screen. I scan the hallway, first looking overhead at the ceiling, before gradually moving down to the floor. "There's several cigarette butts in the corner," I say. "They feel important."

"Okay, you're doing very well. What else can you see?"

"The house is changing. It's becoming brighter, clearer, as if it's from an earlier time."

"Keep focused on the screen."

"I feel as if it's sucking me in."

"It's okay, Isabella, you're separate from it. You're safe."

"There are voices."

"What kind of voices?"

"Male voices. There's more than one."

"Anything else?"

"I can't see them. They must be in a different room. I think it's one off the hallway."

"Listen hard."

I do as Eoghan asks, but then I realise the sound of male voices is blocking something else out. What is it?

I must look scared, because Eoghan asks again if I'm okay.

"I hear something else."

"What?"

"Someone's crying."

"Who?"

"That girl from the garden and the woods, the older girl. She's calling out for someone to help her. She doesn't want to be in that dark room anymore."

"Can you see her?"

"No, she's somewhere else, but I can tell she's frightened. She hates being alone. She hates feeling locked in."

"Do you know where she is in the house? Is the room nearby?"

"I'm not sure. It's impossible to say."

"Okay, concentrate on what you can see."

"I see the hallway, nothing more, although the male voices are getting louder. I think they're leaving whatever room they're in. They're arguing with one another."

"Isabella, I want you to move forward, and when you do, the screen will move to a different part of the house. Can you do that?"

"Yes," I say, and soon, I see into a room off the hallway, but my vision is partly blocked by a half-opened door. "I can't see their faces," I say, "because the room is dark."

"Listen closely."

"They're shouting really loud now. One of them says 'we need to shut that child up.'"

"Can you see their faces?"

"No," I say, unable to take my eyes away from the screen. "Wait," I almost scream, "one of the men is coming out. He's in the hallway."

"What about the other man?"

"I think he's still in the room."

I let out a gasp.

"What's happening, Isabella?"

"The little girl is screaming. The man is shouting at her. He's telling her to shut up, that no one cares about her, not her family, not her mother, not anyone. He says he's the only one who can help her now, and if she doesn't stop snivelling, he'll give her something to cry about."

"What's happening now?"

"Her cries are softer, almost silent. The man is walking back, only, he's keeping his face downward."

"Where's he now?"

"He's back in the room, and the other man is laughing, so loud, the little girl must hear it too."

"Isabella, I'm going to take you back."

"No, wait. He's saying something to the other man, the one who was shouting at the little girl."

"What's he saying?"

"He's calling him a prick."

"What else?"

"There's something about playing the big detective . . ."

"I need to take you back, Isabella."

"Please, I want to stay, that little girl needs me."

"Isabella, you're not part of this memory. Remember, you're only a spectator watching it unfold. I want you to leave the room."

"Okay," I say, and like before, Eoghan guides me outside, through the hallway, all the way to the staircase leading to the garden, and finally back to the room with the dimmed light and the smell of vanilla wax. Soon, outside noises return, the sounds of the here and now.

Eoghan asks me to remain seated. He wants to reassure me that I'm safe, and that whatever I saw or heard is separate from me now. It's in the past.

"Only," I say, "it's not separate, is it? It's part of who I am, and that little girl, the one crying at that house, is scared, because she doesn't know what to do. She doesn't know if her family still loves her, or if what that man says is true."

For a moment, Eoghan doesn't reply, but then he says. "During the regression, you said one of the men said something about a detective."

"He did, didn't he," I say, sitting up.

"What do you think it means?"

"I don't know, but it might tie in."

"To what?"

"Things I discovered since my parents' deaths."

"Go on."

"My parents went to England for a while. When they returned, I was with them, but my birth certificate says my place of birth is Dublin and puts my parents' names, or rather the people I thought were my parents, under the headings 'Name of Mother' and 'Name of Father.' I think it was some kind of illegal adoption, which would have needed someone in authority, perhaps someone in the police, to authorise the fake papers. I think all of it is somehow linked to a man called James Lennox, and the address on that piece of paper my mother was trying to get rid of before she died."

"The house on Charlesworth Avenue?"

"Yes, and that might be where the detective comes in."

He shakes his head, unsure. "It's still possible, Isabella, your imagination is invading your regression."

"But that reference to a detective makes sense. Maybe whoever it was, was involved with the falsification of the birth records, with that other man, James Lennox, the criminal I told you about. Assuming, he didn't offend again, or was never caught, he could have rebuilt a different life, become someone else, but there were definitely two men in that room."

"Again, I caution you, your imagination, because of the connection to the house, could be interfering."

I think about what he's saying, and I know he isn't telling me anything I haven't thought about myself, that somehow, I might be imagining all of this, jumping to conclusions to make sense of all the missing bits.

"The smell of nicotine," I say then.

"What about it?"

"During the regression, it felt important."

"Yes, you did say that."

"I mentioned the smell of nicotine the last time too, when I heard the footsteps approaching me in the woods."

He nods his head in agreement. "But still, Isabella, as I said, I advise caution."

"Because you think what I saw on the television screen could be memory, or possibly, my imagination interfering? Superimposing a false memory if you like."

"Indeed."

"So, how do I know what's real and what isn't?"

"You don't. With regression, you're trawling backward. Some of the memory, or the recall, is trustworthy, but other elements may be obscuring the truth, including one's own imagination."

51

NICK

THE MISSING SKETCH FROM THE EVIDENCE BOXES IS STILL TROUBLING Nick, as is the lack of any official report on Elizabeth Harte's original assault, nor any notes from his father, other than Elizabeth's own witness statements, referencing the sexual assault. He hadn't planned to meet Elizabeth Harte for a second time, but the need to revisit what could be one of the killer's earlier attacks, along with the missing items from the case files, can no longer be ignored.

The location is the same as before. This time, he arrives first. On the interview techniques front, Nick's usual call is to give the interviewee enough rope to hang themselves, but Elizabeth isn't a suspect, nor as yet, an official witness, and even "helping the police with their enquiries" is a stretch. No, she's something else entirely. She's part of his father's old life, his police career, everything he staked his reputation on, and the idea that, at best, his father might have been sloppy in Nina Harte's missing person case, was reason alone to keep Nick awake at night. But coupled with the rumours, and now, the mess of the case files, and potentially James Lennox being overlooked, Nick's going to meet it head on if Elizabeth Harte is the key to finding answers.

Waiting for her at the Black Sheep restaurant, the air-conditioning is acting up, creating an edgy humidity. Around him, punters are chatting, catching up with old news, regular talk, unlike the one he's about to have with Elizabeth Harte. She didn't have to agree to meet him, but there was something about her response that made him wonder once again if Elizabeth has an agenda of her own, greeting his call with more relief than he'd expected.

Either way, he doesn't have to wait long, because soon he sees her, moving faster this time, as if there's a fresh urgency at play.

After formalities, he cuts to the chase.

"As I said earlier, Elizabeth, there are aspects of your daughter's case that are troubling me."

"Right," she replies, before repeating the word "right" again, as if nervous, trying to steady herself.

"You mentioned the man who attacked you may also be your daughter's abductor."

"I feared it, as soon as it happened."

"I've reviewed some of the old case files in Santry."

She shifts in her seat, as if the mention of the case files has spiked her interest. He wonders if he should tell her about the sloppiness of some of the evidence boxes, or that the sketch of her attacker is missing. He decides against both.

"We spoke before, Elizabeth, about my father making that connection too, the attacker and the abductor being the same man."

"Your father's advice to me was to leave the police to do what they do best."

"That's a standard line," he agrees, "leave it to us, and have the confidence we're doing everything we can."

"It got to the point where I felt I was an interference."

"I'm sorry about that."

"You don't have to be. God knows, I've beaten myself up enough about it over the years, my decision to step back, to leave things to others."

"Elizabeth, does the name James Lennox mean anything to you?"

"No, I don't think so. Should it?"

"I'm not sure, not yet."

"Did you find it in Nina's case file?"

"It's probably not connected," he says, attempting to backtrack, only wanting to feed her information, like his father, on a need-to-know basis. He doesn't want Elizabeth going off on some crusade. "The name came up within another search around cases I'm working on," he says, "but mainly, I was curious if it meant anything to you."

"Sorry," she says, deflated, "I thought it might have been a fresh lead."

"I wanted to talk to you about your original assault too."

"Why?"

"I read your witness statements."

"Then, you know everything."

"You said your attacker knew things about you."

"Yes, he did. He studied me."

"Do you know why?"

"Because I was chosen."

"But why you?"

"I don't know, but it should have taught me to be more careful, because people like him are obsessed, and with that obsession comes a form of ownership."

"Ownership?"

"He felt he owned me, everything about me, including, I believe, my daughter Nina."

"Elizabeth, why did you really come back here?"

"At first, I thought it was to try again, to attempt to remember all the bits that got lost the first time around. I thought, even if I could remember, or find, one small thing, it might be enough. They say that, don't they? That all it takes is a missing link slotting into place."

"And have you found it?"

"No, not yet, but I guess, with certain plans, life can have other ideas. I know now, I had several reasons for returning."

"Meaning?"

"It's hard to explain."

"Take your time."

"When you're someone like me, Nick, someone whose daughter vanished, it makes you different to other people. You spend years trying to work out where she is, if she's okay, or even worse, if she's dead. That sort of difference makes you insular. You look inside yourself, instead of looking out, mainly because no one else understands what you're going through. Only, by looking inward, you stop living, at least not properly. That happened to me. I became a non-living thing, and also, someone with no idea how to change things."

"And what about now? Has coming back changed you?"

She doesn't answer straightaway. Instead, she looks out onto the street.

"It's complicated," she finally says, "because changes can happen in tiny ways, so tiny you barely notice them, until one day you wake up and something has shifted. You're different, and you're not altogether sure why, and sometimes those changes surprise you, especially when you find them in unexpected places."

"I'm not sure what you mean."

"It doesn't matter. Call it the ramblings of an older person."

She sips her tea. This time, the sleeve of her shirt rises upward. When she places her cup back down, it's then Nick notices the faint markings around her wrists.

"Did he cause those," he asks, "your attacker?"

She looks downward, the tips of her fingers touching the faint white lines, where likely, her blood was once restricted, the ropes cutting into the skin.

He can't take his eyes off the marks, so faint you would almost miss them unless you knew exactly what you're looking for.

"I used to hate these," she says then. "I used to want them to disappear completely."

"And now?"

"Now," she replies, straightening her back as if placing her body in a position of resolve, "they're all I have of my daughter, the reason she came to be, the reason I need to hang on to the belief that she's still out there somewhere."

"Elizabeth, can I ask you something else?"

"What?"

"Why didn't you report the original assault."

She stares at him blankly.

"I know lots of women find it hard to report these things. The system is fucked up for a start, and there's always the fear you won't be believed, but the break-in at the house, the fact that you were tied up, including the obvious proof," he says, pointing to her wrists, "meant no one would doubt the attack."

"What makes you think I didn't report it?"

"There's nothing on file."

"Just because you didn't find it, doesn't mean it doesn't exist."

"Well, did you?"

"Yes," she says, assured, "I reported it."

"When?"

"The day after the attack."

"Where to?"

"Your father's old station, the one in Irishtown near Sandymount."

Nick hesitates before asking his next question, aware, if no record of Elizabeth's original statement exists, the one reporting her assault, this could be the moment he finds out it wasn't sloppy police work on his father's part, but rather, suppression of evidence.

"Who did you make the statement to?"

"David Carroll. He was a young police officer, and I remember his name very clearly. He was kind too. He took all the details."

"And then?"

"Then nothing. I mean, I didn't see my attacker's face. I couldn't identify him from any lineup or anything."

"But you must have been subject to medical checks?"

"Oh yes. They were done at the hospital."

"And?"

"As you said, Nick, there wasn't any doubt about the assault, but the identity of the attacker was another thing entirely."

"I guess semen samples weren't any use back then," he says, thinking aloud. "We didn't have the technology."

"They got a blood type. I do remember that. Type O."

"The most common variety."

"I'd say that bothered him."

"Why do you say that?"

"Because he thinks he's special."

Nick does a quick countdown to the date of Elizabeth's attack. His father would have already reached the rank of senior detective. "Did my father know about the assault when you originally reported it?"

"I don't know. Back then, I didn't even know he was stationed there. It was only afterward, when Nina went missing, he mentioned working at the same station."

Nick weighs this last piece of information up for size. It's possible, he thinks, his father was out on leave, or at a conference. But it's also possible his father knew about Elizabeth Harte long before she knew about him.

"Along with your statements, Elizabeth, the case files mentioned that facial sketch, the one you spoke about, of your attacker's eyes. Was my father involved with that?"

"Yes," she says, "it was his idea, although he warned me the value of a sketch after six years would be suspect, especially only a partial sketch."

Nick makes a mental note to find out where that police officer, David Carroll, is now. And another mental note about the blood type of Elizabeth's attacker—blood type O. It's the same blood type, albeit associated with 35 percent of the population, as a sample found on Rachel Meadows's clothing. Another tentative, although broad, link.

"Elizabeth?"

"Yes."

"I've another question."

"What?"

"Where do you think your attacker is now?"

She doesn't answer straightaway, pausing as if looking inward, before saying, "He never goes away. He's nowhere and everywhere all at the same time."

52

HIM

He needs to be extremely careful with Elizabeth, because as a previous target, if he's not careful, there's always the risk that a second assault could lead back to him. It's daring, but exciting too. Before Charlotte, things had started to become monotonous, even if he hadn't realised it until now, and perhaps serendipity is playing a part too. He likes the idea of serendipity, him being a believer in both destiny and timing.

Also, that old cash cow, the one who fed him extra money for years, allowing him to avail of resources that otherwise would have been out of reach, is dead—killed in that car crash, along with his wife. The news of this had forced him to think about the child again, now an adult, and another reason why the prospect of Elizabeth's death is playing on his mind, like a melody that doesn't want to stop. After all, as of now, neither Elizabeth nor Nina are aware of the other's existence; at least, not for certain. At any point, that could change, which would complicate matters. He can't risk them working things out, as again, that might lead back to him. Meaning, Elizabeth's time has come to an end, but as always, it will happen on his terms.

He's worked out all the critical factors. The normal act of surprise is one, the ability to gain access and exit with ease from the target's premises is another, quickly followed by the need to disarm the target in some way, making her easier to manage and control. Outside of these considerations, there's also the complication of that child, April. He's a lot of things, but he's not one of those bastards who get kicks from messing with children. Besides, children, especially those of April's age, are messy, not to mention the shitload of extra attention that would ensue. He's been through that before with little Nina, and it's not a pathway he wishes to revisit.

He's been thinking about that afternoon in the woods again too, when he snatched the child while she was playing hide-and-seek, and how easy it was, despite the unwanted attention that followed. All of it was inevitable from the moment he saw Nina, when, like now, an unsuspecting friend led him back to Elizabeth.

At first, as he had done years before, planning his original assault, breaking into Elizabeth's old family home, he kept his distance. He wasn't even sure if it was his child, but then he moved in closer, seeing the chiselled cheekbones of his mother, that uncanny resemblance, so clear, it was like history was repeating itself.

The child belonged to him as much as Elizabeth. Maybe even more so, because all the actions that led to her creation were orchestrated and controlled by him. It gave him rights, and within his hands, her fate would be decided. His decision to sell the child proved lucrative for years, until that car crash, when payments to his private account, the one in a false name, ceased.

Even if Elizabeth, or the child she bore, hadn't realised it just yet, all these years, he's been controlling their lives. Elizabeth suffering the anguish of a missing child, unaware of Nina's fate. While Nina lived a life bought for her, one of privilege, but not without complications.

He's always known exactly where to find Nina. A new name doesn't change that. The same way, at any point, he has always had the power to release Elizabeth from her misery, and by not doing that, keeping her in the dark about whether her child was alive or dead, like the money from Nina's adoptive parents, it paid its own dividends. Only, Elizabeth has been playing her own version of hide-and-seek. Initially, moving away from her old family home, then marrying that wimp of a husband, pretending happy families, pretending he didn't exist, before changing address yet again after Nina went missing. Finally, taking up residency with her younger daughter, Alison. All the time, foolishly thinking she was slipping further into obscurity. He knows everything about Elizabeth, because he's made it his business to know. And yes, over the years, he's often thought about seeking her out, but the time never felt right until now.

He never imagined she would come back here, but yet, here she is, having retraced her steps right back to the scene of the crime, the street she lived on before Nina's abduction, almost taunting him in plain sight.

Perhaps Elizabeth wants this as much as he does. Perhaps she wants it even more.

53

ELIZABETH

LEAVING THE RESTAURANT, I'M CHURNING THE CONVERSATION WITH Nick Matthews over in my mind. Who is James Lennox? Could he be my attacker? Nick Matthews tried to put me off, dismissing it as something irrelevant, but he wasn't fooling me. When you're used to being fed crumbs of information, you can tell when something is important. But also now, I'm thinking about all the questions I didn't ask. I was nervous, yes, but then near the end, when he asked about my attacker, about where he might be, it set my mind racing, because no matter how many years have passed, he's still out there. He was able to slip into my life not only once, but twice before, and that cliché of third time lucky is ringing in my head, feeling more like a prediction than a distant dread.

I should be happy Nick Matthews is at least digging into the old case files, even if I'd wager it's mostly because of his father. I guess I'm not the only one with unanswered questions. I could have at least asked him that. Why, exactly, he was suddenly so curious. I mean, sure, I'd spiked his interest, alluding to his father's death not being a suicide, but I'd wager there's something else playing out in the background. Maybe it's those rumours about his father taking bribes, in themselves full of unanswered questions, or perhaps it's the possible connection to his cold cases. Either way, he was keeping his cards very close to his chest.

I didn't tell him about my recent concerns either—the movements in the dark, or even that jogger who I've become increasingly suspicious of, and I already know why. It's because there are different types of fears. The first, sadly, is the possibility that I won't be believed again, and potentially labelled paranoid. I think about all the times I contacted the police over the years, when I thought *he* was watching the house, or that someone was following me home. In the beginning, they'd been sympathetic, but later, when they kept calling Alison to pick me up, I knew I was being dismissed as someone more to be pitied than believed.

The second fear has a different shape. It's the fear that I might actually be right, that I'm justified in being afraid. Only, a part of me isn't ready to fully face up to that truth, even if I'm still aware of the power he has over me, and with him, it's all about power and control.

I knew it from the evening of the assault, his desire to own my fear, to be in control of it. Which is why I should have known he would never go away, not completely. Just like I should have trusted my instincts years before, sensing danger before the assault. And how, after Nina went missing, even though I didn't have any idea how he found us, or learned of her existence, once he found out about Nina, everything would have changed for him.

My assault, and Nina's subsequent disappearance, sent my life on a forced trajectory, no matter how much I wanted it to be different. Because when someone like him has you in their sights, you are left with the knowledge that certain things are inevitable, and living a life of fear is one of them.

Arriving home, other thoughts invade my head, remembering how, after the assault, my whole world was turned upside down. I became lost, frightened, like some kind of blind thing without any clear idea which direction to follow. Later, when the pregnancy was confirmed, I felt violated all over again, catapulted into an even scarier place. Mainly because I knew if I kept the child, he would always be part of our lives, but if I didn't, I'd lose yet another part of me.

There were other fears too. Fears of being looked down upon, those sideway glances from people seeing me as some kind of fallen woman. It wasn't easy in the '90s in Holy Catholic Ireland, having an unplanned pregnancy, being a single mother. In work, at my job in the bank, customers would look at my bump, before glancing down at my wedding finger, seeing it didn't have a wedding band. After that, there were never any congratulations given. Friends too would give me odd looks, saying things like it's such a tragedy, or others, overly curious, wanting to know about the father. The Magdalene Laundries, places where so-called "fallen women" were put away into servitude, were still in existence back then, offering violence and oppression by the same Catholic Church I grew up with. I guess, if I'm being honest, when I met Tom, the prospect of playing happy families wasn't my only goal. I also wanted to hide my shame, for people to stop looking at me, thinking I was some kind of sinner, when my only sin was stupidity, not recognising the danger.

After Nina went missing, when Tom found out the truth, that it wasn't simply a one-night stand, a brief encounter meaning nothing, as I had led him to believe, along with the hurt and anguish over Nina, he'd also felt cheated, and used too. Not only had I lied to him, but I'd hurt him badly, because, obviously, I didn't trust him, and if I didn't tell him the truth about Nina, what other lies had I told him, making him doubt everything, including my love for him. Which in hindsight, despite me desperately wanting our marriage to work, perhaps he was right, even if I didn't want to admit it at the time.

Now, as I check all the doors and windows at home, feeling even more anxious, I'm totally regretting not telling Nick about my current fears: that someone might be watching the house, that someone unlocked the kitchen window, or that something has gone missing, even if the item, the top of a perfume bottle, isn't exactly valuable. And as I'm thinking this, I'm also wondering if perhaps he's different than his father. Perhaps he's someone I can really trust. But trust is something earned, and right now there are few people, if any, in that group.

Feeling exhausted, I curl up on the couch again, my mind shifting to April, and to what I said to Nick Matthews about how I've changed. How sometimes you find changes in the most unexpected places. The child is like some kind of blazing light in the middle of all this darkness. Someone I neither expected nor initially understood, but she has changed me for sure, and what I said to her yesterday, about how much she's helped me too, doesn't even cover it.

I hear singing coming from outside, and I already know it's April in the next-door garden, blasting out some made-up song about life. I love her ability to find joy in the moment, despite all the challenges she faces, and I think I know why. It's because her inner world is somewhere she's content with. I'd like to be like that again, make my inner world somewhere I'm happy to be.

A couple of days ago, I found her cupping her hands around a ladybird who managed to get inside the house. She made it her newfound mission to return it safely to the garden. I watched as ever so gently she encouraged the tiny creature onto her hands from the window, before telling the ladybird everything would be okay, as she nudged the back door open. I told her she was very caring, helping the tiny creature, and how it was lovely to see how gentle she was, bending over backward to bring the ladybird to safety.

"No, Elizabeth," she replied, "I didn't bend backward. I was completely straight." And then I laughed, a big belly laugh, the kind

I used to laugh before my life changed, when I was the younger me, before the assault.

I continued smiling for a very long time before the guilt hit home, before I thought, *I should probably be too sad to be happy.* But April makes me think differently. With her, I let my guard down. I fret and delight in the knowledge that some of her enthusiasm might be rubbing off.

I pull a blanket over me on the couch, still thinking about all the unasked questions from today, knowing there's another reason why I held back from asking them, and it's likely the same reason April, at ten years of age, has shifted so many other things in my head. It's because I've come to realise, despite the difficulties and challenges of April's world, despite her various meltdowns and temporary doubts, she has something I've lost. She has a sense of her own worth. And that's something I need to crawl my way back to.

54

HIM

He listens to Mozart's concerto number 3, playing from the music centre in the attic room, soft and slow at first, as he savours the rise of the orchestra, the tempo slowly building, before retreating back, moving from joy to sorrow, until finally, the speed is so fast, he can barely draw breath.

When he was younger, he'd marvelled how Mozart created such an intricate reflection of life when he was so young. This put fire in his soul, and he became determined, if nothing else, he'd never be ordinary, but rather, the very opposite—extraordinary.

Closing his eyes, he brings his mind back to Elizabeth, savouring every last detail, remembering again their first encounter, the sky a dazzling pink flush before sunset. He'd waited as he'd done previously, for darkness, the slither of moon shining down. His footsteps were silent on the tarmac, watching her, sitting at her upstairs window, focusing hard. He recalls how her hair was still wet, having only stepped out of the shower, and how some strands clung to her face.

He lodges the scene to memory one more time—the opened window, the sweet scent of rose petals billowing in a light breeze, the birds in perfect harmony, reaching their crescendo. Him knowing exactly what he'd do next.

As he waited, somewhere inside him he repeated her name, animal-like, and even before he reached the back door, it had started to rain. He pulled his jacket collar up, and the balaclava down. The lock on the door was easily done away with. He stepped in fast—silent. She was upstairs, unaware, happy. He eased the door closed, shutting out the rain.

His mind is back there now, transfixed, the wooden floorboards beneath him, silent too. He'd placed his boots, the laces undone, by the back door, ready for a speedy exit.

It was then he spotted the car lights slide across the downstairs window as he took the first step on the staircase, illuminating his shadow.

Moving upward, the rain hammered against the skylight window. He turned the doorknob to her bedroom, and she saw him. It was soon followed by that confused look on her face, the nervousness, the shock, the attempt at understanding. It all pleased him.

It was when he moved closer that he saw the flicker of denial in her eyes, the desperate need for this to be something different, before the realisation that it was already too late, as she worked out faster than most that one wrong decision could cost her everything.

The sound of the concerto playing in the music centre comes to an end as he thinks again how her life, once he crossed her path, had always belonged to him.

The only question now is whether or not her killing will be enough, or does he need something more? Is there another chapter to consider, one that could include that precious and valuable commodity, their daughter, Nina.

55

NICK

SEVERAL THOUGHTS ARE COLLIDING IN NICK'S HEAD AFTER MEETING with Elizabeth Harte—firstly, contacting David Carroll, the police officer who took her statement when she originally reported the assault, and secondly, the ongoing uncertainty about his father's reputation, including, where in the hell is James Lennox.

His father wasn't a man who liked loose ends. He would hunt them down, examine them for all they were worth, and make sense of them no matter what. Is that why the Nina Harte's investigation plagued him so much, or should Nick turn that question on its head, and ask, what if the loose ends were something his father needed to get rid of?

He thinks about talking to the assistant deputy commissioner again, but decides against it; besides, he's probably up to his eyeballs with the impending presidential visit—a smooth-running operation a feather in everyone's cap, especially the higher brass.

No, his focus right now needs to be on the loose ends and half-truths floating in this mess—the sloppy case files, the missing sketch, the potential connection of Elizabeth Harte and her daughter Nina to Operation Shadow—as well as on talking to David Carroll and locating James Lennox. All of which might lead him back to his father's suicide and potentially, the latest missing woman, Charlotte

Marry. Somewhere in all of it, there's a common denominator. Find that, and other things will slip into place.

It doesn't take him long to locate David Carroll, now an ex-member of the police force. His career in the force was short-lived. The stories on the grapevine were that David was a troublemaker and someone who wouldn't play ball. However, there was many a decent officer turned whistle-blower tarnished with the same negative tag, and one hour after digging into David's career, Nick has a mobile number for him—a direct line to his private investigator practice.

As Nick punches in his number, he's not placing any bets on what to expect, but the phone only rings out twice before the male voice answers.

"Nick Matthews here, I sent you a message earlier."

"I got it—you're working on a cold case?"

"Yep. I've been going through case files, and your name cropped up."

"In what context?"

"A sexual assault and break-in over thirty years ago."

"Is it on PULSE?"

"That's the thing. It's not on the database. It happened when you were stationed in Irishtown. The victim's name was Elizabeth Harte, or rather, Elizabeth Conway, as she was known then."

There's silence at the end of the line.

"Do you remember her, David?"

"I know the name Elizabeth Harte, sure. She's the mother of that missing girl."

"Yep."

"I'm also assuming, Nick, there's likely a family connection here. Your father was DI Matthews."

"If this were Mastermind, David, you'd be scoring high."

He laughs, and it seems to break the ice.

"Look, Nick, I never had any issues with your father. From what I saw, he was likely a straight-up kind of guy."

"Likely?"

"You know the way it is. I doubt the force has changed much over the years. Lots of things happen behind closed doors, things a newbie, which I'd have been at the time, wouldn't have been aware of."

"I'll cut to the chase, David. You met Elizabeth Harte long before her daughter went missing."

"What are you asking, exactly?"

"She reported being sexually assaulted over thirty years ago. Which, according to her, she reported the very next day, in Irish-town, and to you."

"Okay."

"I can't locate the case file. So, what I want to know is, what happened to it?"

"It's complicated."

"Look, David, I know she went to the hospital after the assault, so some kind of medical records should exist in the database, but as yet, I can't locate them."

"I'm not disagreeing with you, and I really wish I could tell you more, but . . ."

"Her attacker used ropes."

There's another silence.

"You do remember her, David, don't you?"

"It was a long time ago, and . . ."

"And what?"

"It was a different time."

"So, where are the official records?"

"Nick, I'm not going to give you any bullshit, but in the '90s computerisation was in its infancy. There was often paperwork, scraps of paper, lying around the place. With no computerisation, things went missing all the time. And if you're asking me if some crimes slipped through the cracks, then the answer is yes. Or if there's a possibility paperwork went missing too, then yes again. There were lots of flaws in the system, with huge pressure on resources. It's partly why there are so many gangland crimes today. Everyone had their eyes on the troubles, the IRA, and any other illegal military activity. Bank raids, raids on vans transporting money, you name it, were ten-a-penny before the Good Friday Agreement, and corners were constantly being cut."

"So, Elizabeth's statement and hospital details got lost?"

"Probably, yes."

"I'm going to ask you again, David, and this time, don't pawn me off."

"I'm not . . ."

"Do you remember her?"

"I do."

"Then you'll also likely remember which hospital she was referred to."

"It was the Rotunda in the centre of town. SATU, the Sexual Assault Unit, was set up there in 1985. It was the first dedicated unit of its kind established in Europe."

"Okay, that's something."

"She's been through a lot. And I met her more than once."

"Oh?"

"She came back into the station years later, after she was married, with her two little girls. She told me that she was in a good place and had moved to a new house on Serpent Drive, and thanked me for my kindness that day."

"The good place didn't last."

"No, it didn't."

"I've one more question, David."

"What?"

"My father."

"What about him?"

"Did you trust him?"

"I was only there a couple of years."

"You must have formed an opinion."

David draws in breath. "From what I remember, your father wasn't a man to be messed with. It was his way or the highway, a quality that can be both admirable and questionable."

Hanging up, Nick isn't sure he's any the wiser about his father's part in anything shady, but at least now, he's a potential reason for Elizabeth's assault report being missing—total incompetence. Is that why the sketch went missing too, inappropriate handling of evidence, nothing more? David seemed tight-lipped about Nick's father, a fact that makes him wonder if his father was responsible for David's name tag of being a troublemaker, especially based on his description in David's eyes as being a man who held the view that it was his way or the highway.

Either way, now at least, he has another detail on Elizabeth's assault. Even if the police fucked up, losing the records, he's hoping SATU haven't. He's about to put a call through to the unit at the Rotunda when his phone rings. It's the assistant deputy commissioner, Norris. The contact surprises him, especially with all the activity around the presidential visit, so he immediately assumes it's bad news.

"Nick, there's been a development."

Nick holds his breath. "What?"

"We've found Charlotte Marry's body."

56

ELIZABETH

AS NIGHT FALLS, I'M ALONE IN THE DARK AGAIN. THE STREET SOUNDS from outside intermingle with one another, a distant engine, a car pulling out of a drive, along with a leaking gutter two doors up, while a dog whines into the night.

I'm still on edge, but I also tell myself I need to stay calm and avoid jumping to any crazy conclusions too soon. I should feel somewhat better too. After all, I've met with Alison, and although a huge amount of hurt still exists, we'd reached some kind of *something*, and that alone is good. I spoke with her again today. My comments about Ciaran, about how she doesn't have to stay with him, living a life she's no longer happy with, seem to have taken seed. She didn't exactly say things were over between them, but I feel, at least, something has shifted.

It also seems, of late, that my mind has become sharper and more focused. The decision to come here, even if it didn't work out exactly as I planned, I believe was the right one. April has helped me find all sorts of clarity. Although I'd wager I've still a lot more to learn.

The real question right now is whether I should be frightened. A movement in the shadows, a forgotten unlocked window, or even a gut feeling, one that's been growing by the day, on their own, may not be enough. But still, I failed to trust my instincts before, and I've lived to regret it. It's the missing top of the perfume bottle that potentially moves things from possible paranoia to something of real concern. Something went missing before my assault all those years ago too. A cheap bracelet, a pink one with a silver edge. It never turned up, and I had my suspicions, as I told the police officer after the assault, that my attacker had taken it. Nobody probably remembers that detail, except for me.

This time, it's not a thing exactly. Well, I guess, in truth, it is a thing, but does the missing lid from a perfume bottle, one with a fake pink bow, justify consideration? It doesn't have any value, although being the same colour, pink, freaks me out a little. What was it April said the other day? Details are important.

I hear a car door closing, followed by voices—regular people greeting one another. Their cheerfulness makes me feel worse. I want to scream—*I can't stay hidden in the dark forever.* Sooner or later, I'll need to do something more. Being stuck, my previous "go-to" option, has already been ruled out. I was that way when Nina went missing, feeling stuck, helpless, and even before that, after the assault, and then later still, when I discovered I was pregnant.

Why do I keep going back to the pregnancy?

Because it's where everything started, my inner voice screams back at me. The same voice that used to ask me where I'd gone, when I stared at the bedroom wallpaper for far too long. I used to think everything changed with the assault, but it didn't, not entirely. The feeling of terror may have begun then, but the pregnancy changed so much more, because my decision to keep Nina meant I would be linked to my attacker forever.

Carrying her, I thought life couldn't be more tilted or terrifying—how wrong was I? I didn't see what lay ahead. Neither the joy of having Nina, nor the anguish of losing her.

It was in the heady days after she was born, when I was out of my mind with lack of sleep and confusion, and I thought it was only a matter of time before I would lose it completely, that I had visions of leaving Nina on a doorstep, feeling the need to seek out a better mother for her, and certainly, a better father, wanting the truth in all its ugliness to be something different.

In the end, I never left her on any doorstep. I held her close to me, and soon the thought of losing or abandoning her felt so alien, I even convinced myself I never thought about it. Only, that memory returned when Nina was finally taken—*be careful what you wish for.*

It was as if "he," the man who attacked me, wanted to test me even more. As if he could somehow read my thoughts, and within them, he found a new way to destroy me, because by destroying me, he elevated himself.

If he has returned after all this time, what does he want now? To finish off what he started years before—to kill me? As always, there are more questions than answers, including, if he did take Nina, the biggest one of all: Is she still alive? Or has all this time, all this waiting, the unknowing, the unrelenting guilt, been nothing more than a wasteland of regret?

57

NICK

THE FIRST THING NICK NOTICES ABOUT THE CRIME SCENE IS THE yellow-and-black tape wrapped around several trees, with a uniformed police officer at the opening nearest the road, guarding it. A second officer is farther up the terrain. Both in place to prevent unwelcome visitors. Only authorised personnel can enter the crime scene, something he hopes Assistant Deputy Commissioner Norris will approve for him.

He's already noted the terrain is difficult to manoeuvre. Therefore, whoever brought Charlotte's body here was either physically fit, or had an accomplice, and based on the killer's profile, the former was the most likely. He pauses before moving farther up, taking in more details—the dense woodland, the area mountainous and rural, yet close enough to the city to be easily accessed by road. The heavy rain over recent nights and the time lag between death and discovery will have reduced the odds of picking up tyre tracks; it's a sad truth that most trace evidence is lost within the first few hours. Still, as he sees Assistant Deputy Commissioner Norris walk in his direction, like other officers, he holds firm to Locard's Exchange Principle in forensics: every contact leaves a trace, and failure to find it, even within meagre pickings, will be down to those currently scanning every inch of the crime scene.

"Nick," Christopher Norris says, when he's within earshot.

"What's it like up there?" Nick asks, pointing toward the tip of the white tent, the one sheltering Charlotte Marry's remains.

"You know yourself, Nick, every damn one of them is different, but each of them is our beginning."

"Do we know cause of death?"

"Preliminary examination by the pathologist notes an incision to the neck, damaging the inner wall of the carotid artery, which may have led to her suffering a stroke."

"It would have been fast, then."

"Most probably, but we'll need a full autopsy. Anyhow, now, we've a full-scale murder enquiry on our hands. The Incident Room in Tallaght is being set up as we speak."

"The investigation always follows the body," Nick says, taking in more of the terrain. "How far will the guys expand the scene?"

"Difficult to know. It depends on what we find farther out from the body, but so far, the area is looking too bloody clean."

"Another hallmark of our guy."

"Maybe, but we've a different game on our hands now. Missing person to murder investigation is a huge shift. I've twenty officers allocated already. No stone will be left unturned."

"It's linked; I know it."

"Too early to be conclusive."

"And what about me? What role will I play?"

"Advisory, but distant."

"For Christ's sake, why?"

"Nick, you know the score. Right now, you're a cold case investigator."

"So?"

"I need the guys to look at this clean. Fresh eyes, without any influence from previous fuckups."

"I want to see the body."

"I'll make sure you get crime scene images. You know the protocol, Nick. Minimise the risk of contamination. Only those who need to be there get access."

"You owe me."

"Do I?"

"This is the same guy," Nick says, repeating his earlier point.

Norris takes a step closer. "From the sound of it, Nick, you're already jumping to a lot of conclusions. We don't know anything for sure, not yet."

"Then fill me in. How long has she been in the ground?"

"Several days, maybe five."

"But the missing person report was only filed eight days ago."

"I know that."

"Then the killer acted fast, too fast."

"Your point?"

"If it's our guy, from what we know, he's only ever moved this quickly once before, with Marie Byrne."

"So?"

"She didn't follow the same pattern as the others, as it was a shorter time frame between abduction and death."

"What are you thinking?"

"The same thing I thought in the Marie Byrne case, that any of three possible scenarios could apply, although one of them, in Marie's case, was eventually ruled out because of the extended time lag between her death and his next victim."

"The scenarios?"

"Firstly, something happened during the abduction that forced the killer's hand, and because of that, the victim met her demise faster than the others. Or secondly, the victim disappointed him, and without him gaining whatever fucked-up pleasure he needed, the target was quickly disposed of. The third scenario, the one ruled out with Marie Byrne, was that the killer had already identified a fresh target."

"But there's never been two killings that close together, Nick. There's always been a time span of years."

"A fresh target can be a trigger."

"It's not part of his MO."

"Not yet, but part of this guy's success is his ability to adapt."

"One more thing, Nick."

"What?"

"We *may* have a partial tyre print."

"Really?"

"A tyre mark from a Škoda Kodiaq SUV was found near the roadside, but it could be anyone's, and for all we know, totally unconnected."

"Or, if Charlotte Marry is tied to *Operation Shadow*, it could be his first mistake."

Norris looks up at the crime scene. "I'm giving you ten minutes, Nick, and no more."

"Got it."

"Be fully protected, and don't fuck up."

"I won't."

APPROACHING THE WHITE TENT, NICK BRACES HIMSELF. NORRIS IS right, no two crime scenes are the same, and as he gets closer, the images of Rachel, Lisa, Marie, and Kimberly form in his mind. All lives, like Charlotte Marry's, cut short. All lives, who in death need answers, and currently, every person charged with bringing their perpetrator to justice, including him, has failed them. The knowledge of this alone is enough to make his mood sombre, but reaching the entrance to the tent, the first thing that hits him is the stench, and inside, he sees why. Insects have already hatched on the corpse, feeding on the dead tissue, meaning the sooner the body is released, the better.

Hunkering down, covering his mouth and nostrils, he examines Charlotte's face, the skin grey-blue, with much of it no longer intact. His eyes move downward, seeing the incision to the neck. Most of the answers regarding cause of death, he figures, will now come from the internal organs.

Scanning the rest of her body, laid out as if in a coffin, he notes, her clothing is covered with heavy muck. Her footwear, a pair of white runners, are muddied too, as he recalls how jogging was a new hobby of hers.

"Did *he* do this to you?" he whispers, wanting to somehow bring her back to life, to a time before evil crossed her path. Her silence is both humbling and huge. Somewhere inside him, he wants to scream because of the pure waste of it all, and the awful fact that in this world, there are far too many people with evil in their heart, and far too many victims who suffer because of them.

He doesn't shed a tear. He's beyond tears. Instead, despite his lack of religion, he says a brief prayer for Charlotte, her family, and for those who will live this hell for the rest of their lives.

Leaving the tent, he signs the exit sheet with one of the uniformed officers before making his way down to the main road where his car is parked. As he turns the key in the ignition, his phone rings. It's the Sexual Assault Unit in the Rotunda hospital, the Archive Division to be exact, Nick having logged their number in his phone earlier.

Seconds later, the information he receives is scant, name, date, type of examination, blood test results, name of medical examiner, all confirming what Elizabeth told him, that she reported the assault the following day. Only, with the police report missing, he hadn't even known some basic information, like her home address. He could have asked her for it when they met, but now, from the hospital, he has the exact location of her assault from all those years before.

58

ISABELLA

(Present Day)

APPROACHING EOGHAN'S PLACE, THE WEATHER IS TURNING. OVERHEAD the heavens open again, the rain suddenly bucketing down. I speed up, crossing the road. Suddenly, a car, appearing out of nowhere, brakes. The driver, a man, smiles at me, indicating I should continue. Only, there's something about the way he looks at me that feels unsettling, making me anxious, reminding me that my need to find the truth is so huge now, it's almost bigger than me.

I haven't discussed the sessions with anyone, fearing their response, but the truth is, the sessions are the only thing that's helping me.

Entering Eoghan's office, straightaway, he picks up on my mood.

"It's hard, Isabella," he says, "I know it is. Regression brings up all kind of confusing emotions and questions."

"I still want to continue."

"You're sure?"

"Completely."

"Fine, but before we start, can I ask you something."

"Of course."

"Since the last time we met, have your feelings changed? I'm assuming you've been thinking about the sessions."

I breathe out long and hard, already knowing parts of this will be difficult to explain.

"Take your time," he says, as if again, he's partly reading my thoughts.

"Okay," I say, pausing, before saying, "each of the sessions have been different and yet similar."

"Go on."

"The first time, it was the picnic in the woods with my parents, and then later, I was in that garden with the woman and the two little girls."

"That's right."

"After that, I was hiding in the woods, and I heard the footsteps approach me, and finally, the last time, when I regressed to that house, the one I had such a strong connection with, there were the two men, and the little girl I thought needed help."

"And both of us," he says, "were unsure how much of the regression was real or imagined."

"I know, but even though each regression was different, certain things remained the same."

"What?"

"The obstacles."

"Obstacles?"

"That first time, during the picnic in the woods, even though a part of me wanted to run into the woods and hide, the little-girl me couldn't do it. The next time, no matter how hard I tried, I wasn't able to make that woman turn around, to look at me, so I couldn't see her face. Then, hiding in the woods, I felt held back, as if something was stopping me."

"Okay."

"A similar thing happened in the final session, when we attempted to regress to that house on Charlesworth Avenue, and I heard the two men speak. I thought one of them moved out of the room, but yet I couldn't see his face, or the man in the shadows. I couldn't look at them directly, or enter the woods, or convince that woman in the garden to turn around."

"I know."

"But the thing is, Eoghan, I don't know why."

"It could be, as I said before, your subconscious protecting you."

"From what?"

"I don't know."

"And whatever about the regression to that garden, or the picnic in the woods, those last two sessions felt different, like some kind of nightmare I couldn't wake up from."

"As I said before, some, or none, of those sessions may be trustworthy. The last time we met, we spoke about imagination playing its part. You mentioned that while researching that address, at one point, you discovered it was owned by a convicted criminal."

"That's right."

"That one fact alone could have stimulated all sorts of imaginary outcomes in your mind. And we also have to consider the possibility of a recurring dream from childhood, something so vivid in your memory, it feels real. You said yourself; you had night terrors when you were younger."

"But the regression felt so specific."

"Dreams feel real when they're happening, especially reoccurring ones."

"I suppose."

"The tricky thing about memory, Isabella, is that some of it can be tainted in the retrieval of it."

"But, Eoghan, you said, with regression, you can go back to that true event, and be an adult watching your child self."

"Yes, you can, but it gets complicated if your subconscious mind insists on protecting you."

"From the memory?"

"Yes."

"So, how do we move on? How do we unblock it."

Eoghan doesn't answer straightaway, and I sense his silence reflects an apprehension about future risks involved, which is why I say, "I need to do this, Eoghan, whatever it takes."

"I think, Isabella, we should go back to that house again."

"The one in Charlesworth Avenue?"

"Yes, only this time, let's go back to the 'adult you' being there."

"Why?"

"Because sometimes, when our thoughts are racing fast, especially when it comes to deep-rooted emotional fears, our mind is so busy trying to work it all out, important details get lost within the memory."

"Like what?"

"You said, when you were there, you felt fear."

"Yes."

"But yet, there was no logical reason why you should have felt that way. There wasn't any immediate physical threat to indicate you could come to any harm."

"No, there wasn't."

"Nor did the level of concern and the fear you experienced make any logical sense. You see, Isabella, fear is arguably the most powerful emotion we have. Fear results in massive changes in the body, including blood flow. There are many evolutionary reasons for this, but mainly, because it assists our survival."

"Okay."

"And by going back to the fear you felt there, by regressing to that memory, we may be able to pinpoint some of the thoughts racing through your mind when you felt that way."

"Okay," I say, "let's do it."

Moments later, as before, I'm making my way through the garden and then the staircase, but this time, instead of finding myself in the hallway of doors, I'm outside, and walking toward the house on Charlesworth Avenue. When I reach the front door, Eoghan asks me to open it.

"Where are you now, Isabella?"

"I'm inside the house."

"What can you see?"

"The staircase, and the rooms off the hallway."

"I want you to walk as far as the staircase."

"Okay."

"Are you at the bottom of the stairs?"

"Yes."

"How do you feel?"

"Afraid."

"Are you alone?"

"Yes."

"Look around you and describe anything important."

My eyes scan the floor before crawling up the walls. I tilt my head backward to study the ceiling before finally looking downward again.

"I can't see anything important," I say.

"Look again."

"There's something on the floor."

"What?"

"That cigarette butt, the one I saw in a photograph, when I was here weeks ago."

"Why in particular does it interest you?"

"It's triggering something."

"What?"

"Terror."

"Okay."

"I think it belongs to one of the men from the room."

"Are they there now?"

"No."

"Okay, move closer to it."

I do as he asks.

"I'm beside it now. I'm sure it belongs to the man," I say, "the one who left the room."

"The man from your childhood dream or memory?"

"Yes."

"Okay."

"I'm feeling more frightened now. It's getting darker. The darkness makes me uneasy. I'm worried he's going to return."

"Who?"

"The man. I want to leave, but I can't."

"Why not?"

"He won't let me."

"Isabella?"

"Yes."

"Your voice is different."

"Is it?"

"It sounds younger."

I realise Eoghan's right. My voice is high-pitched, like a child's.

"He's so mean," I say then, "and I hate his smell. I don't like him."

"What age are you, Isabella?"

"I'm five."

"Can you remember anything else about the man?"

"He wears something over his face. All I can see are his eyes."

"Anything else?"

"His hands."

"What about them?"

"He wears gloves. He keeps checking the ropes."

"What ropes?"

"The ones around my chest and waist, tying me to a chair."

"I want you to concentrate hard. What else can you see?"

"There's a ring on his left hand."

"Are you sure?"

"Yes. I feel it when he's tightening the ropes."

"Which finger?"

"The one beside the little one."

"The fourth finger on the left?"

"Yes, but he's leaving now."

"What else can you see?"

"It's so dark, and there are no windows. I want . . ."

"What do you want?"

"I want my mommy." And it's only then I start to cry, little-girl sobs.

"Are you still in the dark?"

"Yes."

"What about the man?"

"He's gone."

"Okay, I'm bringing you back."

As the numbers change, so too do I, initially finding myself in the hallway of the house on Charlesworth Avenue, and then, I'm on the street outside, before finally reaching the staircase and the garden, and then, as the smell of vanilla candles return, Eoghan's office.

I feel more exhausted than any of the other times.

"Don't move for a while," Eoghan instructs.

I'm not sure how much time passes, but finally, Eoghan brightens the room, easing the chair back to the upright position. "Are you okay?"

"I think so."

"Your regression was very specific this time."

"Is that good or bad?"

"Neither."

"I don't understand."

"It's a bit like solving a mystery."

"What do you mean?"

"Working out which bits lead you to answers, and which bits send you entirely in the wrong direction."

"Either way, as you said, Eoghan, it was very specific."

"It was, and you became your child self again too."

"There's something else."

"What?"

"This time when I regressed, when I was alone in that dark space, I remembered more."

"What?"

"Something else about being in the woods."

59

ELIZABETH

I'M AWAKE EARLY, HAVING TOSSED AND TURNED IN THE BED ALL night, considering all my options. If he has come back, what then? Am I setting myself up as some kind of bait? That would be stupid, wouldn't it? Yet, here I am, sitting by the upstairs bedroom window, studying the street below. I know most people's routine by now—the forty-something male at the top of the street who works nights. He usually arrives back by 6 a.m. looking tired, as most of the world greets a new day. Then there's the older woman living in number 19. I'm guessing, she must be in her late eighties. She likes to let her cat out at 7 a.m., although sometimes, it can vary by a few minutes. Now, it's gone eight o'clock, and it's the turn of the regular day workers and families dropping off children at school, April being one of them. I think about my grandchildren, Emily, Oscar, and Katie, as April waves up at me, enthusiastic. I do miss them. I wave back with extra gusto. She has another twenty minutes before she needs to get into the car with her mother, but April likes to be ready early, avoiding, she once told me, any unexpected catastrophes.

As April translates my enthusiasm into an instruction to knock on the front door, I think about the jogger again too. I keep noticing him in the evenings, after it gets dark, only I still haven't worked out which house he lives in.

Soon, April is standing in my hallway, looking expectant, as if the wave on my part was also an indicator of news.

"What is it?" she asks, barely inside the door, and already taking out her Harry Potter notebook, opening it on a blank page marked with a black ribbon, her pen at the ready.

"I've noticed a jogger lately, a male, do you know him?"

"What are his details?"

"Details?"

"Yes, height, age, build."

"Oh, I see." I think for a minute. "He's definitely male, lean build, about six feet tall, although hard to pinpoint an age, as he always has his head down."

"Can I have his height in metres. I don't do Imperial."

"Right," I say, doing a quick calculation, "1.8 metres, maybe a little more."

"Hmm," she says, concentrating hard. "I need to go to the closet," her voice sounding slightly panicked, "*straightaway*."

"Closet?"

"Yes, the one at the back of Ellie's wardrobe. I used to go there a lot."

"Why?"

"I like it. It's really dark inside, which helps me to think, and to self-regulate, like the blackout tent in the sensory room at school. I've often sat in there for hours. Ellie never minds, only now, I've less than fifteen minutes before I need to leave for school, so I have to be *fast*."

I follow her upstairs, watching her dart into the bedroom. She doesn't even look back as she wades through the clothes on the hangers, pulling them aside the way you'd pull back a set of curtains, and before I know it, she's gone.

"Hello," I call out, "are you okay?"

"Yes," she says from behind some kind of wooden divide.

I look a little closer, pulling the clothes back myself, as April's body did only seconds before. I see two hinges on the sides, and in the centre, a narrow slit, with a tiny hole, big enough for a finger to slip through. Which I assume must have been how April opened the secret door.

"I didn't know that was here," I say, still studying the hidden doorway.

"It's my favourite part of Ellie's house. It's a great place to think."

"Are you thinking about the jogger?"

"Not yet, as you keep interrupting."

"Sorry," I say then, "I won't say a word."

After a few minutes, she says, "I'm worried about you, Elizabeth."

"Me?"

"Yes. You seem anxious. I understand being anxious, because it's part of being me."

"I guess I'm a little overwhelmed," I reply, still talking in the direction of the back of the wardrobe.

"Is it because of the jogger?"

"Maybe."

"You don't have to worry about him."

"Why not?"

"He's from the next street. He likes to start jogging when autumn comes, and he's very nice."

"How long has he lived here?"

"Years."

"Okay then, I guess I'm overreacting."

"Is it shadow man?" she asks then. "Is he the one worrying you?"

"Who?"

"I've seen him a couple of times."

"When?"

"If I tell you, you have to pinkie promise you won't tell anyone, especially my parents."

"I pinkie promise," I say, my own anxiety levels rising by the millisecond.

"There are some nights I stay awake *all night*."

"Okay."

"And when I get bored, I look out the window."

"Right."

"One night, I thought I saw aliens. I mean real aliens, not the ones going around in my head."

"And?"

"Mam said my eyes were playing tricks in the dark."

"What did you say?"

"I told her my eyes weren't playing tricks in the dark. They were with me, in my head, the whole time."

"Right."

"But the aliens haven't come back in ages."

"That's good."

"Shadow man is there now. He's new."

"How new?"

"He was there a couple of nights ago. I saw him last night too."

"Why do you call him shadow man?"

"Because he stays in the shadows. I can't see his face."

"No?"

"Do you think . . . ," she says then, her voice elevated to panic mode, "he could be like that guy who went around killing people."

"Who?"

"The Golden State Killer, Joseph James DeAngelo Junior."

"How do you know about him?"

"From the television. My parents watched a documentary . . ."

"They let you watch it?" I ask, startled.

"No, no, I listened from upstairs when they thought I was asleep. He killed loads of people, and the police didn't track him down for years. He was only discovered because of DNA evidence using genealogy records."

"Right," I say again as I watch April opening the secret door from the inside, her finger wriggling through the hole and pushing the door out.

"Will shadow man kill me, Elizabeth?" she roars, looking absolutely terrified.

"No," I say, "you probably imagined him."

"No," she says straight back, "I didn't. What should we do, Elizabeth? Should I be worried? I don't want to DIE."

"You're not going to die," I say, needing to calm her. "It's nothing to worry about."

"You promise."

"I promise," I say, lying, because what else can I do.

"Oh God," she says then, "I think I'm going to puke."

"You won't."

"Are you sure?"

"I'm sure."

"Okay then," she says, calmer.

"You better go back downstairs," I tell her. "Your mother will be looking for you."

"Right," she says, slamming her Harry Potter notebook shut, leaving the bedroom as fast as she entered it.

From the doorway downstairs, she shouts up. "You're sure, Elizabeth, I won't puke?"

"Positive."

"And there's nothing to worry about?"

"Nothing," I reply, but as she slams the front door shut, I'm anything but sure, even if it's hard to trust a ten-year-old who regularly sees aliens.

60

HIM

Arriving home from work, he finds it hard to keep his anger in check. So many people don't get it. They haven't lived his life. None of them appreciate how difficult it's been. They didn't have to learn resilience as a boy, the way he had to, locked in that cellar by his mother, hungry and frightened, the darkness becoming his only friend.

At first, he didn't understand why his mother did it, but then finally, he worked it out. It was the prospect of him growing up, getting older, and going through puberty that changed everything between them—her bitterness fuelled with regret, partly because she was abandoned by her husband, his father, and left with him, a boy who constantly reminded her of the man who rejected her.

It took a long time for him to work out that "regret and anger" were the cause of her actions, her warped way of thinking, being enraged that he was changing from a little boy into a man. Which was why she started early, when he was aged nine, to go down a pathway of life lessons, to show him the errors of his ways, and why, as he developed as a teenager, his body reacting to his changing hormones, he disgusted her even more.

Only, it wasn't just being locked away in the darkness, it was the beatings too. He clenches his fists, remembering the rage inside her, uncontrolled, unguarded.

But in the end, her treatment of him cemented, rather than eradicated, his manly thoughts. If people knew the truth about his life, it might surprise them. It shouldn't. Families do the worst things to one another.

Upstairs, he locks the attic door behind him, remembering too, how his confinement, the uncertainty of whether or not freedom would ever return, taught him new ways of endurance. On its own, being locked up is tricky, not least because of the difficulty to determine time. Five minutes can feel like an hour, and an hour, forever. But that need to survive not only made him resolute, it defined him. He learned that the choice is simple. Either allow himself to be crushed, or ensure the opposite occurs. And control, the ability to determine what happens next, is always key.

He watches Elizabeth via the camera in her living room. His mind is shifting again. Next time he visits, he'll place more cameras upstairs. The last time, that young girl, April, disturbed him. But mainly, as he studies Elizabeth, his fresh anger is now firmly placed on her. She messed up big time having that child, and now, that child is a woman. It's only lately he's come to realise that Elizabeth and Nina are part of some kind of prophecy. A form of life-test he needs to pass, which also means how he handles it is important too.

As his wife entertains downstairs, he hears laughter. She and her friends are drinking. He wants to roar at them, but he stays silent, his mask needing to remain in place.

He checks his private bank account online. Funds are declining. This is important, because the hand that giveth is no more, which means a reappraisal of the status quo is required. The decision of whether or not Nina survives is back on the table, but it's not a decision about that alone, because Elizabeth is part of it too.

Now that the cash cow is gone, he's no qualms about killing his daughter. She was Elizabeth's idea, not his. And he's been watching Nina too, following her, even when Charlotte was still in the frame. He knows about her miscarriage, because he was there, standing outside the maternity hospital, when she came out crying. He'd followed her too, when she went back a second time, for her post-miscarriage final exam. And then, later still, after the car crash, he watched her again, visiting her dying mother. He even knows about that quack of a hypnotist, remembering how his car turned the corner, and he'd braked, giving her a fright. He'd smiled at her, indicating she should cross the road. More than once, he sensed she knew he was there. He admired that about her, her ability to detect—maybe she has more in common with him than he first thought.

And then there's Elizabeth, having lived half a lifetime with so many unanswered questions. Surely, it's time she learns the truth. How crushing it would be for her to finally realise her precious Nina has been alive all this time, out of her reach, only for that life, the one she has missed out on for so long, to be taken from her again, but this time, for good.

He's never killed two women at the one time before. It will be another progression. The thought excites him. He could take them to the lock-up, but maybe this time, he should handle it differently. Maybe he should go back to the place he held Nina as a child, before she was sold off. After all, 62 Charlesworth Avenue is not only empty, but that soundproof cellar is also there, the key to it, like all his prized possessions, still close at hand.

The more he considers it, the more perfect he thinks it might be. He'll take Nina first, and spend some time with her, an opportunity to talk to his daughter face-to-face. Besides, she needs to get to know him. Everyone has the right to the truth, no matter how difficult it might be. Others would be appalled by the idea of killing their own flesh and blood, but they forget, those amongst us who are the most damaged, are also the most dangerous.

61

ISABELLA

"ISABELLA," EOGHAN ASKS, "WHAT ELSE DID YOU REMEMBER ABOUT the woods?"

I close my eyes, thinking hard. "We were playing a game."

"Who?"

"Myself and my little sister."

"What else?"

"The game was hide-and-seek. She was hiding and I was trying to find her."

"Go on."

"We both had dolls, and our mother was there too."

"Your mother?"

"Yes. She's the woman from the garden, the one with the two little girls on the swings."

"Isabella, are you absolutely sure?"

"I think so," I say, still trying to concentrate. "The memory came back, as I said, Eoghan, during the regression, when I became that little girl locked in the dark room. As if somehow, even without regressing to that particular memory, it still appeared."

"Your mind unlocked it."

"I remember other bits too."

"What?"

"There was a man."

"Who?"

"I don't know, but he's the same man from that house, the one who tied me up."

"What else can you remember?"

"He's called me by name. I didn't want to go to him, so he came closer."

"What did you do next?"

"I froze, and then . . ."

"What?"

"He grabbed me. He put a hand over my mouth to stop me screaming."

"Can you remember what he looked like, his face?"

"No, he wore a cap down low, shadowing his face."

"Anything else?"

"After he grabbed me, everything started to whiz past at speed."

"Were you running? Was he carrying you?"

"At first, yes, but then, we were in a car. I was looking up at the trees, all of them moving so fast . . . and . . ."

"What?"

"Everything went black."

Eoghan stares at me, and for a second, I wonder if he thinks I've gone completely mad.

"Isabella, you're shaking. I'll get you a blanket."

"No, no," I say, "I'm fine, but I need you to tell me, is the memory real, or imagined?"

"I'm not sure," he says, standing up and walking around.

But as he walks, I'm thinking again about how my parents dressed me as a boy for years, the homeschooling, not mixing with other children, the early years, the ones I've no memory of, when my aunt told me I was in the UK. Then, there was the night terrors, my mother telling me all the bad dreams would go away, only they didn't, because they're still inside my head.

"Isabella, you mentioned something else in that memory."

"What?"

"You said the man called you by name."

"Yes."

"What did he call you?"

I close my eyes again, tight, willing myself back to the memory. In the woods, the sun is making everything hazy. I see him standing close by, calling me, hunkering down, willing me to go toward him. He gestures with his hands, calling me again . . .

I look toward Eoghan. "I can't remember," I say, frustrated, because it feels like I'm so close to something, I can almost touch it.

"Isabella, I've an idea."

"What?"

"It might be important for you to write down everything you think you remember, whether it was through our regression sessions, or what seem like unlocked memories, even if you doubt yourself. Somewhere within it, the regression, the potential restored memory, even those old nightmares, whether it's your subconscious mind, or your imagination mixing things up, there's a truth, but right now, only you can find it."

I feel like I'm two people at once. Firstly, the Isabella who up till a few months ago felt she lived a particular life, and the second, the new me, the changed Isabella, searching for all the missing pieces, the ones inside of me, if only I could unlock them.

Leaving Eoghan's, instead of going home, I go to my parents' house in Killiney again, pulling down all the photo albums one more time. This time, I study the images carefully, one at a time, as if within any one of them, the truth may lie hidden. Then, I do what Eoghan suggested. I take out a pen and paper and I start writing everything down. I've reams of scribbled notes in front of me. I flick through them, seeing the name James Lennox over and over. I do a quick run-through of the facts—not the regression, or the nightmares, or even the recent memory recall, which may be flawed, but the facts. Fact one, my mother had the address of that house in Charlesworth Avenue in her bag. Fact two, the piece of paper was old, folded and refolded, but kept. Fact three, James Lennox is associated with that house. He's a convicted criminal, one who seems to have dropped off the radar. Fact four, my mother told me not to look back. She said there was danger there. Fact five, according to my aunt, I was adopted in the UK, but my birth certificate says my birthplace is Dublin, and my supposedly adoptive parents are registered as my natural mother and father. The final piece I'm sure of is that my parents lied to me, and obviously, somehow, they managed to get false paperwork.

I push all the papers aside and open my laptop. It feels crazy even typing the words into the Google search bar, but yet, I find myself doing exactly that, starting again with James Lennox, convicted criminal, then moving to the address on Charlesworth Avenue, and finally, writing the words "missing child," "child abduction," "child lost in the woods." One case keeps reappearing over and over. I look at the image of the missing girl, wondering if it could be me, all the time telling myself this is completely crazy, this can't be happening, but then I spot a link to a press conference. I see the distraught mother of the little girl, and a man sitting beside her. There are police officers on either side of them. I replay the video of the press conference a second time, this time with the volume turned down. Could this be my mother?

I try to concentrate hard, remembering Eoghan's words about the truth being inside of me, locked away, waiting for me to find it, only it's hard to keep focused, because someone is ringing at the front door. I want them to go away, but they're persistent. I need to get rid of them.

"Coming," I shout out, as the ringtone is repeated over and over, getting faster and faster the closer I get to the door.

62

NICK

IT'S LATE AFTERNOON BY THE TIME NICK REACHES SANDYMOUNT Strand. The sea is out, and the strand looks endless, the horizon so far beyond reach, he could probably walk for miles without touching water. He takes in the red-and-white chimneys of Poolbeg too, as a hazy sky hangs low, and seagulls swoon, eager for leftover pickings.

Turning the car to the right, he follows the sat-nav directions, taking another left, slowing down, searching for number nine. It doesn't take him long to find it, and when he does, he parks opposite. It's a small house, painted in cream. It might be thirty-one years later, but despite the intervening years, he stares at the house, studying it as if it were a crime scene, reenacting in his mind the horror Elizabeth went through.

He takes in the side entrance with a wooden gate. One which could be easily jumped. He makes a mental note of the number of windows, wondering if Elizabeth's attacker entered from the front or the rear. The front garden is now overgrown, unloved, but under the main window downstairs, there's a white rosebush. The roses are large, some still in bloom. A pebbled pathway, barely visible, with tall shoots of grass, sits behind a small rusting wrought iron gate, with low concrete pillars on either side. Beyond the gate is the front door, which, like the window frames, looks uncared for, the paint peeling, revealing a light blue underneath.

Getting out of the car, he walks toward the house, and the closer he gets to it, the more run-down it looks. The gate squeaks as he pushes it open, the noise forcing him to look around, to see if anyone is watching. There isn't a soul about. Quiet neighbourhood, he thinks, but as he takes in the row of houses, he realises some of them are boarded up, and most likely awaiting demolition. Whoever owns them is probably sitting on a small fortune, waiting for property prices to peak before developing their asset.

The side gate isn't locked, so he keeps on going, finally reaching an overgrown back garden at least sixty feet in length. He peers into one of the back windows. The interior looks abandoned too, with layers of dust everywhere, and a broken chair on the floor below an old table, as if at some point, perhaps a family, Elizabeth and her parents, might have shared meals in this now discarded room. The second window on the ground floor likely belongs to the kitchen, but it's covered with black plastic bin bags, and no matter how hard he tries, he can't make out anything behind them. His eyes scan the two neighbouring houses, their back gardens also a massive wilderness. If someone knocked down all three houses, he surmises, making his way to the end of the garden, they'd be able to build a small apartment block.

Reaching the rear wall, he turns and looks back at the house, staring now at the main bedroom window upstairs. The one Elizabeth would have sat at, the day of her assault. He wonders what she was thinking before the attack took place, and if her attacker had stood exactly where Nick is standing now.

For a second, he considers breaking in, having a good look at the place from the inside, but decides against it, not wanting to add unlawful breaking and entering onto his already damaged reputation. What had he hoped for by coming here? A sense of place, yes. A link to the past, maybe? But as he walks back through the long grass, he's also thinking about Elizabeth's attacker. If Nick is right, and this was one of his earlier assaults, perhaps even his first, could this place be important? Statistically, in the beginning, many offenders keep close to home. Something or someone attracts them, and the attraction fast becomes an obsession. Did that happen here, with Elizabeth? Could her attacker have lived nearby?

Back at the car, Nick decides to take a closer look at the surrounding area, to get a sense of the kind of people who live there. Despite the boarded-up houses on Elizabeth's old street, it's obviously an affluent area, confirmed by the various new models of cars he spots as he cruises around. Nowadays, you'd need to be flush with money to live in this neck of the woods.

It's only as he nears the main road, leading out onto the strand, that he notices one car in particular parked in a driveway, as another vehicle, a navy Škoda Kodiaq SUV, exits from the same drive.

The SUV moves fast, but still, Nick notes the registration. Only, it's the registration of the other vehicle, the one still parked in the drive, that has his brain ticking over, as he frantically tries to work out why it looks familiar. It doesn't take him long. Years in the force have a habit of training your brain to remember far too many random details. The car, and its proximity to Elizabeth's old house, including who he suspects is the owner, has him thinking. More importantly, though, it's that navy Škoda Kodiaq, the one that just left, that's really causing his brain to do somersaults, because he already has suspicions as to who the driver might be.

It feels like one of those moments in an investigation when something almost random happens, and a part of your brain is telling you, this is important, even before you fully work out why. He remembers something else too, something his father told him about cracking a case. "Call it an itch that requires scratching," he'd said, "something in your gut telling you to delve deeper, and to be open to *all possibilities*."

Nick runs both number plates to make sure he's right, and seconds later, the owner of both vehicles is confirmed. On its own, Christopher Norris being the owner of the car parked in the drive, and living close to the house where Elizabeth was assaulted, doesn't prove anything. Only, there's also the connection to that navy Škoda Kodiaq SUV. The tyre prints near Charlotte Marry's burial site belonged to the same type of vehicle. And again, on its own, it's flimsy, but the person fast climbing the ranks of potential suspects didn't mention he owned the same type of car. And that is the itch that's currently scratching at his brain, a part of him already asking, could this be the link? Has he been barking up the wrong tree all this time, so focused on looking out, he failed to look in?

He thinks about Operation Shadow, Nina's abduction, and even Elizabeth's original assault, all rushing through his brain like a form of tsunami. He's also thinking about those dark thoughts he had about his father, wondering if this latest gem fits in or not, remembering again, how his father hated loose ends, how he always wanted to hunt them down. What if he did just that? What if he followed the same steps Nick had done all the way back to Elizabeth's old house, and in this perfectly quiet Dublin suburb, where everything seems so peaceful and normal, he'd wondered, if the reason the investigation kept hitting a brick wall was because someone, possibly someone high up, had interfered with evidence? Sloppy police work only went so far, but with so many other errors, could his father have finally found proof of evidence tampering, or something linking Norris to Nina's abduction? He might have even approached Norris about it. Nick remembers his previous conversation with Elizabeth, how she alluded to something similar, that his father might have uncovered a fresh lead and ended up dead because of it. So, what if, like Nick, he had tried the same scenario on for size, and ended up thinking the same thing?

Could this be the man who's eluded the police for so long? Could he have, as Nick often suspected, started his career of violence and destruction close to home? If he had, the risk would have excited him, youthful arrogance playing its part. And if this potential scenario finally ends up making sense, Nick's now wondering if it could explain not only the mess of those old police files, but also the lack of DNA evidence with each of the murders, and the ability to be one step ahead of the police every time, eluding, creating smoke screens, even around Elizabeth. . . . Because if the potential pieces do slot into place, faking an ex–police officer's suicide would have been child's play for a man like him. What was it Christopher Norris had said to him about Elizabeth? That she wasn't a woman to be trusted, a nutjob. He'd tried to stop him looking at his father's suicide too, telling him to stop chasing ghosts.

Does Norris fit the profile? On intelligence—yes. Organisational skills and planning—yes to that too. He's also a man capable of not only interfering with an investigation, but being ahead of it, along with the very real possibility that if Nick's father had been onto him, Norris wouldn't have had any qualms about taking him down. But, if this madness does prove to be true, why did Christopher Norris place Nick in charge of Operation Shadow? Perhaps to control him. The need to keep Nick close by, another way of being always one step ahead. And all that bullshit he told him, about believing in him, how he was a detective who could think outside the box, might be nothing more than another smoke screen to control the drip feed of information, and up until now, Nick had been too stupid to see it.

63

HIM

The house in Killiney is exactly how he remembers it, tall, elegant, as if organically grown from the hillside. Its individuality is further enhanced by the ornate Gothic design, setting it apart from the other large, detached homes, making the property a loud financial statement of wealth. The elevated position overlooking the bay is important too. It tells visitors the people living there aren't only rich, but powerful too. He smiles to himself thinking about how much money he'd gotten out of the sad sucker over the years. The husband was a right pain, the wife less so, but needy in that obnoxious emotional way.

Disconnecting the CCTV wasn't difficult, the wiring being of the older kind, and not operated by Bluetooth. The alarm system is controlled by Wi-Fi, although he's assuming it's currently off, with Nina inside. Either way, the ID and password are likely on a label underneath the modem, or at least, they used to be, and people seldom change their habits.

Once inside, he'll check this out, in case there's an additional panic button to deal with. He feels a mix of comfort and pleasure. A combination he often senses before he harms another person. He won't kill her straightaway. As he decided earlier, she will be for savouring, but right now, he's also wondering about her reaction. It's unlikely she'll make the connection immediately, but she might, with all that regression therapy playing around in her head. He'd done his own research on regression therapy through hypnosis, and on that hypnotist too. The guy had even written papers on it, explaining how difficult it can be to determine which elements of the regression are actual memories, or fabricated ones. This dilemma most likely sent poor Nina's head into a tailspin. One he'll gladly relieve her of as soon as they get closer.

Over the years, she was never far out of his sight, but lately, he's paid her much more attention, especially after the pregnancy and subsequent miscarriage, followed by that car crash. Her pathetic father, or rather, her pretend father, tried to control everything about her—the way she looked, her chosen friends, the type of school he finally allowed her to go to, but he could see from the beginning the father's plan was destined for failure. She had far too much spirit in her to be held back. A little bit like him, he thinks, and with this thought, he allows himself a moment of fatherly pride.

Today, he's wearing an outfit that wouldn't look out of place on the golf course, like many of the members of this pristine and bright community, wanting to melt into the crowd. Still, it doesn't pay to take risks, so he keeps his head down, avoiding any unnecessary attention getting out of the vehicle, which is parked at the rear entrance to the property, ensuring swift departure, once himself and Nina get reacquainted. He's already combed the area via Google maps, working out the ideal getaway routes, those away from police prying eyes. There's a positive celebratory pep in his step as he makes his way around to the front door to ring the bell, one hand blocking the camera above the bell push, the other, pressing "ring" over and over, getting faster all the time, until Nina answers, and she gets to know her daddy all over again.

64

ELIZABETH

EVER SINCE APRIL LEFT FOR SCHOOL, I'VE BEEN ON A HEIGHTENED sense of alert. It could be a coincidence. I mean, sure, I thought I saw someone in the shadows, and yes, in my gut, I'd the sense that it might be him. But now, April has seen him too, this mystery man, not once, but twice. I think about contacting Nick Matthews, but what good would that do. The police might send around a squad car, but probably nothing more. Then there's the top of the perfume bottle still being missing, only that might be nothing. But, if it is him, I'm also wondering how he discovered I was back here. The only people who knew my exact whereabouts are Ellie, Alison, Ciaran, and Lynda Keating, the family liaison officer, who hasn't yet turned up. Still, it's often hard to work out how information gets out, and I didn't exactly instruct people to keep my location a secret. So, it's very possible he heard about me returning to this street from somewhere.

I consider phoning Alison, but if I contact her, telling her I'm anxious, she'll probably tell me it's partly my own fault for returning to the street we lived on before Nina's abduction. And she'd probably be right.

All day, I keep looking out the windows to see if I might catch a glimpse of him, starting with the windows downstairs, then working my way upward. After several attempts of trying to catch sight of him, by late afternoon, I pull the curtains closed. At one point, I contemplate hiding in that tiny closet behind Ellie's wardrobe upstairs, only, I dismiss the idea as ridiculous. I need to get a grip, but still, I leave the curtains pulled over, considering my next move.

By the time I hear April's voice bellowing through the letter box, I'm a nervous wreck. "Elizabeth, are you okay? Why are all your curtains closed?"

I think about making some excuse, like I'm resting, or I've a headache, but because she keeps calling my name, having moved from talking now to singing, I open the front door.

"What is it?" she asks, talking fast. "Is it shadow man? Is he spying on you? Are we in danger?"

"No, of course not," I say, "we're completely safe," hoping my words might settle the two of us, and that by saying them out loud, it will make them truer.

She looks at the pulled curtains suspiciously. "You know," she says, "if someone wanted to keep an eye on you, they might put a spy camera inside your house."

"Where in the heck did you learn about them?"

"A show on Netflix called *The InBESTigators*."

"I see," I say, because I can't think what else to say.

"After that, I looked them up on Google. The spy cameras, I mean."

"Right."

"It turns out there are any number of ways you can detect hidden cameras."

"Right," I say again, as if I've no longer any other words in my vocabulary.

"You need to look for suspicious objects."

"What makes them suspicious?"

"By checking to see if anything has been moved or rearranged."

"I don't think anything's been touched," I say, looking around the room.

She takes out her notebook, flicking back through the pages, and lands on one titled HIDDEN CAMERAS in block letters. "Another way is to check for lights, because some LED spy cameras have a small light that blinks or shines in the dark."

"Okay."

"You've already got the curtains pulled, so that will help, although it would be much better if it were nighttime."

"I'll do upstairs," I say.

"Good," she says, "because I've already started looking down here."

After searching for nearly twenty minutes, I decide this whole thing is ridiculous, and my paranoia, boosted by April's enthusiasm, needs to take a well-earned break.

"I'm going to open the curtains," I declare, as an official end to both of us playing amateur detectives.

"No wait," April says. Then, "Do you have a flashlight?"

"Yes, there's one under the sink in the kitchen."

Before I've a chance to stop her, she darts out of the room, and is back within seconds. "In some cases, you can find hidden cameras by using a flashlight," she declares, far too enthusiastically for my liking. "You need to shine the flashlight around the room and check carefully for tiny reflections."

I decide to leave the detective work to April, as she's obviously enjoying herself, eagerly searching the living room from floor to ceiling, explaining how you can also detect hidden cameras behind a two-way mirror. I've almost eased myself back into a mental position of safety when she lets out an enormous scream.

"What is it?" I cry, seeing the child freeze on the spot, but there's no need for her to answer, because already, above a landscape painting hanging on the living room wall, I see a tiny reflection twinkling back at us.

My immediate response is to panic, but I fast realise, if this is a camera, and he's placed it there, I'm not the only one in danger.

"You have to leave, now," I tell April, almost shouting.

I can see she's stressed, already thinking she might be in danger, likely caused by both my facial expression and my raised tone.

"It's okay, April," I say, lowering my voice, "it's probably part of the alarm system. I'll check it out with Ellie."

"But Ellie doesn't have an alarm."

"Well, maybe she's getting one fitted."

"I don't . . ."

I cut her off. "Look, April, I'll look after it, but I need you to go. Your mother will be worried about you."

"She's won't. I told her I was calling in to you . . ."

"I've a really bad migraine coming on," I say then, needing to lie.

"Will you be all right?"

"Fine. I'll be fine," and as I'm saying this, I'm opening the front door, looking up and down the street, making sure the way to next door is safe.

I know she doesn't want to leave, but as I put my hand to my head, indicating my migraine is worsening, finally, she does, possibly wondering if migraines are a new area of research for her. Whatever the reason, I'm relieved she gone, and once she is, my mind goes into overdrive. The first physical thing I do is pull the tiny camera, if that's what it is, out from its position, and fire it in the bin. The second thing I do is search the house, using the flashlight for any more devices. I don't find any. The third and final thing I do is phone Nick Matthews, only, his direct line is engaged. I should simply pack my bags, I think, and get the hell out of here, only I can't do that, because if I'm right, and something bad is happening, leaving, doesn't mean others aren't at risk. I still remember how much *he* talked after the assault, speaking about personal things for hours, when I realised he knew everything about me, and if he's the same person who took Nina, I'd wager he knew everything about Nina too. Which also means he now knows about April.

If I leave, she could still be in danger, and I can't have another child suffer because I didn't do the right thing.

65

ISABELLA

AT THE FRONT DOOR, BEFORE OPENING IT, I TAKE A QUICK LOOK VIA the camera on my phone to see who it is, but there's only a blank screen. "Damn it," I say aloud, wanting to get rid of this interruption as fast as possible, which is why, when I open the door, and see a man dressed as if he's about to do a couple of rounds of golf, his official Garda Síochána ID surprises me. He also hands me his card, Assistant Deputy Commissioner Christopher Norris.

"Is this about my parents," I ask, "the car crash?"

"Not directly, but if we could chat inside, I promise you, I'll explain in full."

I step back, allowing him to enter. He eyes the place as if he's somehow familiar with it, directing me toward the main living room, despite the door being closed. There's something about him that unnerves me, but I'm not sure why.

"I knew your parents very well," he says, sitting down in my father's favourite chair.

"Did you? I don't remember them ever mentioning you."

"There's actually a few reasons why I'm here," he says, ignoring my last remark. "You may have heard of a missing person's case, that of young Nina Harte."

I can hardly believe he's talking about the case I've just been reading about online.

"Are you okay, Isabella? You look quite pale."

"It just . . ." I can't finish my sentence, trying to put all the pieces together. If he's here about the missing girl case, then maybe I'm right. Maybe I am Nina Harte.

"I'll get you some water from the kitchen," he says, and weirdly, he seems to know where to go. Perhaps he did know my parents, and was even a visitor to the house. There's certainly something familiar about him, only, I can't quite put my finger on it.

His absence gives me time to think. I mean, it's possible, isn't it. But, God, all those lies from my parents, and even worse, did they know the truth? Did they realise I might be that missing girl? Did both of them know?

"I can see you've a lot of questions," he says, handing me a glass filled with water, and sitting down again.

"I want to know everything," I say. "I want the truth."

"Are you sure?" he asks in a way that makes me feel slightly uncomfortable again.

"I'm Nina Harte," I blurt out. "I'm her."

He lets out a long sigh, as if all the years of police work are finally culminating in this. "Yes," he says, "I believe you are."

I think about the night terrors again, the regression, the falsification of papers, the truth tumbling down like a large boulder from up high, huge and fast.

"I had night terrors as a child," I say, "worrying about being locked up."

He nods sympathetically.

"And I've been doing regression too, a form of hypnotherapy, which is why I need to ask you . . ." I pause, unsure how to frame the question, but then I say, "I think two men were involved. One of them did the abduction, and the other, I'm not sure of his role, but I was wondering if it's possible one of the suspects might be a police officer."

"You must be reading my mind," he says. "I was about to come to that. You see, the reason why the investigation into your abduction partly stalled so much over the years is because a high-ranking official in the force was covering things up."

"Who?"

"Detective Inspector Matthews."

I repeat the name in my head, but it means nothing. Only then do I remember the police press conference. "I've just seen him online," I say, "he was the lead detective." And as I'm saying this, I'm also realising the distraught woman who pleaded into the camera is my real mother.

"He was a blight on the force. It only came to light after his retirement, and soon after that, he committed suicide."

"Oh, how awful."

"Yes," he says.

"That's probably how he was able to falsify records too," I say. "I read about that, how there might have been collusion in the past between the police and the religious orders."

"Indeed, but I don't think there was any church interference here."

"No," I say, still trying to get all this fresh information into perspective, "but if as you say, I might be Nina Harte, then it was an abduction, which goes way past falsifying records."

"Indeed."

"And you say he's dead, the police officer."

"Yes."

"What about James Lennox?" I ask then.

"What about him?"

"Was he involved?" My mention of James Lennox seems to take him by surprise, but surely, if he's part of the investigation team, he should know about him.

"How did you find out about James Lennox?"

"I found an address in my mother's belongings after she died. I went to the house. It was owned by James Lennox up to 2009, after which it was put down as vacant, at least until 2011. That's when the library copies of Thom's directory ran out. When I went to the house, I felt an immediate connection, but not in a good way. He was a criminal, wasn't he?"

"Clever girl," he says.

And again, that uneasy feeling returns.

"I'm afraid James Lennox is also dead, killed in a car crash. He was drunk behind the wheel, nearly two decades ago, shortly after his release from prison. The impact meant his death was instantaneous."

I don't know how to feel about this last piece of information, that the two men involved in my abduction are both dead.

Assistant Deputy Commissioner Christopher Norris leans forward. "So, you see, Nina, you are the only witness."

As he says this, there's something sinister hovering around his words. I look down at his fingers, seeing nicotine stains, remembering my abductor was a smoker. "Did they smoke?" I ask then. "Did either of the men involved in my abduction smoke?"

"No, I don't believe so."

"You're married," I say then, looking at his ring finger.

"Yes, very much so," he laughs, only his humour isn't making me feel any more at ease—quite the opposite.

"We think," he continues, "your father paid money to both men. And the cost of a child, you must agree, Nina, is priceless."

I don't answer him, because another thought is jumping into my head, remembering where I saw him before. It was outside Eoghan's place. I was crossing the road, and his car came out of nowhere. He stopped and smiled at me, indicating I should cross. I remember now, because the way he looked at me back then had felt unsettling too.

"I'm sorry," he says then, looking down at my stomach, "for your recent loss."

"How do you know about that?" I ask, shocked, because no one other than the hospital staff should know.

"Because, Nina, I know about everything."

He's on his feet now, fast, the way a panther might strike, and the sudden movement causes me to instantly freeze. Before I realise what's happening, he's grabbing me from behind, heaving me up like I'm an old sack, and it's only then, as a cloth goes over my mouth, and other memories come flooding back, that I realise this man, Assistant Deputy Commissioner Christopher Norris, is my abductor, before everything goes black.

66

HIM

It couldn't have been more perfect, Nina at the point of working out her true identity, and him, her biological father with her, to share the precious moment. Her knowledge of James Lennox surprised him, but then again, it shouldn't. No doubt, she has some of his intelligence.

A pity the library copies of the Thom's directories ended in 2011, because if Nina had gone a little further, she'd have found his name as the new owner of the property at Charlesworth Avenue, and maybe things would have turned out differently. A rookie mistake, her believing that once she found a criminal associated with the house, he must be the real bad guy. He'd seen it happen a million times in the force. A suspect gains the attention of an overzealous police officer, and he or she closes their eye to looking any further.

James Lennox had been useful for a time, especially having a home with a cellar. The logistics were more demanding too, requiring a second pair of hands, but he never liked working with others, which is why, eventually, after James got out of prison, he had to get rid of him. His death was easy. Not too many people care about a convicted rapist falling off the radar. They never found the body; he made sure of that.

But DI Matthews's death required a lot more sensitivity. The problem with him was the same as with Nick: never wanting to let go. He chiselled away at Nina's abduction, constantly going back to it, even when it had moved to the Cold Case teams. That sort of dedication can get you into a lot of trouble, especially if you land on certain truths, and especially if you decide to have it out with the suspect before sharing the information with anyone else. It was Nick's father who finally worked out someone must have interfered with evidence, initially, when it came to checking vehicle registrations parked near Massey Woods. It was only one line of enquiry amongst a sea of them, and the investigation's senior police officer, Matthews, although in charge, couldn't single-handedly check everything. Particular details had to be taken at face value. Once Matthews discovered this particular nugget, that somehow Lennox had slipped through the radar, he kept on digging, like some kind of lone warrior, finding out other things that had been overlooked, initially believing the errors could be down to police stupidity, but finally realising it was something more. And very few officers were capable of pulling off something like that, unless, of course, you were someone who not only had the opportunity to interfere with evidence, but someone who could also quash any inconvenient questions being raised, making sure others looked the other way. And sadly for Matthews, all those unanswered questions finally led him to the truth. His stupid decision to approach the subject, without getting others involved, was born out of his personal arrogance, and cost him his life. It had been easy, back in the day, to start those rumours, undermining his investigation right from the get-go. Easier again when later, after his death, suicide was assumed. All it took were a few clever building blocks.

Now, with Nina safely secured in the back of his Škoda, he turns the corner near the rear of Charlesworth Avenue, having decided he'll enter via the back laneway. He'd done a quick recognisance of the area to be sure none of the neighbours had installed devices, not that it mattered. They too are easily interfered with.

Finally, he reviews all the details of the plan in his mind. Firstly, put darling Nina in the cellar, something he's sure will evoke plenty of memories. Then secondly, get Elizabeth.

It was thanks to Lynda Keating, the family liaison officer, that he learnt of Elizabeth's current whereabouts. Lynda wanting to put him in the picture, being concerned that Elizabeth Harte had returned, and feeling she might be having some kind of emotional breakdown. He eased her fears of course, long enough for him to get close. It was a fellow officer who'd tipped him off the first time too, when he was able to abduct Nina. David Carroll going on about how Elizabeth had come into the station to thank him, telling him all about her new life.

Yes, he thinks, soon it will be happy families: him, Elizabeth, and their precious daughter, Nina.

67

NICK

WITH ALL THE VARIOUS DETAILS FLYING AROUND IN HIS HEAD, NICK decides to make a visit to Norris's home. If his hunch is right, and the SUV was driven away by Norris, his wife may still be at home. They've only met a few times at police gatherings, but it wouldn't be the first time he had to wing a situation.

He buzzes the intercom. A female voice answers. "Yes."

"It's DI Nick Matthews. Can I have a word with Christopher?"

"You've just missed him," she says, opening the door.

"That's a pity, but I wonder, Mrs. Norris," he asks, looking slightly embarrassed, "if I could use your bathroom?"

"Of course," she says, stepping back to let a colleague of her husband's in, "it's upstairs."

"Great."

Once inside, Nick takes in the surroundings, everything looking pristine, with nothing out of place. "You keep a tidy house."

"It's the way Christopher likes it, and you know what he's like when he wants things a certain way."

"Believe me, I do."

She points upstairs.

"Thank you, Mrs. Norris. I won't be long."

"Take your time, only don't venture near the attic room. It's Christopher's office, and he's very particular about it."

"No problem."

It doesn't take Nick long to find the bathroom, which he opens and immediately closes again without going inside. The bit about the attic room has intrigued him, and likely something Mrs. Norris needs to tell every visitor for fear, even by accident, someone might sneak a look. Nick knows, legally, he should have a search warrant, but even a police officer can accidentally go in the wrong direction. Only, when he reaches the attic door, it's locked, and forcing it open could hardly be viewed as legal. He puts his ear to the door—nothing. So, he gets down on his hunkers and looks underneath. Through a narrow-sliced view of the floor, he spots what looks like a spy camera box. Is it enough to argue due cause? He decides, for now, it is, rooting in his pocket for anything he can use to open the lock. It's a toss-up between a paper clip or his nail clips. The paper clip wins out, and although it takes some wiggling, soon, he hears the click of the lock. Before entering, he puts on a set of blue gloves and booties, just in case.

Eyeing the room, multiple objects jump out at him. More boxes of equipment for spy cameras, and on a desk, a laptop with a large screen attached, along with a set of earphones, an empty wineglass, and two cigarette butts in a black marbled ashtray. There's an old square tin can on the desk too, with Action Man on the front in camouflage gear. A piece of memorabilia from childhood, he thinks, before opening it, seeing a mix of things, including what looks like the top of a perfume bottle in the shape of a pink bow. Under it, there's tissue with some red lipstick, but what really grabs his attention are the two dried-up miniature perfume samples that most likely belonged to Rachel Meadows. He hears, before he sees, Mrs. Norris behind him.

"What are you doing?" she asks, indignant.

"Finding answers," he says as he places the empty wineglass in an evidence bag, and the cigarette butts in another.

68

NINA

I'M DRIFTING IN AND OUT OF CONSCIOUSNESS, BUT I'M AWARE I'M IN a vehicle, one that is moving at varying speeds, probably because of city traffic. Right now, the vehicle is moving fast. I can't see any light, so I must be underneath something blocking my view. Memories of another time seep in, feeling very young and alone and frightened. Back then I didn't know where I was being taken either, but now I know the driver is the same man, the man from the woods. I repeat the name Nina, over and over. My mind drifts back to the woods. There was a strange silence before the man called out my name, but now I hear him. "Nina, Nina, come to me." I hadn't wanted to go with him. I wanted to scream for my mother, but like earlier, before he grabbed me, I froze, and that's all it took for him to have control over me.

The road gets bumpier. I figure I must be somewhere near the floor of the car. My mind is still racing back through time, to being that little girl again, the one who wanted to scream out, but couldn't, because like me, right now, her mouth was gagged. And like me, she too was tied up. The same little girl who woke up with all those night terrors, the ones my new mother, not my real mother, told me would go away with time. How could that little girl have forgotten? Is Eoghan right about the mind being capable of almost anything, possibly even reinventing a different history? Only, there wasn't a different history. There was a void, an emptiness, blocked by the terror and the trauma, and a need for her to know that she had been loved and cared for, that her real mother desperately wanted her back.

I must have slipped in and out of consciousness again, because now, when I open my eyes, I realise the car is stopped. I think the man is gone, but I can't be sure. I listen hard. I hear traffic sounds coming from outside and voices too. Is he waiting until dark? I try to scream but it's no use. With the gag, all that comes out are low muffled sounds. I have no choice but to wait for him to return, but then what? I already know the answer to that. I've seen his face. He's told me his name. He's given me enough information to know, if it was up to him, I will not survive this.

I close my eyes again, seeing that woman at the police public appeal, my mother, my real mother. Her name is Elizabeth Harte, and what that man told me as a child, about her not loving me, wasn't true, because I saw it in her face at that news conference, the loss and devastation my abduction caused her.

I hear someone opening a car door to the front. The car is put in reverse. We're moving again, slowly, perhaps up a narrow road or laneway. When the car stops, I hear him open the car door again, before closing it shut. I hear footsteps. They're getting closer. Something creaks open, a car boot perhaps, as a breeze wafts in. A layer of darkness is lifted, and in the distance, as my eyes adjust to the light, behind a large dark shadow, I see an oak tree, its leaves yellow, brittle, faded, and about to fall.

"Another one for the road, Nina," he says, pulling the gag out of my mouth and replacing it. And again, I'm knocked out cold.

The next time, when I come to, I'm no longer in the car. I'm inside that house. It's dark, pitch black, but I know I'm right about the location, because everything about it feels far too familiar for it to be anywhere else. This is where he took me as a child. This is where he locked me up, where he and, most likely, James Lennox waited, until my pretend father came up with enough money to buy himself a daughter.

I need to think. I must be below ground level, because all the noises I hear are coming from above. Will he leave me here to rot, or does he have other ideas in mind.

I'm still gagged and tied up, but neither of these things can stop me from crying, for the fact that I've ended up back here again, for the terror my little-girl self must have gone through, for my earlier life, the one my memory shut down, and also for the life I never got to live. Right now, if this is actually happening, all of it may have been for nothing, because this time, he won't let me go.

I've stopped crying by the time I hear him opening a door above me, the same way he did over twenty-five years before. Soon, he'll walk down the steps, and then he'll tell me I've to do exactly as he instructs, that I'm his now, and everything is within his power. He might try to tell me again that I'm unloved, that my mother doesn't want me anymore, words that as a child tore me apart. Only I'm not a child, and along with the knowledge of who he is, I also know that all those years ago, not only did he lie to me, he also took pleasure from it.

69

HIM

He's glad Nina is alert when he arrives.

"I'll be removing the gag now," he says, "but it will be pointless screaming as no one will hear you. This cellar is completely soundproofed."

She stares at him as if weighing up his words, wondering if she might test the soundproofing out for size.

"Don't bother trying," he says. "I've hardly gone to all this trouble to allow you to alert the neighbours."

"What do you want?" she asks, but he can tell by her eyes the stark truth is well within her grasp.

"We're overdue a long chat."

"Again why?"

"Questions, questions, questions. Your mother is the same, always looking for answers to things beyond her reach."

She doesn't reply. She probably trying to work out the odds of getting out of here. He could take her out of her misery, but time is of the essence, and besides, he's so much to say.

"You must be wondering, Nina, who your father is, now that you realise your pretend mother and father were simply that."

"Is he the police officer at the press conference, the one sitting beside my MOTHER." She says the last word louder than the others, as if she wants him to take note of her emphasising it.

"Wrong, Nina, and if I had more time, I'd tell you the whole sordid story, but your real father is sitting in front of you."

"No," she says, shaking her head in denial, "you're lying again."

"Believe what you want."

"You lied before, when you took me here as a child. I know where we are," she says then, defiant. "We're in that house on Charlesworth Avenue, only when I came here a couple of months ago, I'd forgotten about that trap door."

"You were only five the first time, so you're forgiven," he says, mocking.

"You said the man who used to live here is dead."

"Yes, so he won't be bothering us. This place is mine now. I bought it outright a while back, thanks to your parents, or should I say your pretend parents. Your father, for want of a better description, paid like clockwork every month, until his accident."

"Did you cause it, the accident?"

"Don't ask silly questions. Why would I cut off such a lucrative supply."

"If it wasn't for the accident, I wouldn't have discovered the truth," she says, "I'd have kept living the lie."

"That's the thing about truth, Nina, once you realise you've been tricked, it becomes impossible not to seek it out."

"Did they collect me from here?"

"Yes. They thought James Lennox operated alone, and that the bank details given to them were his in a false name. The false name part is true, although the bank account was mine."

"Did they know I was abducted?"

"We didn't swap details, but your father, the man who bought you, wanted a clean transaction, nothing complicated."

"You make me sick."

"Tut, tut," he says, "that's what my own mother used to say to me, and it's no way to talk to your father." He moves toward her, taking a closer look at her facial features now the gag is out of her mouth. "You definitely have my mother's chin."

She says nothing, but the family resemblance, he thinks, is another bonus.

"You're going to kill me, aren't you?"

"Yes," he says, "but not yet. First, I need to tell you about my childhood."

"I don't care about that."

"And I don't care that you don't care. You're going to listen, because now there is no longer anyone else to bother us. There's only the two of us."

Silence.

"Good," he says, sucking in air, feeling the breath fill his chest. "My mother did terrible things to me growing up. She had a difficult time with men. One in particular, my father, treated her badly, and she didn't want me becoming one of those BAD men, not before she taught me a great many lessons. She used to lock me up too. She said it was her way of getting my attention, and her cruelty had few boundaries, especially when excess alcohol was involved. It's why I never wanted children of my own. I hoped to stop history repeating itself. They say that happens within families, unless you kill it off at the source."

"Did you kill her, your mother?" Nina asks.

"No," he says, remembering how he found her years before. "She got very drunk one night, and she choked on her own vomit. She denied me even that, the opportunity to kill her, but every time I kill, and believe me, Nina, I've killed a lot, I relive it just a little, reimagining I'm killing her over and over."

"You're mad."

"I probably am, but you've only heard some of the story, so I suggest you hold judgment until you've a better grasp of all the facts."

"Why did you have me, if you didn't want children."

"That was your mother's idea, not mine. Would you like me to tell you how you were conceived?"

"I don't want to hear anything from you," she says with such venom, it's almost admirable.

"Your mother," he hisses, "tried to hide you from me. She tried to trick me, but she underestimated my resolve."

She doesn't respond, but he can see now, she's listening attentively, searching for, like Elizabeth, that broken bond between mother and daughter.

"It's partly, Nina, why I had to take you from her, to punish her for the deceit."

"Why didn't you just kill me then?"

"There's a time and place for everything, and besides, you were worth far more to me alive than dead."

She tries to pull at the ropes behind her back in frustration.

"Have I made you angry?" he asks. "Are you cross with me?"

She pulls at the ropes again.

He laughs at her valiant efforts.

"Save your energy," he says, stepping back, "because now it's time for us to really play happy families."

70

ELIZABETH

I FINALLY GET THROUGH TO NICK MATTHEWS. "NICK," I SAY, MY throat tense, croaky, "I think I might be in danger."

"Elizabeth . . ."

"Don't try to shut me up," I say, talking extremely fast, like April often does, "or appease me, even if this sounds *crazy*, but I think he's back. I found a hidden camera in the living room, well not me, it was . . . look, it doesn't matter who found it, the point is, someone put one there."

"Are you at home?"

"I'm at my friend Ellie's house."

"YOU NEED TO GET OUT OF THERE."

"I can't."

"Why not?"

"Because, I can't." There's no way I'm leaving with April so close.

"ELIZABETH, IF YOU'RE RIGHT, YOU'RE NOT SAFE."

"There's a young girl, April, who lives next door. We're friends, and if that man has placed the camera here, if it is him, he'll know about her too. He knows everything. I can't risk the same thing happening to her that happened to Nina."

"YOU'RE NOT GOING TO BE ABLE TO . . ."

"I'M NOT LEAVING."

"Okay, I'm on my way, but I need to ask you something."

"What?"

"Has anything gone missing from your place, anything, no matter how small."

"A top off a perfume bottle, in the shape of a . . ."

"Pink bow," he replies, finishing my words.

"How did you know?"

"I'll explain when I get there, but first, I'm going to send you an image of the man I think attacked you, and likely, the same person who took Nina."

"You know who he is?" I ask, my words high-pitched, unable to believe it's possible, that after all this time, the man I've feared for so long actually has an identity, a name. He will no longer be elusive, but still, oh my God, dangerous, and also possibly close by.

"Yes," he says, "now give me your address."

He hangs up after I give it to him, and within seconds, my phone bleeps a WhatsApp message from Nick with the image. My hands shake as I'm opening it, and then I see him, this unknown face, this stranger. I zoom in on the eyes, knowing immediately Nick's right, it is him. I keep staring, studying other aspects of his face, when suddenly, I want to cry, because a part of him also looks like my daughter Nina.

I'm so fixated on the image, I don't hear the low sound at first, a kind of tap-tapping, like someone has a tiny hammer and is trying to drive home a nail. Then it gets louder, and it takes me a second to locate its direction. Someone is knocking at the back door.

"Shit," I say aloud, what if it's him. What if he's already here.

The tapping intensifies, but then I hear a voice. "Elizabeth, it's me, April. Let me in."

"Shit," I say for a second time, rushing to the back door to unlock it. "I told you to go home, April. GO HOME AND STAY HOME."

Her eyes look panicked, both of them bulging from their sockets, as she shakes her head so fast, I think she's going to let out an almighty scream. I pull her inside, realising I'll need to calm her, and somehow get her to self-regulate, or all of this could go terribly wrong, and one or both of us could end up dead.

"You're okay," I say, my voice softer.

"I had to warn you," she says, her voice a mix of screaming and crying.

"Warn me of what?"

"He's here."

"Who?"

"Shadow man."

"Where?"

"I saw him park a big car up the road. It's navy. I put the registration number in my book. I like to collect registrations, and . . ."

"STOP IT, APRIL. You need to tell me why you're so sure it's him."

"The way he moves."

"How?"

"Like he's gliding."

I'm still trying to take in her words, a flash of old memory leaping forward, of how my attacker moved, knowing April's description is exactly right, when I hear the front garden gate opening. It could be Nick, but what if it isn't? My eyes dart around the room, looking for somewhere safe. "Quick," I say, to April, "we'll need to hide."

"Where?"

"The upstairs closet, behind the wardrobe in Ellie's bedroom," I say, putting my finger to my mouth, warning her to be quiet.

Part of me is surprised when she doesn't question me, because she questions everything.

"You go first," I whisper, following behind her, into the darkness.

71

NICK

DRIVING TO ELIZABETH'S HOUSE, LOTS OF SCENARIOS ARE JUMPING around in Nick's head, but if he gets that DNA result, and they're able to link it to the partial profile from the Marie Byrne case, all hell will break loose. In the meantime, a mini-hell is already gaining momentum. Mrs. Norris may not have been able to get through to her husband, but she has plenty of other high-profile players to rant and complain to.

He reaches a tailback of traffic in Templeogue village, so he uses the police siren to save time, gaining extra speed. One thing he knows for sure, if he's right, it's the breakthrough that has been years coming, but if he's wrong, any amount of shit will hit the proverbial fan. Right now, as the siren blares, apart from awaiting the DNA results from the glass and the cigarette butts he managed to get to forensics, he has Elizabeth Harte in his sights. That SUV was going somewhere, and until he has ironclad proof linking Norris to at least Marie Byrne's killing, no one is going to issue a warrant for Assistant Deputy Commissioner Christopher Norris.

He mentally reviews all the links in his mind as his car overtakes several others pulled to the side—the sloppy police work, the missing sketch, the ability of someone like Christopher Norris, a police officer, to not only mess with evidence, but working odd hours, to carry out crimes without others asking too many questions. If he's working at two o'clock in the morning, no one queries it, including his wife, allowing him the ability to hide in plain sight. But there's something else too, and it wasn't just Norris's advice not to look back, or to stop chasing ghosts, or even the SUV, it's the physical resemblance that has eluded Nick until now. Because unless you're actively seeking it out, you could easily miss it—the facial resemblance to the missing girl, Nina Harte, especially the images from the later reconstructions. It was as if Nina's attractive features had been superimposed on Christopher Norris's face, only in a less successful way. His eyes farther apart, but with a similar mouth. His lips positioned above a square-shaped chin, while her chin was more chiselled, feminine, and attractive.

His phone rings out, and recognising it as the number of one of the higher-ups, he lets it go to voicemail, having no intention of listening to an earful until he's something solid behind him.

Reaching the bridge, driving even faster, cars swerve to avoid him. Elizabeth's safety is on the line, and the only thing on his mind right now is getting to her, but when his phone rings out again, and he sees it's from one of the forensic team, this time he answers.

"What news?"

"It's a match, absolutely no doubt about it."

"Okay," he says, the momentum of this hitting home as he hangs up, knowing now he's a zillion calls to make. But his first call needs to be for backup, as he heads toward Elizabeth Harte's place.

72

ELIZABETH

HIDING WITH APRIL IN THE DARK, I WHISPER, "WE NEED TO STAY completely quiet." She doesn't answer, so I'm thinking, *Okay, she's got the message*, only it's never that straightforward with April.

"Do you want to know some facts about killer whales?" she whispers.

"No, April, not right now."

"I either tell you, or I'll have to scream."

Shit. "Okay, but be fast," I whisper. "And please, April, keep your voice so low, I can barely hear it."

"Okay," she says. "Fact one, they measure nearly ten metres in length and weight up to 5,500 kilograms. Fact two, females are usually smaller than males. Fact three, the male's fin can be up to 1.8 metres, making it the largest of all the cetaceans—that's marine mammals, including whales, dolphins, and porpoises. Fact four, you don't want to see them smile, because they have a hundred pointy teeth to grasp and kill their prey. Fact five, they can live up to ninety years of age. Fact six, the female killer whale is pregnant for seventeen months. Fact seven, they're really called orcas, not killer whales. Fact eight, they've their own language, a series of clicks, whistles, squeals, squeaks, and screams. Fact nine, they're not whales at all. They're actually dolphins, only a lot bigger . . ."

"Shush," I say.

"But I haven't told you fact ten."

"Sweetheart, listen to me like you've never listened to anyone before. Right now, we both need to be completely quiet. Do you think you can do that?"

"Okay, but will I puke?" she asks, as I realise, even in the dark, her eyes are bulging out of their sockets.

"No," I say, as I hear the lock on the front door clicking open.

I've no idea if April is going to play ball, but what I do know is that the front door has been opened and closed, and if it was Nick Matthews, he'd be calling out for me, unlike the person who has just entered the house. The only thing more frightening than hearing sounds you don't want to hear is hearing nothing, except for April's low breathing, as my heart thumps faster in my chest.

Shit, I hear something else now. It's from upstairs, as if drawers are being opened and closed. I think April is going to say something, but she doesn't, and I realise she's self-regulating, breathing in and out, and I think, *Thank God.*

My eyes are peering out of the tiny finger hole, through the gap in the clothes, and the narrow slit in the wardrobe door—a slit of light, until it goes dark, and then I realise, someone is there. He's in the room, walking past, blocking out the light.

April grabs my right hand with both of hers so tight it hurts. I want to tell her everything's going to be okay, but I can't risk speaking. The slit of light keeps going in and out of sight—light, darkness, light, darkness. He must be right outside the wardrobe. I think about my old childhood nightmares, worrying about monsters hiding under the bed, or a wicked witch who might sneak into my room and kill me. And then the light comes back, and the next sound I hear is farther away. He could be downstairs. What if he notices the spy camera is missing? Maybe he'll think

I've left, running away from him again, only my car is still parked in the drive.

"Elizabeth," April whispers, "I'm going to puke."

"No, you won't," I reply, still wondering if he might be downstairs, or if he's already left.

"I'll scream then."

"*No, you won't*," I repeat. "Don't you dare scream."

But as the sound of police sirens grows louder in the distance, April screams so loud, and so desperately, I'm not sure she's ever going to stop.

73

NINA

IN THE DARK, MY LEGS AND HANDS ARE TIED EVEN TIGHTER. HE made sure of that earlier. He's gone for now, but I know he will return. I also know he is quite prepared to kill me, because unless some miracle happens, no one even knows I'm here. By the time anyone raises an alarm, or starts to wonder about my whereabouts, I'll already be dead.

And now, there's another sickening reality curling around inside of me. A truth that's too hard to bear, that this man, not James Lennox, may be my father. Of course, he could be lying, but there was something about the way he said it that made me believe him. What does that make me? The daughter of a monster? And if it's true, what does it even matter now? The only thing that matters is somehow getting out of here, but then I remember, he made me a promise. He said he'd bring Elizabeth, my birth mother, here. If he's doing that, I doubt it's by choice. She might not even know I'm still alive. Did she keep on looking for me, even after the police messed up, or is the reason she never found me because she gave up hope?

I pull at the ropes around my wrists and ankles, but it's no use. Again, I call for help, screaming the word "HELP" over and over, only it's useless. In this darkened cellar, underneath this house, a place no one knows about except for him, no one is going to hear me.

Perhaps Eoghan will piece it all together the way I did. He might even contact the police, but if he does work it out, what then? He could tell them about the house. I'm sure I gave him the address, but did I tell him which number? I can't remember. And even if I did, it would only work if time was on my side, which it isn't.

Thinking about the regression, I consider all the bits I finally remembered, including how I not only lost a mother, I lost a sister too. Her name is Alison. I repeat the name, as if by saying it, I might be able to somehow reach her. What must it have been like for her? Does she even remember I existed? An image of her forms in my mind, a little blonde girl with thick curls, like the little girl I saw on the beach a couple of months back, with her pink shoes and bathing suit, her mother holding her hand tight. Now, when I visualise Alison, I see her walking with her doll, the one with blonde hair just like hers, grabbing it by the hair with her tiny fists, the doll bobbing up and down, every so often dragging its plastic feet along the ground.

I think about all those weeks I felt I was being watched too, a form of paranoia I put down to stress and grief, but now knowing it was him all this time. He must have followed me to the hospital, somehow working out about the miscarriage. He's been watching me all along, even on my visits to Eoghan, like some sick pervert, sneaking around in other people's lives.

And more than anything right now, I know if I had to, I would kill him. I ask myself the question again, what does that make me? A monster, just like him.

74

NICK

NICK ARRIVES AT ELIZABETH'S PLACE BEFORE THE BACKUP SQUAD cars. Both Elizabeth and the young girl April look visibly shaken. April's mother is there too, hugging her daughter as Elizabeth fills Nick in.

"He was here," she says, "in the house. He came in through the front door. I think he was searching the house for me, but we were hidden."

"Where?"

"There's a kind of secret closet, a void behind the wardrobe upstairs. I only knew about it because of April. Oh my God," Elizabeth says, holding her hands tight to her chest, "I was convinced he'd find us."

"Maybe the sound of the squad car spooked him," Nick says, "or, he was just checking the place out."

"NO," Elizabeth replies, adamant, "he was looking for me, and April nearly got caught up in it. She saw him. She even got his registration number. It's in that little notebook of hers."

"I'll look at it," he says, "but if it's him, I think I already know the registration."

The little girl, April, walks over to hug Elizabeth, and she seems to hug her so tight, Nick's unsure if she'll ever let her go.

"I never got to tell you, Elizabeth," April says, finally releasing her grip, "about fact number ten."

"No," Elizabeth says, smiling, "you never did. What is it?"

"There are around fifty thousand killer whales in existence. They can't be completely certain of the number, because it's hard to count them, being killers and all, but it's probably about right. Fact ten, they're considered an endangered species, even though they're extremely dangerous."

"That's good to know," Elizabeth replies, "and especially good to know about those teeth too."

April beams up at her, as if she's already put the whole scary experience of recent events behind her. He doubts Elizabeth has told her everything, but she's probably told her enough.

Nick takes Elizabeth aside. "We've matched his DNA to at least one of the four murder victims. There are possibly more women out there, although we've nothing as yet to link him to your attack, other than I'm pretty sure I found the top of your perfume bottle, along with a whole lot of other stuff."

"I don't need forensic proof," she says, "to know it's him. I've seen his photograph now, and despite the horror of finally seeing his face, I also saw my daughter Nina in that image too."

"I'm surprised you never met him, Elizabeth, during the investigation into Nina's abduction. He works in the force."

"What's his name?"

"Christopher Norris."

She looks as if she's repeating the name in her head, trying to find it somewhere in a lost memory, before saying, "He's the guy who put you in charge of investigating Rachel Meadows's murder, and the others."

"Yes," he says, "how did you know that?"

"I overheard someone say it at your station."

Nick stares at her in disbelief before she asks, "Did he work with your father?"

"At one point, but not during Nina's investigation, apart from probably interfering with evidence."

"What now, Nick?"

"There's an alert out for his arrest. Don't worry, Elizabeth, we'll find him. We're running a search on properties in his name as we speak. He held his victims somewhere before death, and likely Nina too, as a child."

A look of horror comes on Elizabeth's face, making her suddenly look older.

"Do you think he killed her?"

"I don't know, Elizabeth, but we're closer to him now than we've ever been."

Nick's phone rings out. "Hold on a second," he says, "I have to take this."

"Okay," he says into the phone. "We'll need to check all three locations. I'll take the last one, but make sure we've plenty of backup. We can't risk not finding him."

"Do you know where he is?" Elizabeth asks.

"We've an address for a lockup in Lucan, along with a set of houses, including the one you used to live in, where you were attacked, and a house on the north side of the city, on Charlesworth Avenue."

"How did he acquire so much property?"

"That's one of the questions we'll be putting to him as soon as we track him down."

"Which address are you going to?"

"The one farthest away, 62 Charlesworth Avenue. We've a search warrant for all three locations, but I better go."

"Okay."

"You're sure you're all right?"

She nods.

"I'm going to leave two officers here, Elizabeth, just in case."

"Thanks, Nick," she calls after him, as he reaches the front door, "it feels good to finally be believed. Your father would be proud of you."

"I know that," he says, looking back, and for the first time since his father's alleged suicide, many of the dark questions he's had inside his head subside, even if others still linger.

75

HIM

He knows, driving away from Elizabeth's, turning to avoid the line of the squad cars, that it's happening now. He knew it even before his wife called and told him that his various contacts in the force, high-brass officials, are all refusing to talk to her. He let her rant on and on, talking about Nick Matthews being in the attic room, barely listening to her, because this is the moment he thought would never happen, even if he spent most of his adult life imagining it—the fallout. The shocked faces, the disbelief, the shame within the force, a bloody mess that human resources and the media teams will have to handle—the low morale, the notoriety in the newspapers, on TV, radio, and online. Right now, out there, someone has yet to decide if they'll write a book about him, while another is unaware of the documentary they might make. All of it is suspended in time, in this moment, as he goes back to see his daughter one last time.

He doesn't rush when he reaches Charlesworth Avenue, having parked the Škoda several streets away, knowing by now, there's likely an all-out alert for the registration plate. He even smiles at the next-door neighbour he spoke with a few months back, talking about putting the house up for sale. She doesn't know as yet about any of it, and that's when it hits him, how he's spent a lifetime pretending to other people, putting his normalised front out in the world for all to see, to bear witness, while inside, where it counts, his mind is anything but normal, it's enraged.

Walking down the cellar steps for the last time, he's already decided he can't face prison. He's crossed too many paths with criminals and made far too many enemies. Even those who don't know about him will hear of him, and they'll hate him the same way his mother hated him. They'll look down on him, set themselves up as judge and jury, and decide his fate. No, he's not going to allow that to happen, but first, he says, "Hello, Nina," flashing a torchlight in her direction. "Your mother wasn't home," he says. "She ruins everything." He notes the disappointment in her face, a face he remembers from years before, when the younger Nina was scared because the bad man wouldn't set her free. He'd explained everything to her, about how he'd found her a new set of parents, people who would really love her, now that her real mother didn't want her anymore. Through the tears and misery, she had broken down completely, and now, as he looks at her, Nina the adult, he sees a different face looking back at him, the face of someone who would kill him given half a chance. It's not all black and white, *he thinks. There's grey in every one of us. We're all capable of killing, given the right set of circumstances.*

Circling the torch on her face, he removes the gag, thinking about all the women he's killed, reliving the moment of death with each one of them. He thinks about the supposed suicide of Nick's father, and his partner in crime, James Lennox. He visualises his mother too, lying on the bed, dead within her own vomit, and the irony of it all isn't lost on him. "You make me sick," she used to say, over and over. A part of him smiles, wondering if somehow, in her disappointment with him, he'd killed her after all.

"You look just like her," he tells Nina again. "The same facial features, the way you hold yourself, the way you stare, as if you despise me."

She goes to speak but stops herself.

"The police," he says, "likely have enough evidence to convict me. I thought you should know that, and I doubt one more killing will change things very much."

Again, she says nothing.

"I thought it would be perfect, Nina, with you, me, and Elizabeth here, but you see, I was wrong about that. It's best it's just the two of us, as now, I've the pleasure of pretending one last time that as I kill you, I'm killing my mother instead. Finally, I have the perfect replica."

76

NICK

NICK KNOCKS ON THE DOOR OF NUMBER 62 CHARLESWORTH AVENUE, not expecting an answer. After the second attempt, he kicks it in. With most of the wood in the door already rotten, it doesn't take a lot of effort, and he enters the hallway with a crew of officers behind him, and another team entering from the rear.

Minutes later, they establish the premises are empty, and Nick is already checking in with the other teams. Both the lockup in Lucan and the string of houses in Sandymount have come up blank. Reluctant to accept Christopher Norris may have slipped out of their grasp, he reexamines the rooms downstairs one more time.

The house is old, Georgian, but as he's looking around, he takes in more details about the interior. Some of the original features are badly damaged, but still in place. The rooms aren't large, heating being an issue when these homes were originally built, and as he's thinking this, he's also thinking about how so many of these houses had cellars, a place to store fuel, coal mostly, for the winter months.

He looks out back, having kicked that door down too, searching for any access to a cellar from the rear, but there's nothing. Once inside again, he examines the floor for a trapdoor, starting in the back kitchen, then moving to the two reception rooms at the front. As he's standing in the hallway, with his back to the front door, and the staircase in front of him, with his foot he shifts the Persian rug on the floor to the side. When he sees the trapdoor, he raises his hand, getting the attention of two of the officers. He puts his finger to his lips to warn them not to make a sound. This message is communicated in near silence to the rest of the team, as they each check their firearms are exactly where they should be, their bulletproof vests also in place.

Nick lifts the trapdoor. "Norris," he roars, "it's over."

"Not until I say so," comes a swift reply.

77

HIM

He's surprised when he hears the police move above him, especially because he never really thought Nick Matthews would work it all out, but then again, he was banking on the alcohol taking its toll on him, drinking so heavily after his father's death, before going cold turkey and spoiling everything.

Just like his father, when on his game, Nick's too good a detective for his own good. Now, the odds are more stacked in his opponent's favour, and he's not feeling confident.

He can see in Nina's face a combination of hope that she'll be saved and horror that he'll pull the trigger of his SIG Sauer, the one he's now pointing right at her.

He's not sure what's holding him back, being aware time isn't on his side, but there's something else he's seeing in her face now, the resemblance not only to his mother, but to himself.

When he's gone, he thinks, there'll be plenty of news reports about him, most likely calling him the "Shadow Man," or something else equally alarming, considering he code-named the investigation into the cold cases of his victims: Operation Shadow. But does he really want it all to end here? He knows he's going to kill himself, as prison isn't an option, and the question now is whether he'll die with Nina's body lying beside his, or if he wants another outcome, one where the embodiment of him, in his child, survives.

He hears the trapdoor opening. He counts the seconds in his head, as Nick roars, "Norris, it's over," and he replies, "Not until I say so."

His fingers are tightening on the trigger. This is it, *he thinks. All the fucked-up history, the harm done to him, and to others, all the pretence, the lies, the endless planning, and even his sorry excuse of a marriage, it all ends here, as he pulls the trigger, with no chance of missing the target.*

78

NINA

AS SOON AS I HEAR MOVEMENT ABOVE THE CELLAR, I HAVE HOPE, but there's no way of knowing for sure that they'll find the trapdoor. What if they're like me, and check the place from top to bottom, and find nothing. There's no reason to think they'll work it out, and right now, my captor looks far too controlled, with an expression on his face I can't quite make out. Is it arrogance, or something else? Whatever it is, it's as if he's so caught up inside his own thoughts, there's no way of knowing what he'll do next.

I hear more movement above. There are definitely a lot of footsteps. Could it be the police? Is that possible, that miraculously, they've worked out I'm here? But then I remind myself, no one knows I'm here, except for him. If it is the police, they're looking for him, not me.

What if they start shooting? What if I'm caught in the crossfire? But as I'm thinking this, he's double-checking his gun, making sure it's fully loaded. If someone comes through that trapdoor, he's going to shoot them for sure. I've no idea what to do next. Then, I see him raise the gun and take aim at me. He's going to kill me. He's going to pull that trigger and end everything. What's another lost life to someone like him—nothing.

I hear the trapdoor opening, and a male voice roars down. My captor smiles as he answers him. He's completely mad, I think. He's capable of doing almost anything. His hand tightens on the trigger. I scream out, "Please, DON'T!"

He smiles again.

I see movement from behind, bodies rushing down into the darkness. The first man through the trapdoor reaches out to try to stop my captor from shooting, but he's not close enough to him, and as he moves, the gun changes direction, from facing me to his forehead. He fires, a direct shot to the head, his expression changing to one of almost surprise, before his body drops to the ground.

I scream again, as loud as I've ever screamed in my whole life. The man, the one who tried to stop him pulling the trigger, stares at me.

"My name is Nina Harte," I say. "I've been missing for over twenty-five years, and that man, my abductor, is my father."

"Nina," the man says, his voice gentle amid all the noise, "we're going to take you home. Everything's going to be okay."

"Is he dead?" I ask then, seeing the man feel for a pulse on my abductor's neck.

"Yes," he says, "he's gone. He won't be hurting anyone anymore."

79

ELIZABETH

IT FEELS LIKE AN ETERNITY WAITING FOR NEWS, BUT FINALLY THE call comes through from Nick, telling me I've nothing to worry about, that they've caught up with him. Nick also tells me, this man, the one I've lived in fear of for so long, has taken his own life. The world feels different as soon as I hear that, as if even I underestimated the terror I carried around inside of me, now this horrible shackle has been lifted. I hear my voice from a different time, from the young woman I used to be before his horror came into my life. *It's okay*, she says. *I've been here all this time, waiting for you.*

"There's something else," Nick says then.

I grip the phone tight. "What?"

"We've found Nina. She's alive."

His words stun me. The world stops. There's no other way to describe it, and for a second I can't even breathe. I've dreamt about hearing those words for so long, repeating them in my mind over and over, through all the decades of uncertainty, doubts, and unknowing, often grasping in desperation but never giving up hope, when almost everyone else had.

"Are you sure?" my voice asks, as timid as a mouse, as if I need to shrink in size, make myself smaller, become of less consequence, for fear, even now, it could all be some big mistake.

"I'm sure," Nick says. "*Elizabeth*, we've found her. We've found your daughter."

Everything stands still, my mind and heart wanting to take that leap of fate, to really believe it, to hold the joy of it, as tears well up inside, a release of years of anguish and pain, as I ask, "Is she okay?" hanging on for his every word.

"She's been through an ordeal, Elizabeth, but she's doing well. She's made of tough stuff, like her mother."

"Thank you," I say, clutching the phone, my knees wobbly, as I lean against the wall and breathe, long deep breaths of acceptance.

"Nick?"

"Yes."

"Did he have her all this time?"

"No. She was somewhere else, but I'll explain everything once I wrap things up here. But she's okay, Elizabeth. Your daughter is okay."

"Can I see her?"

"Of course, very, very soon."

I finish the call with Nick, after he tells me he'll be here in a couple of hours. I must still be in shock, because for a very long time, I sit and do nothing. I would probably still be doing nothing, only for the sound of *tap-tap*ping on the back door again. When I open it, April asks, "Are you okay?"

"I think so," I reply, somewhat amazed that I'm even able to speak.

"I can't stay long. My mam says I can only stay for a minute, and twenty seconds has already gone by, and—"

"The police found Nina," I say, interrupting her, realising April is the first person I'm telling.

Her eyes open wider than I've ever seen them. "That's *amazing*, Elizabeth." She smiles. "Are you happy?"

"I'm very happy."

"Then, I'm happy too."

I take her hands in mine, remembering her hard grip when the two of us were hiding in that closet upstairs. "What about you," I ask, "how are you doing?"

"I'm okay. I'm glad you're not sad anymore."

"I'm glad about that too."

"Elizabeth?"

"Yeah?"

"Can I have another hug?"

"Sure."

I hold her, and she holds me right back, tight, trusting and tender.

"April," I say, "I'm so glad I got to meet you."

"Me too," she says, loosening her grip. "Will you still want to be my friend, Elizabeth, now you have Nina back?"

"One hundred percent."

"Do you think my teddy might turn up too, the one I lost on holiday?"

"Never give up hope, April."

"I won't," she says, so sincerely I almost want to cry again.

A FEW HOURS LATER NICK MATTHEWS CALLS TO THE HOUSE TO FILL me in. I can't quite believe Nina has been living a separate life all this time, or even, how over the years, our paths might have crossed without us knowing.

"Well, Elizabeth," he says, "soon you'll see Nina again. You got what you came back here for."

"I got a lot more than that."

"I don't understand."

"I found something else very precious," I say, staring out the window, hearing April sing a made-up song at the top of her voice, oblivious to the rest of the world. "I met a real treasure, Nick."

"Treasure?"

"April. She helped me with so many things, but mostly, she helped me to refind myself."

After he leaves, I stand at the kitchen window for a very long time, remembering all the sadness and joy over the last couple of months. I think about that day weeks ago, swinging with April in her back garden, and how at first I felt ridiculous, but then I let go of worrying about such nonsense. I allowed myself to enjoy it, to enjoy this most ordinary yet somehow extraordinary thing, two people talking and caring for one another.

I let out a long sigh, thinking again about this clever, funny, sincere, beautiful young girl. Complicated but simple, different but true, and most of all, just as Ellie described her, an utter joy. I never expected to meet someone like her, but she taught me so many things during the darkest of times, including, even if you're sad, it's still okay to smile. And when things are hard, giving up is far worse than losing.

I often felt like giving up, hiding myself away, living a lie, but not anymore. I guess life is a mixture of all kinds of stuff, and even when it's hard, or you've reached the worst of places, not only do you still have to try, you have to like yourself too. At times, we all need a piece of magic, someone like April to help us find our true selves, separate from other people's opinions of us, or any other inaccurate conclusions others might make. Because finding yourself is actually all about returning to the person you used to be. You may be older, more bruised and battered, but you're still you.

EPILOGUE

TODAY I GET TO SEE MY DAUGHTER NINA. THE LAST TIME I SAW HER was that afternoon in the woods when she was only five years old. We've both done a lot of living since then. We've both changed. We both have a quarter of a century of memories that don't include one another, but today, we can begin making new memories, because today, we'll be together again.

I walk toward the place we're supposed to meet. Everything feels so vivid and alive, just like the day Nina disappeared—the sky clear and blue, the air crisp, almost as if the world is attempting to return us to something stolen from us, far too long ago.

I study the faces of people walking past, no longer searching for my daughter in them. I marvel at the rush of dry leaves rising from the ground as I breathe in the smell of city footpaths after a light spell of rain, and the aroma of spices and cheeses as I pass a delicatessen. I hear children laughing close by, no doubt eager and excited, having finished another school day. All of it feels refreshingly normal, alive and without fear.

I pass two young men strumming guitars, street buskers, and I drop twenty euro in their hat as a donation. They both look so engrossed in what they're doing, it feels joyous, as I manoeuvre my way past a woman with a small child in a buggy before reaching the flower sellers near the top of Grafton Street. The flowers bring back memories too: the blue iris of my grandfather's garden, the sunflowers from that last holiday in France with my parents, the white roses with their large blooms from the house I grew up in, and where time stood still on that fatal night, creating so many ripples that afterward I thought I'd never find myself again. And then later still, when I lost Nina, how I wasn't even sure I wanted to try.

A lot of time has passed since then. I know I've changed, but somewhere deep inside I've come to realise that young woman, the woman I was before the assault, before all of it, is still there. Despite the onset of years, and all the things that have happened, she's the reason, little by little, I fought back, and somehow, while finding myself, I found my daughter Nina too.

As I pick out a bunch of white lilies, Alison's favourites, I wonder if Nina might like them too, and smile. Alison and I have talked a lot over the last few days. She was the next person, after April, I spoke to about the police finding Nina. It was during that conversation she told me that her and Ciaran were splitting up. She'd found a second mobile phone and challenged him on it. Eventually, he admitted to having an affair, a truth that meant lots of other lies unravelled. The deception, along with all its ramifications, hurt her deeply, but little by little I know we'll work through it together.

Farther up the street, at a shop window, I stop and catch my reflection looking back at me, a well-dressed older woman who still looks a little unsure, but then I tell myself today is a new beginning.

Before I left, April gave me some serious words of advice. "Don't talk too fast, or too much. Don't get overly anxious, because if you do, you might knock something over. Don't ask too many questions, and remember, you've waited a long time for this, so be happy."

I turn the corner and walk toward the Shelbourne Hotel. One of the Nubian princesses looks down on me as her hands reach up to the sky. I breathe in deep, and soon I arrive at the red Georgian door of the address I've received from Nick. The noises of the city go silent. I push the door open and climb the staircase, hearing the creaking of wood beneath my feet. The backs of my knees feel weak, my breath now short, as I hear my heart thumping fast. I pause before knocking on the panelled door of the room, the one with the number twenty-five near the top. I realise I'm shaking, as if I'm no longer familiar with my limbs, like I'm a small child again, learning to walk for the very first time. I stretch out my arm, clenching my fist tight, knocking hard on the door.

When it opens, the social worker, the woman who is going to help me and Nina get reacquainted, greets me. She looks kind, and I'm about to introduce myself when across the room, I see a young woman reflected in the mirror, her hair dark, her complexion flawless, staring back at me. I gasp, breathing in deep again, seeing the eyes of my daughter Nina, older now, no longer the eyes of a child, the little girl lost in the woods who, through some miracle, has been found.

She turns toward me, this beautiful creature, our eyes locking together as I say, "Hello, Nina."

THE END

ACKNOWLEDGMENTS

THREE YEARS AGO, SOMEONE VERY CLOSE TO ME WAS DIAGNOSED with clinical depression. It hit them hard, and by extension, it hit me too. At the same time, a close family member struggled with post-traumatic stress, and very soon after that, our empty nest became a very busy place indeed, as our eldest daughter and her two children came to live with us. Both our grandchildren are autistic, and while navigating the many changes in our lives, this story, and the fictional character of Elizabeth Harte, came to be. Elizabeth is very different from me, but as she grew on the page, this woman who'd gone through such extreme trauma, who was determined not to live out the third act of her life without discovering the truth about what happened to her missing daughter, Nina, I fell in love with her. I loved her honesty, her unguardedness and self-questioning, her warmth and self-effacing bravery, all set against a backdrop of huge emotional struggles.

One of my aims for this novel was to look at the "missing person" story from a fresh perspective. Through previous research, I'd worked closely with Irish detectives attached to the 1986 missing child investigation for Philip Cairns, and also the case of Mary Boyle, who was six when she went missing in 1977. One of the detectives was the family liaison officer attached to Philip Cairns's family—a lifelong relationship that only ends when the missing person is found. Sadly, in both Philip's and Mary's cases, that never happened. The devastating effect such an enormous emotional loss can have on a family and those connected to them, often lasting for decades, soon became another driving force in the creation of this fictional story, and I thank everyone who has helped me along the way.

The writing and publication of a novel needs the support of a great many people, so I would also like to thank my wonderful agent, Gráinne Fox of United Talent Agency (UTA), New York, for her passion and support for me every step of the way. Also, thanks to Claire Wachtel of Union Square & Co., who was so passionate about this novel from the beginning. Many thanks also to Madison Hernick at UTA and all the team at Union Square & Co., for their work and enthusiasm while working on *Nina*.

In the area of research, I am forever grateful to those within An Garda Síochána, including ex-detectives Pat Marry and Tom Doyle, both of whom have worked on a great many high-profile criminal investigations in Ireland. They assisted me with all aspects of police procedure, and if an error exists, it is mine alone and is not connected to these wonderful experts who gave their precious time and knowledge.

I am also grateful to the amazing author Patricia Gibney, who read this novel in advance, and to whom I give my heartfelt thanks. Special thanks also to the Irish Writers Centre in Dublin, and the Tyrone Guthrie Centre in Monaghan, who awarded me the "Jack Harte Award" for an early draft of this novel. Also, thanks to the Arts Council of Ireland, who supported the writing of this work by granting me an Arts Bursary for Literature.

Sincere thanks to my family, whose love and support have encouraged me all the way through my writing journey, particularly my husband, Robert; our children, Jennifer, Lorraine, and Graham; and our grandchildren, Caitríona, Carrig, James, and Jack. A special thanks to Caitríona, who inspired the wonderful character April.

Finally, I would like to thank you, the reader, for travelling this journey with me. I hope it was an enjoyable one.

ABOUT THE AUTHOR

Dublin-born crime author **Louise Phillips** is an *Irish Times* best-selling author of six crime novels, five of which were shortlisted for the Best Irish Crime Novel of the Year in the Irish Book Awards. Her second novel, *The Doll's House*, won the award. She has also been long-listed for the Crime Writers Association (CWA) Dagger in the Library Award in the UK for her body of work, and is the recipient of several literary awards, arts bursaries, and residences.

RAISING READERS

Books Build Bright Futures

Thank you for reading this book and for being a reader of books in general. As an author, I am so grateful to share being part of a community of readers with you, and I hope you will join me in passing our love of books on to the next generation of readers.

Did you know that reading for enjoyment is the single biggest predictor of a child's future happiness and success?

More than family circumstances, parents' educational background, or income, reading impacts a child's future academic performance, emotional well-being, communication skills, economic security, ambition, and happiness.

Studies show that kids reading for enjoyment in the US is in rapid decline:

- In 2012, 53% of 9-year-olds read almost every day. Just 10 years later, in 2022, the number had fallen to 39%.
- In 2012, 27% of 13-year-olds read for fun daily. By 2023, that number was just 14%.

Together, we can commit to **Raising Readers** and change this trend. How?

- Read to children in your life daily.
- Model reading as a fun activity.
- Reduce screen time.
- Start a family, school, or community book club.
- Visit bookstores and libraries regularly.
- Listen to audiobooks.
- Read the book before you see the movie.
- Encourage your child to read aloud to a pet or stuffed animal.
- Give books as gifts.
- Donate books to families and communities in need.

BOB1217

Books build bright futures, and **Raising Readers** is our shared responsibility.

For more information, visit **JoinRaisingReaders.com**

Sources: National Endowment for the Arts, National Assessment of Educational Progress, WorldBookDay.org, Nielsen BookData's 2023 "Understanding the Children's Book Consumer"